Edmund Clarence Stedman

The poetical works

Edmund Clarence Stedman

The poetical works

ISBN/EAN: 9783743463653

Manufactured in Europe, USA, Canada, Australia, Japa

Cover: Foto ©Andreas Hilbeck / pixelio.de

Manufactured and distributed by brebook publishing software (www.brebook.com)

Edmund Clarence Stedman

The poetical works

Edmund Clarence Stedman

THE

POETICAL WORKS

OF

EDMUND CLARENCE STEDMAN

𝕳ousehold 𝕰dition

WITH ILLUSTRATIONS

BOSTON
HOUGHTON, MIFFLIN AND COMPANY
NEW YORK: 11 EAST SEVENTEENTH STREET

The Riverside Press, Cambridge :
Electrotyped and Printed by H. O. Houghton & Co.

THIS COLLECTION

IS AFFECTIONATELY AND REVERENTLY

𝔇edicated

TO MY MOTHER.

CONTENTS.

X CONTENTS.

LIST OF ILLUSTRATIONS.

EARLY POEMS.

EARLY POEMS.

BOHEMIA.

A PILGRIMAGE.

I.

WHEN buttercups are blossoming,
    The poets sang, *'t is best to wed :*
So all for love we paired in Spring —
Blanche and I — ere youth had sped,
For Autumn's wealth brings Autumn's wane.
Sworn fealty to royal Art
Was ours, and doubly linked the chain,
With symbols of her high domain,
That twined us ever heart to heart ;
   And onward, like the Babes in the Wood,
   We rambled, till before us stood
    The outposts of Bohemia.

II.

For, roaming blithely many a day,
Eftsoons our little hoard of gold,
Like Christian's follies, slipt away,
Unloosened from the pilgrim's hold,
But left us just as blithe and free ;

Whereat our footsteps turned aside
From lord and lady of degree,
And bore us to that brave countree
Where merrily we now abide, —
  That proud and humble, poor and grand,
  Enchanted, golden Gypsy-Land,
    The Valley of Bohemia.

III.

Together from the higher clime,
By terraced cliff and copse along,
Adown the slant we stept, in time
To many another pilgrim's song,
And came where faded far away,
Each side, the kingdom's ancient wall,
From breaking unto dying day ;
Beyond, the magic valley lay,
With glimpse of shimmering stream and fall ;
  And here, between twin turrets, ran,
  Built o'er with arch and barbacan,
    The entrance to Bohemia.

IV.

Beneath the lichened parapet
Grim-sculptured Gog and Magog bore
The Royal Arms, — Hope's Anchor, set
In azure, on a field of *or*,
With pendent mugs, and hands that wield
A lute and tambour, graven clear ;
What seemed a poet's scroll revealed
The antique legend of the shield :
Cambrinus. Rex. helde.Wassaille.here.
  Joyned. with. ye. Kinge. of. Poetot.
    O. worlde-worne. Pilgrim. passe. belowe.
      To. entre. fayre. Bohemia.

V.

No churlish warder barred the gate,
Nor other pass was needed there
Than equal heart for either fate,
And barren scrip, and hope to spare.
Through the gray archway, hand in hand,
We walked, beneath the rampart high,
And on within the wondrous land ;
There, changed as by enchanter's wand,
My sweetheart, fairer to the eye
    Than ever, moved along serene
    In hood and cloak, — a gypsy queen,
        Born princess of Bohemia !

VI.

A fairy realm ! where slope and stream,
Champaign and upland, town and grange,
Like shadowy shiftings of a dream,
Forever blend and interchange ;
A magic clime ! where, hour by hour,
Storm, cloud, and sunshine, fleeting by,
Commingle, and, through shine and shower,
Bright castles, lit with rainbows, tower,
Emblazoning the distant sky
    With glimmering glories of a land
    Far off, yet ever close at hand
        As hope, in brave Bohemia.

VII.

On either side the travelled way,
Encamped along the sunny downs,
The blithesome, bold Bohemians lay ;
Or hid, in quaintly-gabled towns,
At smoke-stained inns of musty date,

And spider-haunted attic nooks
In empty houses of the great,
Still smacking of their ancient state, —
Strewn round with pipes and mouldy books,
  And robes and buskins over-worn,
    That well become the careless scorn
      And freedom of Bohemia.

VIII.

For, loving Beauty, and, by chance,
Too poor to make her all in all,
They spurn her half-way maintenance,
And let things mingle as they fall ;
Dissevered from all other climes,
Yet compassing the whole round world,
Where'er are jests, and jousts at rhymes,
True love, and careless, jovial times,
Great souls by jilting Fortune whirled,
  Men that were born before their day,
    Kingly, without a realm to sway,
      Yet monarchs in Bohemia ;

IX.

And errant wielders of the quill ;
And old-world princes, strayed afar,
In thread-bare exile chasing still
The glimpses of a natal star ;
And Woman — taking refuge there
With woman's toil, and trust, and song,
And something of a piquant air
Defiant, as who must and dare
Steer her own shallop, right or wrong.
  A certain noble nature schools,
    In scorn of smaller, mincing rules,
      The maidens of Bohemia.

X.

But we pursued our pilgrimage
Far on, through hazy lengths of road,
Or crumbling cities gray with age ;
And stayed in many a queer abode,
Days, seasons, years, — wherein were born
Of infant pilgrims, one, two, three ;
And ever, though with travel worn,
Nor garnered for the morrow's morn,
We seemed a merry company, —
    We, and the mates whom friendship, or
    What sunshine fell within our door,
        Drew to us in Bohemia.

XI.

For Ambrose — priest without a cure —
Christened our babes, and drank the wine
He blessed, to make the blessing sure ;
And Ralph, the limner — half-divine
The picture of my Blanche he drew,
As Saint Cecilia 'mong the caves, —
She singing ; eyes a holy blue,
Upturned and rapturous ; hair, in hue,
Gold rippled into amber waves.
    There, too, is wayward, wild Annette,
    Danseuse and warbler and grisette,
        True daughter of Bohemia,

XII.

But all by turns and nothing long ;
And Rose, whose needle gains her bread ;
And bookish Sibyl, — she whose tongue
The bees of Hybla must have fed ;
And one — a poet — nowise sage

For self, but gay companion boon
And prophet of the golden age ;
He joined us in our pilgrimage
Long since, one early Autumn noon
  When, faint with journeying, we sate
  Within a wayside hostel-gate
    To rest us in Bohemia.

XIII.

In rusty garb, but with an air
Of grace, that hunger could not whelm,
He told his wants, and — " Could we spare
Aught of the current of the realm —
A shilling ? " — which I gave ; and so
Came talk, and Blanche's kindly smile ;
Whereat he felt his heart aglow,
And said : " Lo, here is silver ! lo,
Mine host hath ale ! and it were vile,
  If so much coin were spent by me
  For bread, when such good company
    Is gathered in Bohemia."

XIV.

Richer than Kaiser on his throne,
A royal stoup he bade them bring ;
And so, with many of mine own,
His shilling vanished on the wing ;
And many a skyward-floating strain
He sang, we chorusing the lay
Till all the hostel rang again ;
But when the day began to wane,
Along the sequel of our way
  He kept us pace ; and, since that time,
  We never lack for song and rhyme
    To cheer us, in Bohemia.

XV.

And once we stopped a twelvemonth, where
Five-score Bohemians began
Their scheme to cheapen bed and fare,
Upon a late-discovered plan;
" For see," they said, " the sum how small
By which one pilgrim's wants are met !
And if a host together fall,
What need of any cash at all?"
Though how it worked I half forget,
   Yet still the same old dance and song
    We found, — the kindly, blithesome throng
      And joyance of Bohemia.

XVI.

Thus onward through the Magic Land,
With varying chance. But once there past
A mystic shadow o'er our band,
Deeper than Want could ever cast,
For, oh, it darkened little eyes !
We saw our youngest darling die,
Then robed her in her palmer's guise,
And crossed the fair hands pilgrim-wise,
And, one by one, so tenderly,
   Came Ambrose, Sibyl, Ralph, and Rose,
    Strewing each sweetest flower that grows
      In wildwoods of Bohemia.

XVII.

But last the Poet, sorrowing, stood
Above the tiny clay, and said :
" Bright little Spirit, pure and good,
Whither so far away hast fled ?
Full soon thou tryest that other sphere :

Whate'er is lacking in our lives
Thou dost attain ; for Heaven is near,
Methinks, to pilgrims wandering here,
As to that one who never strives
  With fortune, — has not come to know
  The pride and pain that dwell so low
    In valleys of Bohemia."

XVIII.

He ceased, and pointed solemnly
Through western windows ; and we saw
That lustrous castle of the sky
Gleam, touched with flame ; and heard with awe,
About us, gentle whisperings
Of unseen watchers hovering near
Our dead, and rustling angel wings !
Now, whether this or that year brings
The valley's end, or, haply, here
  Our pilgrimage for life must last,
  We know not ; but a sacred past
    Has hallowed all Bohemia.

THE DIAMOND WEDDING.

O LOVE ! Love ! Love ! what times were those,
  Long ere the age of belles and beaux
And Brussels lace and silken hose,
When, in the green Arcadian close,
You married Psyche, under the rose,
  With only the grass for bedding !
Heart to heart, and hand in hand,
You followed Nature's sweet command —

Roaming lovingly through the land,
   Nor sighed for a Diamond Wedding.

So have we read, in classic Ovid,
How Hero watched for her beloved,
   Impassioned youth, Leander.
She was the fairest of the fair,
And wrapt him round with her golden hair,
Whenever he landed cold and bare,
With nothing to eat and nothing to wear
   And wetter than any gander;
For Love was Love, and better than money;
The slyer the theft, the sweeter the honey;
And kissing was clover, all the world over,
   Wherever Cupid might wander.

So thousands of years have come and gone,
And still the moon is shining on,
   Still Hymen's torch is lighted;
And hitherto, in this land of the West,
Most couples in love have thought it best
To follow the ancient way of the rest,
   And quietly get united.

But now, True Love, you 're growing old —
Bought and sold, with silver and gold,
   Like a house, or a horse and carriage !
      Midnight talks,
      Moonlight walks,
The glance of the eye and sweetheart sigh,
The shadowy haunts with no one by,
   I do not wish to disparage;
      But every kiss
      Has a price for its bliss,
In the modern code of marriage;

And the compact sweet
Is not complete,
Till the high contracting parties meet
Before the altar of Mammon ;
And the bride must be led to a silver bower,
Where pearls and rubies fall in a shower
That would frighten Jupiter Ammon !

I need not tell
How it befell,
(Since Jenkins has told the story
Over and over and over again,
In a style I cannot hope to attain,
And covered himself with glory !)
How it befell, one Summer's day,
The King of the Cubans strolled this way, —
King January's his name, they say, —
And fell in love with the Princess May,
The reigning belle of Manhattan ;
Nor how he began to smirk and sue,
And dress as lovers who come to woo,
Or as Max Maretzek and Jullien do,
When they sit, full-bloomed, in the ladies' view,
And flourish the wondrous baton.

He was n't one of your Polish nobles,
Whose presence their country somehow troubles,
And so our cities receive them ;
Nor one of your make-believe Spanish grandees,
Who ply our daughters with lies and candies,
Until the poor girls believe them.
No, he was no such charlatan —
Count de Hoboken Flash-in-the-pan,

Full of gasconade and bravado,
But a regular, rich Don Rataplan
Santa Claus de la Muscovado
Señor Grandissimo Bastinado !
His was the rental of half Havana
And all Matanzas ; and Santa Anna,
Rich as he was, could hardly hold
A candle to light the mines of gold
Our Cuban owned, choke-full of diggers ;
And broad plantations, that, in round figures,
Were stocked with at least five thousand niggers !
" Gather ye rosebuds while ye may ! "
The Señor swore to carry the day,
To capture the beautiful Princess May,
   With his battery of treasure ;
Velvet and lace she should not lack ;
Tiffany, Haughwout, Ball & Black,
Genin and Stewart, his suit should back,
   And come and go at her pleasure ;
Jet and lava — silver and gold—
Garnets — emeralds rare to behold —
Diamonds — sapphires — wealth untold —
All were hers, to have and to hold ;
   Enough to fill a peck-measure !

He did n't bring all his forces on
At once, but like a crafty old Don,
Who many a heart had fought and won,
   Kept bidding a little higher ;
And every time he made his bid,
And what she said, and all they did —
     'T was written down,
      For the good of the town,
By Jeems, of *The Daily Flyer.*

A coach and horses, you 'd think, would buy
For the Don an easy victory ;
   But slowly our Princess yielded.
A diamond necklace caught her eye,
But a wreath of pearls first made her sigh.
She knew the worth of each maiden glance,
And, like young colts, that curvet and prance,
She led the Don a deuce of a dance,
   In spite of the wealth he wielded.

She stood such a fire of silks and laces,
Jewels, and golden dressing-cases,
And ruby brooches, and jets and pearls,
That every one of her dainty curls
Brought the price of a hundred common girls ;
   Folks thought the lass demented !
But at last a wonderful diamond ring,
An infant Koh-i-noor, did the thing,
And, sighing with love, or something the same,
     (What 's in a name ?)
  The Princess May consented.

Ring ! ring the bells, and bring
The people to see the marrying !
Let the gaunt and hungry and ragged poor
Throng round the great Cathedral door,
To wonder what all the hubbub 's for,
   And sometimes stupidly wonder
At so much sunshine and brightness, which
Fall from the church upon the rich,
   While the poor get all the thunder.

Ring ! ring, merry bells, ring !
    O fortunate few,
    With letters blue,
Good for a seat and a nearer view !
Fortunate few, whom I dare not name ;
Dilettanti ! Crême de la crême !
We commoners stood by the street façade
And caught a glimpse of the cavalcade ;
    We saw the bride
    In diamonded pride,
With jewelled maidens to guard her side, —

Six lustrous maidens in tarletan.
She led the van of the caravan ;
  Close behind her, her mother
(Dressed in gorgeous *moire antique,*
That told, as plainly as words could speak,
She was more antique than the other,)
  Leaned on the arm of Don Rataplan
Santa Claus de la Muscovado
Señor Grandissimo Bastinado.
    Happy mortal ! fortunate man !
And Marquis of El Dorado !

In they swept, all riches and grace,
Silks and satins, jewels and lace ;
In they swept from the dazzled sun,
And soon in the church the deed was done.
Three prelates stood on the chancel high :
A knot that gold and silver can buy
Gold and silver may yet untie,
  Unless it is tightly fastened ;
What 's worth doing at all 's worth doing well.
And the sale of a young Manhattan belle
  Is not to be pushed or hastened ;

So two Very-Reverends graced the scene,
And the tall Archbishop stood between,
   By prayer and fasting chastened.
The Pope himself would have come from Rome,
But Garibaldi kept him at home.
Haply these robed prelates thought
Their words were the power that tied the knot;
But another power that love-knot tied,
And I saw the chain round the neck of the bride, —
A glistening, priceless, marvellous chain,
Coiled with diamonds again and again,
   As befits a diamond wedding;
Yet still 't was a chain, and I thought she knew it,
And half-way longed for the will to undo it,
   By the secret tears she was shedding.

But is n't it odd, to think whenever
We all go through that terrible River, —
Whose sluggish tide alone can sever
(The Archbishop says) the Church decree,
By floating one into Eternity
And leaving the other alive as ever, —
As each wades through that ghastly stream,
The satins that rustle and gems that gleam
Will grow pale and heavy, and sink away
To the noisome River's bottom-clay;
Then the costly bride and her maidens six
Will shiver upon the banks of the Styx,
Quite as helpless as they were born, —
Naked souls, and very forlorn;
The Princess, then, must shift for herself,
And lay her royalty on the shelf;
She, and the beautiful Empress, yonder,
Whose robes are now the wide world's wonder,

And even ourselves, and our dear little wives,
Who calico wear each morn of their lives,
And the sewing girls, and *les chiffoniers,*
In rags and hunger, — a gaunt array, —
And all the grooms of the caravan —
Ay, even the great Don Rataplan
Santa Claus de la Muscovado
Señor Grandissimo Bastinado —
That gold-encrusted, fortunate man ! —
All will land in naked equality :
The lord of a ribboned principality
   Will mourn the loss of his *cordon.*
Nothing to eat, and nothing to wear
Will certainly be the fashion there !
Ten to one, and I 'll go it alone,
Those most used to a rag and bone,
Though here on earth they labor and groan,
Will stand it best, as they wade abreast
   To the other side of Jordan.

PENELOPE.

NOT thus, Ulysses, with a tender word,
   Pretence of state affairs, soft blandishment,
And halt assurances, canst thou evade
My heart's discernment. Think not such a film
Hath touched these aged eyes, to make them lose
The subtlest mood of those even now adroop,
Self-conscious, darkling from my nearer gaze.
Full well I know thy mind, O man of wiles !

O man of restless yearnings —fate-impelled,
Fate-conquering — like a waif thrown back and forth
O'er many waters !   Oft I see thee stand
At eve, a landmark on the outer cliff,
Looking far westward ; later, when the feast
Smokes in the hall, and nimble servants pass
Great bowls of wine, and ancient Phemeus sings
The deeds of Peleus' son, thy right hand moves
Straight for its sword-hilt, like a ship for home ;
Then, when thou hearest him follow in the song
Thine own miraculous sojourn of long years
Through stormy seas, weird islands, and the land
Of giants, and the gray companions smite
Their shields, and cry, *What do we longer here ?*
Afloat ! and let the great waves bear us on !
I know thou growest weary of the realm,
Thy wife, thy son, the people, and thy fame.

  I too have had my longings.   Am I not
Penelope, who, when Ulysses came
To Sparta, and Icarius bade her choose
Betwixt her sire and wooer, veiled her face
And stept upon the galley silver-oared,
And since hath kept thine Ithacensian halls ?
Then when the hateful Helen fled to Troy
With Paris, and the Argive chieftains sailed
Then ships to Aulis, I would have thee go —
Presaging fame, and power, and spoils of war.
So ten years passed ; meanwhile I reared thy son
To know his father's wisdom, and, apart
Among my maidens, wove the yellow wool.
But then, returning one by one, they came, —
The island-princes ; high-born dames of Crete
And Cephalonia saw again their lords ;

Only Ulyssess came not ; yet the war
Was over, and his vessels, like a troop
Of cranes in file, had spread their wings for home.
More was unknown.   Then many a winter's night
The servants piled great fagots, smeared with tar,
High on the palace-roof ; with mine own hands
I fired the heaps, that, haply, far away
On the dark waters, might my lord take heart
And know the glory of his kingly towers.

   So winter passed ; and summer came and went,
And winter and another summer ; then —
Alas, how many weary months and days !
But he I loved came not.   Meanwhile thou knowest
Pelasgia's noblest chiefs, with kingly gifts
And pledge of dower, gathered in the halls ;
But still this heart kept faithful, knowing yet
Thou wouldst return, though wrecked on alien shores.
And great Athenè often in my dreams
Shone, uttering words of cheer.   But, last of all,
The people rose, swearing a king should rule,
To keep their ancient empery of the isles
Inviolate and thrifty : bade me choose
A mate, nor longer dally.   Then I prayed
Respite, until the web within my loom,
Of gold and purple curiously devised
For old Laertes' shroud, should fall complete
From hands still faithful to his blood.   Thou knowest
How like a ghost I left my couch at night,
Unravelling the labor of the day,
And warded off the fate, till came that time
When my lost sea-king thundered in his halls,
And with long arrows clove the suitors' hearts.
So constant was I ! now not thirty moons

Go by, and thou forgettest all. Alas !
What profit is there any more in love ?
What thankless sequel hath a woman's faith !

Yet if thou wilt, — in these thy golden years,
Safe-housed in royalty, like a god revered
By all the people, — if thou yearnest yet
Once more to dare the deep and Neptune's hate,
I will not linger in a widowed age ;
I will not lose Ulysses, hardly found
After long vigils ; but will cleave about
Thy neck, with more than woman's prayers and tears,
Until thou take me with thee. As I left
My sire, I leave my son, to follow where
Ulysses goeth, dearer for the strength
Of that great heart which ever drives him on
To large experience of newer toils !

Trust me, I will not any hindrance prove,
But, like Athenè's helm, a guiding star,
A glory and a comfort ! O, be sure
My heart shall take its lesson from thine own !
My voice shall cheer the mariners at their oars
In the night watches ; it shall warble songs,
Whose music shall o'erpower the luring airs
Of Nereïd or Siren. If we find
Those isles thou namest, where the golden fount
Gives youth to all who taste it, we will drink
Deep draughts, until the furrows leave thy brow,
And I shall walk in beauty, as when first
I saw thee from afar in Sparta's groves.
But if Charybdis seize our keel, or swift
Black currents bear us down the noisome wave
That leads to Hades, till the vessel sink

In Stygian waters, none the less our souls
Shall gain the farther shore, and, hand in hand,
Walk from the strand across Elysian fields,
'Mong happy thronging shades, that point and say :
" There go the great Ulysses, loved of gods,
And she, his wife, most faithful unto death ! "

THE SINGER.

O LARK ! sweet lark !
   Where learn you all your minstrelsy ?
  What realms are those to which you fly ?
While robins feed their young from dawn till dark,
    You soar on high, —
    Forever in the sky.

   O child ! dear child !
  Above the clouds I lift my wing
  To hear the bells of Heaven ring ;
Some of their music, though my flights be wild,
    To Earth I bring ;
    Then let me soar and sing !

HELIOTROPE.

I WALK in the morning twilight,
   Along a garden-slope,
 To the shield of moss encircling
  My beautiful Heliotrope.

O sweetest of all the flowerets
　　That bloom where angels tread !
But never such marvellous odor
　　From heliotrope was shed,

As the passionate exhalation,
　　The dew of celestial wine,
That floats in tremulous languor
　　Around this darling of mine.

For, only yester-even,
　　I saw the dearest scene !
I heard the delicate footfall,
　　The step of my love, my queen.

Along the walk she glided :
　　I made no sound nor sign,
But ever, at the turning
　　Of her star-white neck divine,

I shrunk in the shade of the cypress,
　　And crouched in the swooning grass,
Like some Arcadian shepherd
　　To see an Oread pass.

But when she came to the border
　　At the end of the garden-slope,
She bent, like a rose-tree, over
　　That beautiful Heliotrope.

The cloud of its subtile fragrance
　　Entwined her in its wreath,
And all the while commingled
　　With the incense of her breath.

And so she glistened onward,
　Far down the long parterre,
Beside the statue of Hesper,
　And a hundred times more fair.

But ah ! her breath had added
　The perfume that I find
In this, the sweetest of flowerets,
　And the paragon of its kind.

I drink deep draughts of its nectar ;
　I faint with love and hope !
Oh, what did she whisper to you,
　My beautiful Heliotrope ?

ROSEMARY.

"There 's Rosemary, that 's for Remembrance."

YEARS ago, when a summer sun
　Warmed the greenwood into life,
I went wandering with one
　Soon to be my wife.

Birds were mating, and Love began
　All the copses to infold ;
Our two souls together ran
　Melting in one mould.

Skies were bluer than ever before :
　It was joy to love you then,
And to know I loved you more
　Than could other men !

Winds were fresh and your heart was brave,
  Sang to mine a sweet refrain,
And for every pledge I gave
  Pledged me back again.

How it happened I cannot tell,
  But there came a cursed hour,
When some hidden shape of hell
  Crept within our bower.

Sudden and sharply either spoke
  Bitter words of doubt and scorn ;
Pride the golden linklets broke, —
  Left us both forlorn.

Seven long years have gone since then,
  And I suffered, but, at last,
Rose and joined my fellow-men,
  Crushing down the past.

Far away over distant hills,
  Now I know your life is led ;
Have you felt the rust that kills ?
  Are your lilies dead ?

Summer and winter you have dwelt,
  Like a statue, cold and white ;
None, of all the crowd who knelt,
  Read your soul aright.

O, I knew the tremulous swell
  Of its secret undertone !
That diviner music fell
  On my ear alone !

Ever in dreams we meet with tears :
　Lake and mountain — all are past :
With the stifled love of seven long years
　Hold each other fast !

Though the glamoury of the night
　Fades with morning far away,
Oftentimes a strange delight
　Haunts the after-day.

Even now, when the summer sun
　Warms the greenwood far within,
Even now my fancies run
　On what might have been.

SUMMER RAIN.

YESTERMORN the air was dry
　As the winds of Araby,
While the sun, with pitiless heat,
Glared upon the glaring street,
And the meadow fountains sealed,
Till the people everywhere,
And the cattle in the field,
　And the birds in middle air,
And the thirsty little flowers,
　Sent to heaven a fainting prayer
For the blessed summer showers.

Not in vain the prayer was said ;
For at sunset, overhead,
Sailing from the gorgeous West,
Came the pioneers, abreast,

2

Of a wondrous argosy, —
The Armada of the sky !
Far along I saw them sail,
Wafted by an upper gale ;
Saw them, on their lustrous route,
Fling a thousand banners out :
Yellow, violet, crimson, blue,
Orange, sapphire, — every hue
That the gates of Heaven put on,
To the sainted eyes of John,
In that hallowed Patmos isle
Their skyey pennons wore ; and while
I drank the glory of the sight
   Sunset faded into night.

Then diverging, far and wide,
To the dim horizon's side,
Silently and swiftly there,
Every galleon of the air,
Manned by some celestial crew,
Out its precious cargo threw,
And the gentle summer rain
Cooled the fevered Earth again.

Through the night I heard it fall
Tenderly and musical ;
And this morning not a sigh
   Of wind uplifts the briony leaves,
But the ashen-tinted sky
   Still for earthly turmoil grieves,
While the melody of the rain,
Dropping on the window-pane,
On the lilac and the rose,
Round us all its pleasance throws,

Till our souls are yielded wholly
To its constant melancholy,
And, like the burden **of its song,**
Passionate moments glide along.

Pinks and hyacinths perfume
All our garden-fronted room ;
Hither, close beside me, Love !
Do not whisper, do not move.
Here we two will softly stay,
Side by side, the livelong day.
Lean thy head upon **my** breast :
Ever shall it give thee rest,
Ever would I gaze to **meet**
Eyes of thine up-glancing, **Sweet !**
What enchanted dreams are ours !
While **the murmur of the showers**
Dropping on the tranquil ground,
Dropping on the leaves and flowers,
Wraps our yearning souls around
In the drapery of its sound.

Still the plenteous streamlets fall :
Here two hearts are all in all
To each other ; and they beat
With no evanescent heat,
But softly, steadily, **hour** by hour,
With the calm, melodious power
·**Of** the gentle **summer rain,**
That in Heaven so long hath lain,
And from out **that shoreless sea**
Pours its blessings tenderly.

Freer yet its currents swell !
Here are streams that flow as well,

Rivulets of the constant heart ;
But a little space apart
Glide they now, and soon **shall run,**
Love-united, into one.
It shall chance, in future days,
That again the lurid rays
Of that hidden sun shall shine
On the floweret and the vine,
And again the meadow-springs
Fly away on misty wings :
But no glare of Fate adverse
Shall on us achieve its curse,
Never any baneful gleam
Waste our clear, perennial stream ;
For its fountains lie below
That malign and **ominous** glow, —
Lie in shadowy grottoes cool,
Where all kindly spirits rule ;
Calmly ever shall it flow
Toward the waters of the sea, —
That serene Eternity !

TOO LATE.

CROUCH no **more by the ivied walls,**
Weep no longer over her grave,
Strew no flowers when evening falls **:**
Idly you lost what angels gave !

Sunbeams cover that silent mound
With a warmer hue than your roses' red ;
To-morrow's rain will **bedew** the ground
With a purer stream than the tears you shed.

But neither the sweets of the scattered flowers,
Nor the morning sunlight's soft command,
Nor all the songs of the summer showers,
Can charm her back from that distant land.

Tenderest vows are ever too late!
She, who has gone, can only know
The cruel sorrow that was her fate,
And the words that were a mortal woe.

Earth to earth, and a vain despair;
For the gentle spirit has flown away,
And you can never her wrongs repair,
Till ye meet again at the Judgment Day.

VOICE OF THE WESTERN WIND.

VOICE of the western wind!
　Thou singest from afar,
Rich with the music of a land
　Where all my memories are;
But in thy song I only hear
　The echo of a tone
That fell divinely on my ear
　In days forever flown.

Star of the western sky!
　Thou beamest from afar,
With lustre caught from eyes I knew,
　Whose orbs were each a star;
But, oh, those orbs — too wildly bright —
　No more eclipse thine own,
And never shall I find the light
　Of days forever flown!

FLOOD-TIDE.

JUST at sunrise, when the land-breeze cooled the
  fevered air once more,
From a restless couch I wandered to the sounding
  ocean shore ;
Strolling down through furrowed sand-hills, while the
  splendor of the day
Flashed across the trembling waters to the West and
  far away.
There I saw, in distant moorings, many an anchored
  vessel tall ;
Heard with cheery morning voices sailor unto sailor
  call.
Crowned with trailing plumes of sable, right afront my
  standing-place
Moved a swarthy ocean-steamer in her storm-resisting
  grace.
Prophet-like, she clove the waters toward the ancient
  mother-land,
And I heard her clamorous engine and the echo of
  command,
While the long Atlantic billows to my feet came rolling
  on,
With the multitudinous music of a thousand ages gone.

There I stood, with careless ankles half in sand and
  half in spray,
Till the baleful mist of midnight from my being passed
  away ;
Then, with eager inhalations opening all my mantle
  wide,

Felt my spirit rise exultant with the rising of the tide;
Felt the joyous morning breezes run afresh through
 every vein,
Till the natural pulse of manhood beat the call-to-arms
 again.
Then came utterance self-condemning, — oh, how wild
 with sudden scorn
Of the chain that held me circling in a little round forlorn !
Of the sloth which, like a vapor, hugs the dull, insensate
 heart,
That can act in meek submission to the lowness of its
 part, —
In the broad terrestrial drama play the herald or the
 clown,
While the warrior wins his garlands and the monarch
 wears his crown !

"Shame" I said, "upon the craven who can rest, con-
 tent to save
Paltry handfuls of the riches that his guardian-angel
 gave !
Shame upon all listless dreamers early hiding from the
 strife,
Sated with some little gleaning of the harvest-fields of
 life !
Shame upon God's toiling thinkers, who make profit of
 their brains,
Getting store of scornful pittance for their slow-decay-
 ing pains !
Give me purpose, steadfast purpose, and the grandeur
 of a soul
Born to lead the van of armies or a people to control.
Let me float away and ever, from this shore of bog and
 mire,

On the mounting waves of effort, buoyed by the **soul's**
　　desire !

Would that it were mine **to govern yon** large wonder
　　of our time :

Such a life were worth the living ! **thus to** sail through
　　every clime,

From a hundred spicy shorelands bearing treasures
　　manifold ;

Foremost to achieve discovery of the peerless lands of
　　gold ;

Or to thrid the crashing hummocks for the silent North-
　　ern Pole,

And those solemn open waters that beyond the ice-
　　plains roll, —

Cold and shining sea of **ages ! like a silver fillet set**

On the Earth's eternal forehead, for her bridal coronet.

Or to close with some tall frigate, for my country and
　　the right,

Gunwale grinding into gunwale through **the** rolling
　　cloud of fight.

When the din of cannonading and the jarring war
　　should cease,

From the lion's mouth of battle there should flow the
　　sweets of peace.

I should count repose in cities from my seventy years
　　a loss, —

Resting only on the waters, like the dusk-winged alba-
　　tross.

I should lay the wire-wrought cable — a ghostly depth
　　below —

Along the marly summit of the plummet-found plateau ;

To the old Antipodes with the olive branch should
　　roam,

Joining swart Mongolian races to the ranks of Chris-
　　tendom.

Oftentimes our stately presence in a tyrant's port should
    save
Captives, rash in freedom-loving, **from the dungeon and**
    the grave ;
And a hymn should greet our coming, far across the
    orient sea,
Like the glad apostles' anthem, when an angel set them
    free.

Such the nobler life heroic ! life which ancient **Homer**
    sung
Of the sinewy Grecian worthies, when the blithesome
    Earth was young,
And a hundred marvellous legends lay about **the misty**
    land
Where the wanton **Sirens carolled and the cliffs of**
    Scylla stand.
How their lusty strokes made answer, when Ulysses
    held the helm,
And with subtle words of wisdom spake of many a
    wondrous realm !
. Neither Circè, nor the languor of enchanted nights
    and days
Soothed their eager-eyed disquiet, — tamed their ventu-
    rous, epic ways ;
And the dread Sicilian **monster, in his cavern by the**
    shore,
Felt the shadow of their coming, **and was blind for**
    evermore.

So lived all those stalwart captains of the loyal Saxon
    blood,
Grasping morsels of adventure as an eagle grasps his
    food ;

Fought till death for queen and country, hating Anti-
    christ and Spain ;

Sacked the rich Castilian cities of the glittering western
    main ;

Hacked and hewed the molten idols of each gray
    cathedral pile,

And with Carthaginian silver dowered the virgin Eng-
    lish isle.

Up and down the proud Antilles still the ringing echoes
    go :

Ho! a Raleigh! Ho! a Drake! — and, forever,
    WESTWARD HO !

Why should not my later pæan catch the swell of that
    refrain,

And, with bursts of fresh endeavor, send it down the
    age again ?

But I know, that, while the mariner wafts along the
    golden year,

Broader continents of action open up in every sphere.

And I deem those noble also, who, with strong persua-
    sive art,

Strike the chords of aspiration in a people's lyric
    heart.

If in mine — of all republics the Atlantis and supreme —

There be little cause for mouthing on the old, undying
    theme —

Yet I falter while I say it : — ours of every crime the
    worst !

For the long revenge of Heaven crying loud and call-
    ing first :

But if fiery Carolina and all the sensual South,

Like the world before the deluge, laugh to scorn the
    warning mouth, —

In the lap of hoary Europe lie her children ill at rest,
Reaching **hands of** supplication **to their brethren of**
      the West ;
Pale about **the** lifeless fountain of their ancient **free-**
      dom, wait
Till **the** angel **move its waters** and avenge their stricken
      state.
Let me then, a new crusader, to the eastward set my
      face,
Wake the fires of old tradition on each sacred altar-
      place,
Till a trodden people rouse them, with a clamor **as**
      divine
As the winds of autumn roaring through the **clumps of**
      forest-pine.
I myself would seize their banner ; **they** should follow
      where it led,
To the triumph of the victors or the pallor of the dead.
It were **better than to conquer — from** the light of life
      to go
With such words as once were uttered, off the isle of
      Floreo :
Here die I, Sir Richard Grenvile, of a free and joyful
      mood :
*Ending earth for God **and** honor, as a valiant soldier*
      should !
But my present life — what **is it ?** mated, housed, like
      other **men ;**
Thoughtful of the cost of feeding, valiant only with **the**
      pen ;
Lying, walled about with custom, on an iron bed of
      creeds ;
Peering out through grated windows at the joy my
      spirit needs.

And I hear the sound of chanting, — mailed men are
 passing by ;
Crumble, walls, and loosen, fetters ! I will join them,
 ere I die ! "

So the sleeping thoughts of boyhood oped their eyes
 and newly stirred,
And my muscles cried for usage, till the man their
 plainings heard :
While the star that lit me ever in the dark and thorny
 ways,
Mine by natal consecration, by the choice of after
 days, —
Seen through all the sorrow thickening round the hopes
 of younger years, —
Rayless grew, and left me groping in the valley of my
 tears.

Seaward now the steamer hovered ; seaward far her
 pennons trailed,
Where the blueness of the heavens at the clear horizon
 paled ;
Where the mingled sky and water faded into fairy-
 land,
Smaller than her tiny model, deftly launched from
 childhood's hand.
With a statelier swell and longer, up the glacis of the
 shore,
Came the waves that leapt so freshly in their youth, an
 hour before.
So I made an end and, turning, reached a scallop-
 crested rock,

In the stormy spring-tides hurling back the tumult of
    their shock.
There reclining, gazed a moment at the pebbles by my
    feet,
Left behind the billowy armies on their oceanward
    retreat ;
Thousands lying close together, where the hosts a pas-
    sage wore,
Many-hued, and tesselated in a quaint mosaic floor.

Thinking then upon their fitness, — each adjusted to
    its place,
Fairly strewn, and smoothed by Nature with her own
    exceeding grace, —
All at once some unseen warder drew the curtains wide
    apart,
That awhile had cast their shadow on the picture of my
    heart ;
Told me — "Thou thyself hast said it ; in thy calling
    be of cheer :
Broader continents of action open up in every sphere !
Hold thy lot as great as any : each shall magnify his
    own,
Each shall find his time to enter, though unheralded.
    and lone,
On the inner life's arena — there to sound his battle-
    cry,
Self with self in secret tourney, underneath the silent
    sky.
Strong of faith in that mute umpire, some have con-
    quered, and withstood
All the pangs of long endurance, the dear pains of
    fortitude ;
Felt a harsh misapprehension gall the wounds of mar-
    tyrdom ;

In the present rancor measured even the scorn of days
    to come ;
Known that never should the whiteness of their virtue
    shine revealed,
Never should the truer Future rub the tarnish from the
    shield.
That diviner abnegation hath not yet been asked of
    thee :
Art thou able to attain it, if perchance it were to be ?
O, our feeble tests of greatness ! Look for one so calm
    of soul
As to take the even chalice of his life and drink the
    whole.
Noble deeds are held in honor, but the wide world sorely
    needs
Hearts of patience to unravel this, — the worth of com-
    mon deeds."

As the darkened earth forever to the morning turns
    again ;
As the dreaming soldier, after all the perilous cam-
    paign,
Struggling long with horse and rider, in his sleep smites
    fiercely out,
And, with sudden pang awaking, through the darkness
    peers about, —
Hearing but the crickets chirrup loud, beneath his
    chimney-stone,
Feeling but the warm heart throbbing, in the form
    beside his own, —
Then to knowledge of his hamlet, dearer for the toil he
    knows,
Comes at last, content to nestle in the sweets of his
    repose,

So fell I, from those high fancies, to the quiet of a
    heart
Knowing well how Duty maketh each one's share the
    better part.
As again I looked about me — North and South, and
    East and West —
Now of all the wide world over still my haven seemed
    the best.

Calm, and slowly lifting upward, rose the eastern glory
    higher,
Gilding sea, and shore, and vessel, and the city-crown-
    ing spire.
Then the sailors shook their canvas to the dryness of
    the sun,
And along the harbor-channel glided schooners, one by
    one.
At the last I sought my cottage; there, before the gar-
    den gate,
By the lilac, stood my darling, looking for her truant
    mate.
Stooping at the porch, we entered ; — where the morn-
    ing meal was laid,
Turning over holy pages, one as pure and holy
    played, —
Little Paul, who links more firmly our two hearts than
    clasp of gold ;
And I caught a blessed sentence, while I took him to
    my hold :
" Peace," it said, " O restless spirit, eager as the climbing
    wave !
With my peace there flows a largesse such as monarchs
    never gave."

    1857.

APOLLO.

VAINLY, O burning Poets!
　　Ye wait for his inspiration,
　Even as kings of old
　Stood by the oracle-gates.
Hasten back, he will say, *hasten back*
　To your provinces far away!
　There, at my own good time,
　Will I send my answer to you.
　　Are ye not kings of song?
　At last the god cometh!
　The air runs over with splendor;
　The fire leaps high on the altar;
Melodious thunders shake the ground.
　Hark to the Delphic responses!
　Hark! it is the god!

THE ORDEAL BY FIRE.

TO many a one there comes a day
　　So black with maledictions, they
Hide every earthly hope away.

In earlier woes the sufferer bore,
Consolement entered at his door,
And raised him gently from the floor.

To this great anguish, newly come,
All former sorrows, in their sum,
Were but a faint exordium.

His days and nights are full of groans ;
Sorely, and with a thousand moans,
For many wanderings he atones.

Old errors, vanquished for a space,
Rise up to smite him in the face
And threaten him with new disgrace.

And others, shadows of the first,
From slanderous charnel-houses burst,
Pursuing, cry, *Thou art accurst !*

Dear, feeble voices ask for bread ;
The dross, for which he bowed his head
So long, has taken wings and fled.

The strong resources of his health
Have softly slipt away by stealth :
No future toil may bring him wealth.

Dreading the shadow of his shame,
False friends, who with the sunshine came,
Forego the mention of his name.

Thus on a fiery altar tost,
The harvests of his life are lost
In one consuming holocaust.

What can he, but to beat the air,
And, from the depth of his despair,
Cry " Is there respite anywhere ?

" Is Life but Death ?   Is God unjust
Shall all the castle of my trust
Dissolve, and crumble into dust ?"

There are, who, with a wild desire
For slumber, blinded by the fire,
Sink in its ashes and expire.

God pity them ! too harsh a test
Has made them falter ; sore distrest,
They barter everything for rest.

But many, of a sterner mould,
Themselves within themselves infold,
Even make Death unloose his hold,

Athough it were a grateful thing
To drain the cup his heralds bring,
And yield them to his ransoming ;

To quaff the calm, Lethean wave, —
In passionless tenure of the grave
Forgetting all they could not save.

What angels hold them up, among
The ruins of their lives, so long ?
What visions make their spirits strong ?

In sackcloth, at the outer gate,
They chant the burden of their fate,
Yet are not wholly desolate.

A blessed ray from darkness won
It may be, even, to know the sun
Hath distant lands he shines upon ;

It may be that they deem it vile
For one to mount his funeral pile,
Because the heavens cease to smile ;

That scorn of cowardice holds fast,
Lighting the forehead to the last,
Though all of bravery's hopes are past.

Perchance the sequence of an art
Leads to a refuge for the heart, —
A sanctuary far apart.

It may be that, in dearest eyes,
They see the light of azure skies,
And keep their faith in Paradise.

Thou, who dost feel Life's vessel strand
Full-length upon the shifting sand,
And hearest breakers close at hand,

Be strong and wait ! nor let the strife,
With which the winds and waves are rife,
Disturb that sacred inner life.

Anon thou shalt regain the shore,
And walk — though naked, maimed, and sore —
A nobler being than before !

No lesser griefs shall work thee ill ;
No malice shall have power to kill :
Of woe thy soul has drunk its fill.

Tempests, that beat us to the clay,
Drive many a lowering cloud away,
And bring a clearer, holier day.

The fire, that every hope consumes,
Either the inmost soul entombs
Or evermore the face illumes !

Robes of asbestos do we wear;
Before the memories we **bear,**
The flames leap backward everywhere.

THE PROTEST OF FAITH.

TO REV. —— ——

DEAR Friend and Teacher, — not by word alone,
But by the plenteous virtues shining out
Along the zodiac of a good man's life ;
Dear gentle friend ! from one so loved as you, —
Because so loving, and so finely apt
In tender ministry to a little flock,
With whom you joy and suffer . . . and, withal,
So constant to the spirit of our time
That I must hold **you** of a different sort
From those dry lichens on the altar steps,
Those mutes in surplices, school-trained to sink
The ashes of their own experience
So low, in doctrinal catacombs, that none
Find token they can love and mourn like us, —
From such an one as **you,** I cannot brook
What from these mummies were a pleasant draught
Of bitter hyssop — pleasant unto me,
Drunk from a chalice worthier men have held
And emptied to the lees.

I cannot brook
The shake o' the head and earnest, sorrowing glance,
Which often seem to say : — "Be wise in time !
Give up the iron key that locks your heart.

1 grant you charity, and patient zeal,
And something of a young, romantic love
For what is good, as children love the fields
And birds and babbling brooks, they know not why.
You have your moral virtues, but you err:
To err is fatal.   O, my heart is faint
Lest that sweet prize I win should not be yours ! "

  In some such wise I read your half-dropped thoughts ;
Yet wondrous compensation falls to all,
And every soul has strongholds of its own,
Invisible, yet answering to its needs.
And even I may have a secret tower
Up storm-cleft Pisgah, whence I see beyond
Jordan, and far across the happy plains,
Where gleams the Holy City, like a queen,
The crown of all our hopes and perfect faith.
I may have gone somewhat within the veil,
Though few repose serenely in the light
Of that divinest splendor, till they shine,
With countenance aglow, like him of old, —
Prophet and priest and warrior, all in one.
But every human path leads on to God ;
He holds a myriad finer threads than gold,
And strong as holy wishes, drawing us
With delicate tension upward to Himself.
You see the strand that reaches down to you ;
Haply I see mine own, and make essay
To trace its glimmerings — up the shadowy hills
Forever narrowing to that unknown sky.

  There grows a hedge about you pulpit-folk :
You reason *ex cathedra.*   Little gain
Have we to clash in tourney on the least

Of points, wherewith you trammel down the Faith,
It being, at outset, understood right well
By lay knights-errant, that their Reverend foes,
Fore-pledged to hold **their own**, will sound their trumps,
Though spearless and unhorsed ! Why take the field,
When, at the best, both sides go bowing **off**
With mutual courtesy, and fair white flags
Afloat at camp, and every fight is drawn?
As soon encounter statues, balanced well
Upon their granite, fashioned not to move,
And drawing all mankind to hold in awe
Their grim persistence.   .

                    If, indeed, I sin
In counting somewhat freely **on that Love**
From which, through rolling ages, worlds have sprung,
And — last and best of all — the lords of worlds,
Through type on type uplifted from the clay;
If I have been exultant in the thought
That such humanity came so near to God,
He held us as His children, and would find
Imperial **progress through the halls of Time**
For every **soul, — why, then, my crescent faith**
Clings round the promise; **if it** spread beyond,
You think, too far, I say that Peter sprang
Upon the waves of surging Galilee,
While all the eleven hugged the ship in fear:
The waters were as stone unto his feet
Until he doubted, even then the Christ
Put forth a blesséd hand, and drew him on
To closer knowledge !

                    So, if it be mine
First of us twain to pass the sable gates,

That guard so well their mysteries, and thou,
With some dear friend, may'st stand beside my grave,
Speak no such words as these : — " Not long ago
His voice rang out as cheerly as mine own ;
And we were friends, and, far into the nights,
Would analyze the wisdom of old days
By all the tests of Science in her prime ;
Anon would tramp afield, to fruits and flowers,
And the long prototypes of trees and beasts
Graven in sandstone ; so, at last, would come,
Through lanes of talk, to that perennial tree, —
The Tree of Life, on which redemption hangs.
But there fell out of tune ; we parted there,
He bolstering up a creed too broad for me !
I held him kindly for an ardent soul,
Who lacked not skill to make his argument
Seem fair and specious.   But he groped in doubt :
His head and heart were young ; he wandered off,
And fell afoul of all those theorists
Who soften down our dear New England faith
With German talk of ' Nature,' ' inner lights
And harmonies ' : so, taken with the wind
Of those high-sounding terms, he spoke at large,
And held discussion bravely till he died.
Here sleep his ashes ; where his soul may be,
Myself, who loved him, do not care to think."

  The ecstasy of Faith has no such fears
As those you nurse for me !   The marvellous love,
Which folds the systems in a flood of light,
Makes no crude works to shatter out of joint
Through all the future.   O, believe, with me,
For every instinct in these hearts of ours
A full fruition hastens !   O, believe

That promise greater than our greatest trust
And loftiest aspiration !   Tell thy friend,
Beside my grave : " He did the best he could,
With earnest spirit polishing the lens
By which he took the heavens in his ken,
And through the empyrean sought for God ;
He caught, or thought he caught, from time to time,
Bright glimpses of the Infinite, on which
He fed in rapturous and quiet joy,
That helped him keep a host of troubles down.
He went his way, — a different path from mine,
But took his place among the ranks of men
Who toil and suffer.   If, in sooth, it be
Religion keeps us up, this man had that.
God grant his yearnings were a living faith !
Heaven lies above us : may we find him there
Beside the waters still, and crowned with palms ! "

THE FRESHET.

A CONNECTICUT IDYL.

L AST August, of a three weeks' country tour,
　　 Five dreamy days were passed amid old elms
And older mansions, and in leafy dales,
That knew us till our elders pushed us forth
To larger life, — as eagles push their young,
New-fledged and wondering, from the eyrie's edge,
To cater for themselves.

　　　　　　　　I fell in, there,
With Gilbert Ripley, once my chum at Yale.
Poor Gilbert groaned along a double year, —

Read, spoke, boxed, fenced, rowed, trod the foot-ball
      ground, —
Loving the college library more than Greek,
His meerschaum most of all. But when we came
Together, gathered from the breathing-time
They give the fellows while the dog-days last,
He found the harness chafe ; then grew morose,
And kicked above the traces, going home
Hardly a Junior, but a sounder man,
In mind and body, than a host who win
Your baccalaureate honors. There he stayed,
Half tired of bookmen, on his father's farm,
And gladly felt the plough-helve. In a year
The old man gave his blessing to the son,
And left his life, as 't were his harvest-field,
When work was over. Gilbert hugged the farm,
Now made his own, besides a pretty sum
In good State Sixes ; partly worked the land,
With separate theories for every field,
And partly led the student-life of old,
Mouthing his Shakespeare's ballads to himself
Among the meadow-mows ; or, when he read
In the evening, found a picture of his bull,
Just brought from Devon, sleek as silk, loom in
Before his vision. Thus he weighed his tastes,
Each against each, in happiest equipoise.
The neighbor farmers seeing he had thrift
That would not run to waste, and pardoning all
Beyond their understanding, wished him well.

But when I saw him stride among his stock, —
Straight-shouldered cattle, breathing of the field, —
Saw him how blowze and hearty ; then, at eve,
Close sitting by his mother in the porch,

    3   D

Heard him discuss the methods of the times,
The need our country has of stalwart men,
Who scorn the counter and will till the land,
Strong-handed, free of thought, — I somehow felt
The man was noble, and his simple life
More like the pattern given in the Mount
Than mine, hedged close about with city life
And grim, conventional manners.

                    So much, then,
For Gilbert Ripley. Not to dwell too long
Upon his doings, let me tell the tale
I got from him, one hazy afternoon,
When he and I had wandered to the bridge,
New-built across our favorite of the streams
That skirt the village, — here three miles apart,
Twin currents, joining in a third below.

  There memory's shallop bore us dreamily,
Through changeful windings, to the long, long days
Of June vacations. How we boys would thrid
The alder thickets at the water's edge,
Conjecturing forward, though the Present lay
Like Eden round us ; for the Future shone —
The sun to which each young heart turned for light !
What wild conceits of great, oracular lives,
Ourselves would equal ! but let that go by :
Each has gone by, in turn, to humbler fates.
Sometimes we angled, and our trolling hooks
Swung the gray pickerel from his reedy shoals.
Beyond a horseshoe bend, the current's force
Wore out a deeper channel, where the shore
Fell off, precipitous, on the western side.
There dived the bathers ; there I learned to swim, —

Flung far into the middle stream by one
Who watched my gaspings, laughing, till my limbs,
Half of themselves, struck out, and held me up.
Far down, a timbered dam, from bank to bank,
Shut back the waters in a shadowy lake,
About a mimic island.   Languidly
The chestnuts still infoliate its space,
And still the whispering flags are intertwined
With whitest water-lilies near the marge.
Close by, the paper-mill, with murmurous wheel,
Still glistens through the branches, while its score
Of laughing maidens throng the copse at noon.

But we, with careless arms upon the rail,
Peered through and through the water; almost saw
Its silvery Naiads, from their wavering depths,
Gleam with strange faces upward; almost heard
Sweet voices carol: "Ah, you all come back!
We charm your childhood; then you roam away,
To float on alien waters, like the winds;
But, ah, you all come back, — come dreaming back!"

At last I broke the silence: "See," I said
To Gilbert, "see how fair our dear old stream!
How calm, beneath the shadow of these piers,
It eddies in and out, and cools itself
In slumberous ripples whispering repose."

But he made answer: "Yes, this August day
The wave is summer-charmed, the fields are hazed;
But in the callow Spring, when Easter winds
Are on us, laden with rain, these fickle streams —
More gentle now than in his cradled sleep
Some Alexander — take up arms, spread wide,

Leap high and cruel in a fierce campaign
Along their valleys. See this trellised bridge,
New-built, and firmer than the one from which
We fellows dropped the line : — *that* went away
Two years ago, like straw before a gale,
In the great April flood, of which you heard,
When George and Lucy Dorrance lost their lives.
I saw them perish. You remember her, —
She that was Lucy Hall, — a charming girl,
The fairest of our schoolmates, with a heart
Light as her smile and fastened all upon
The boy that won her ; yet her glances fell
Among us, right and left, like shooting stars
In clear October nights when winds are still.

"That year our Equinoctial came along
Ere the snow left us. Under mountain pines
White drifts lay frozen like the dead, and down
Through many a gorge the bristling hemlocks crossed
Their spears above the ice-enfettered brooks ;
But the pent river wailed, through prison walls,
For freedom and the time to rend its chains.
At last it came : five days a drenching rain
Flooded the country ; snow-drifts fell away ;
The brooks grew rivers, and the river here —
A ravenous, angry torrent — tore up banks,
And overflowed the meadows, league on league.
Great cakes of ice, four-square, with mounds of hay,
Fence-rails, and scattered drift-wood, and huge beams
From broken dams above us, mill-wheel ties,
Smooth lumber, and the torn-up trunks of trees,
Swept downward, strewing all the land about.
Sometimes the flood surrounded, unawares,
Stray cattle, or a flock of timorous sheep,

And bore them with it, struggling, till **the ice**
Beat shape and being from them. **You know how**
These freshets scour our valleys. So it raged
A night and day ; but when the day grew night
The storm fell off ; lastly, the sun went down
Quite clear of clouds, and ere he came again
The flood began to lower.

                 " Through the rise
We men had been at work, like water-sprites,
Lending a helping hand to cottagers
Along the lowlands.   Now, at early morn,
The banks were sentry-lined with thrifty swains,
Who hauled great stores of drift-wood up the slope.
But toward the bridge our village maidens soon
Came flocking, thick **as swallows after storms,**
When, with light **wing, they skim the happy fields**
And greet the sunshine.   Danger mostly gone,
They watched the thunderous passage of the flood
Between the abutments, while the upper stream,
Far as they saw, lay like a seething strait,
From hill to hill.   Below, with gradual fall
Through narrower channels, all was clash and clang
And inarticulate tumult.   Through the grove
Yonder, our picnic-ground, the driving tide
Struck a new channel, and the craggy **ice**
Scored down its saplings.   Following with the rest
Came George and Lucy, not three honeymoons
Made man and wife, and happier than a pair
Of cooing ring-doves in the early June.

" Two piers, you know, bore up the former bridge,
Cleaving the current, wedge-like, on the north ;
Between them stood our couple, intergrouped

With many others.   On a sudden loomed
An immolating terror from above, —
A floating field of ice, where fifty cakes
Had clung together, mingled with a mass
Of *débris* from the upper conflict, logs
Woven in with planks and fence-rails ; and in front
One huge, old, fallen trunk rose like a wall
Across the channel.   Then arose a cry
From all who saw it, clamoring, *Flee the bridge !*
Run shoreward for your lives ! and all made haste,
Eastward and westward, till they felt the ground
Stand firm beneath them ; but, with close-locked arms,
Lucy and George still looked, from the lower rail,
Toward the promontory where we stood,
Nor saw the death, nor seemed to hear the cry.
Run George ! run Lucy ! shouted all at once :
Too late, too late ! for, with resistless crash,
Against both piers that mighty ruin lay
A space that seemed an hour, yet far too short
For rescue.   Swaying slowly back and forth,
With ponderous tumult, all the bridge went off ;
Piers, beams, planks, railings snapped their groaning
        ties
And fell asunder !

                    " But the middle part,
Wrought with great bolts of iron, like a raft
Held out awhile, whirled onward in the wreck
This way and that, and washed with freezing spray.
Faster than I can tell you, it came down
Beyond our point, and in a flash we saw
George, on his knees, close-clinging for dear life,
One arm around the remnant of the rail,
One clasping Lucy.   We were pale as they,

Powerless to save ; but even as they swept
Across the bend, and twenty stalwart men
Ran to and fro with clamor for *A rope!*
A boat! — their cries together reached the shore :
Save her! Save him! — so true Love conquers all.
Furlongs below they still more closely held
Each other, 'mid a thousand shocks of ice
And seething horrors ; till, at last, the end
Came, where the river, scornful of its bed,
Struck a new channel, roaring through the grove.
There, dashed against a naked beech that stood
Grimly in front, their shattered raft gave up
Its precious charge ; and then a mist of tears   ·
Blinded all eyes, through which we seemed to see
Two forms in death-clasp whirled along the flood,
And all was over.

        " Then from out the crowd
Certain went up the lane, and broke the news
To Lucy's widowed mother ; she spoke not,
Nor wept, nor murmured, but with stony glare
Took in her loss, like Niobe, and to bed
Moved stolidly and never rose again.
Old Farmer Dorrance gave a single groan,
And hurried down among us — all the man,
Though white with anguish — as we took our course
Around the meadows, searching for the dead.

    " An eddying gulf ran up the hither bank,
Close by the paper-mill, and there the flood
Gave back its booty ; there we found them laid,
Covered with floating leaves and twigs of trees,
Not many feet apart : so Love's last clasp
Held lingeringly, until the cruel ice

Battered its fastenings.   On a rustic bier,
Made of loose boughs and strewn with winter ferns,
We placed them, side by side, and bore them home.
The old man walked behind them, by himself,
And wrung his hands and bowed his head in tears."

So Gilbert told his story ; I, meanwhile,
Followed his finger's pointing, as it marked
Each spot he mentioned, like a teacher's wand.
But now the sun hung low ; from many a field
The loitering kine went home with tinkling bells.
Slow-turning, toward the farm we made our way,
And met a host of maidens, merry-eyed,
Whom I knew not, yet caught a frequent glance
I seemed to know, that half-way brought to mind
Sweet eyes I loved to watch in school-boy days, —
Sweet sister-eyes to those that glistened now.

THE SLEIGH-RIDE.

H ARK ! the jingle
   Of the sleigh-bells' song !
Earth and air in snowy sheen commingle ;
      Swiftly throng
Norseland fancies, as we sail along.

      Like the maiden
      Of some fairy-tale,
Lying, spell-bound, in her diamond-laden
      Bridal veil,
Sleeps the Earth beneath a garment pale.

"Hark! the jingle
Of the sleigh-bells' song."   Page 56.

High above us
Gleams the ancient moon,
Gleam the eyes of shining ones that love us :
Could their tune
Only fill our ears at heaven's noon,

You and I, love,
With a wild delight,
Hearing that seraphic strain would die, love,
This same night,
Straight to join them in their starry height !

Closer nestle,
Dearest, to my side.
What enchantment, in our magic vessel
Thus to glide,
Making music, on a silver tide !

Jingle ! jingle !
How the fields go by !
Earth and air in snowy sheen commingle,
Far and nigh ;
Is the ground beneath us, or the sky ?

Heavenward yonder,
In the lurid north,
From Valhalla's gates that roll asunder,
Red and wroth,
Balder's funeral flames are blazing forth.

O, what splendor !
How the hues expire !
All the elves of light their tribute render
To the pyre,
Clad in robes of gold and crimson fire.

3 *

Jingle ! jingle !
Let the Earth go by !
With a wilder thrill our pulses tingle ;
You and I
Will shout our loves, but aye forget to sigh !

THE BALLAD OF LAGER BIER.

IN fallow college days, Tom Harland,
We both have known the ways of Yale,
And talked of many a nigh and far land,
O'er many a famous tap of ale.
There still they sing their Gaudeamus,
And see the road to glory clear ;
But taps, that in our day were famous,
Have given place to Lager Bier.

Now, settled in this island-city,
We let new fashions have their weight ;
Though none too lucky — more 's the pity ! —
Can still beguile our humble state
By finding time to come together,
In every season of the year,
In sunny, wet, or windy weather,
And clink our mugs of Lager Bier.

On winter evenings, cold and blowing,
'T is good to order " 'alf-and-'alf " ;
To watch the fire-lit pewter glowing,
And laugh a hearty English laugh ;

Or even a sip of mountain whiskey
    Can raise a hundred phantoms dear
Of days when boyish blood was frisky,
    And no one heard of Lager Bier.

We 've smoked in summer with Oscanyan,
    Cross-legged in that defunct bazaar,
Until above our heads the banyan
    Or palm-tree seemed to spread afar ;
And, then and there, have drunk his sherbet,
    Tinct with the roses of Cashmere :
That Orient calm ! who would disturb it
    With Norseland calls for Lager Bier ?

There 's Paris chocolate, — nothing sweeter,
    At midnight, when the dying strain,
Just warbled by La Favorita,
    Still hugs the music-haunted brain ;
Yet of all bibulous compoundings,
    Extracts or brewings, mixed or clear,
The best, in substance and surroundings,
    For frequent use, is Lager Bier.

Karl Schæffer is a stalwart brewer,
    Who has above his vaults a hall,
Where — fresh-tapped, foaming, cool, and pure —
    He serves the nectar out to all.
Tom Harland, have you any money ?
    Why, then, we 'll leave this hemisphere,
This western land of milk and honey,
    For one that flows with Lager Bier.

Go, flaxen-haired and blue-eyed maiden,
    My German Hebe ! hasten through

Yon smoke-cloud, and return thou laden
  With bread and cheese and bier for two.
Limburger suits this bearded fellow ;
  His brow is high, his taste severe :
But I 'm for Schweitzer, **mild and yellow,**
  To eat with bread and Lager Bier.

Ah, yes ! the Schweitzer hath a savor
  Of marjoram and mountain thyme,
An odoriferous, Alpine flavor ;
  You almost hear the cow-bells chime
While eating it, or, dying faintly,
  The *Ranz-des-vaches* entrance the ear,
Until you feel quite Swiss and saintly,
  Above your glass of Lager Bier.

Here comes our drink, froth-crowned and sunlit,
  In goblets with high-curving arms,
Drawn from a newly opened runlet,
  As bier must be, to have its **charms.**
This primal portion each shall swallow
  At one draught, for a pioneer ;
And thus a ritual usage **follow**
  Of all who honor **Lager Bier.**

Glass after glass in due succession,
  Till, borne through midriff, heart, and brain,
He mounts his throne and takes possession, —
  The genial Spirit of the grain !
Then comes the old Berserker madness
  To make each man a priest and seer,
And, with a Scandinavian gladness,
  Drink deeper draughts of Lager Bier !

Go, maiden, fill again **our glasses** !
　While, with anointed eyes, **we scan**
The blouse Teutonic lads and lasses,
　The Saxon — Pruss — Bohemian,
The sanded floor, the cross-beamed gables,
　The ancient Flemish paintings queer,
The rusty cup-stains on the tables,
　The terraced kegs of Lager Bier.

And is it Göttingen, or Gotha,
　Or Munich's ancient Wagner **Brei,**
Where each Bavarian drinks his quota,
　And swings a silver tankard high ?
Or some ancestral Gast-Haus lofty
　In Nuremburg — of famous cheer
When Hans Sachs lived, and **where, so oft, he**
　Sang loud the praise of Lager Bier?

For even now some curious glamour
　Has brought about a misty change !
Things look, as in a moonlight dream, or
　Magician's mirror, quaint and strange.
Some weird, phantasmagoric notion
　Impels us backward many a year,
And far across **the northern ocean,**
　To Fatherlands **of Lager** Bier.

As odd a throng **I see before us**
　As ever haunted Brocken's height,
Carousing, with unearthly chorus,
　On any wild Walpurgis-night ;
I see the wondrous art-creations !
　In proper guise they all appear,
And, in their due and several stations,
　Unite in drinking Lager Bier.

I see in yonder nook a trio :
   There 's Doctor Faust, and, by his side,
Not half so love-distraught as Io,
   Is gentle Margaret, heaven-eyed ;
That man in black beyond the waiter —
   I know him by his fiendish leer —
Is Mephistophiles, the traitor !
   And how he swigs his Lager Bier !

Strange if great Goethe should have blundered,
   Who says that Margaret slipt and fell
In Anno Domini Sixteen Hundred,
   Or thereabout ; and Faustus, — well,
We won't deplore his resurrection,
   Since Margaret is with him here,
But, under her serene protection,
   May boldly drink our Lager Bier.

That bare-legged gypsy, small and lithy,
   Tanned like an olive by the sun,
Is little Mignon ; sing us, prithee,
   Kennst du das Land, my pretty one !
Ah, no ! she shakes her southern tresses,
   As half in doubt and more in fear ;
Perhaps the elvish creature guesses
   We 've had too much of Lager Bier.

There moves, full-bodiced, ripe, and human,
   With merry smiles to all who come,
Karl Schæffer's wife, — the very woman
   Whom Rubens drew his Venus from !
But what a host of tricksome graces
   Play round our fairy Undine here,
Who pouts at all the bearded faces,
   And, laughing, brings the Lager Bier.

" Sit down, nor chase the vision farther,
   You 're tied to Yankee cities still ! "
I hear you, but so much the rather
   Should Fancy travel where she will.
Yet let the dim ideals scatter ;
   One puff, and lo ! they disappear ;
The comet, next, or some such matter,
   We 'll talk above our Lager Bier.

Now, then, your eyes begin to brighten,
   And marvellous theories to flow ;
A philosophic theme you light on,
   And, spurred and booted, off you go !
If e'er — to drive Apollo's phaeton—
   I need an earthly charioteer,
This tall-browed genius I will wait on,
   And prime him first with Lager Bier.

But higher yet, in middle Heaven,
   Your steed seems taking flight, my friend ;
You read the secret of the Seven,
   And on through trackless regions wend !
Don't vanish in the Milky Way, for
   This afternoon you 're wanted here ;
Come back ! come back ! and help me pay for
   The bread and cheese and Lager Bier.

HOW OLD BROWN TOOK HARPER'S FERRY.

JOHN BROWN in Kansas settled, like a steadfast
Yankee farmer,
  Brave and godly, with four sons, all stalwart men of
might.
There he spoke aloud for freedom, and the Border-strife
grew warmer,
  Till the Rangers fired his dwelling, in his absence, in
the night ;
             And Old Brown,
             Osawatomie Brown,
Came homeward in the morning — to find his house
burned down.

Then he grasped his trusty rifle and boldly fought for
freedom ;
  Smote from border unto border the fierce, invading
band ;
And he and his brave boys vowed — so might Heaven
help and speed 'em ! —
  They would save those grand old prairies from the
curse that blights the land ;
             And Old Brown,
             Osawatomie Brown,
Said, " Boys, the Lord will aid us ! " and he shoved
his ramrod down.

And the Lord *did* aid these men, and they labored day
and even,
  Saving Kansas from its peril ; and their very lives
seemed charmed,

Till the ruffians killed one son, in the blessed light of
    Heaven, —
  In cold blood the fellows slew him, as he journeyed
    all unarmed ;
          Then Old Brown,
          Osawatomie Brown,
Shed not a tear, but shut his teeth, and frowned a ter-
    rible frown !

Then they seized another brave boy, — not amid the
    heat of battle,
  But in peace, behind his ploughshare, — and they
    loaded him with chains,
And with pikes, before their horses, even as they goad
    their cattle,
  Drove him cruelly, for their sport, and at last blew
    out his brains ;
          Then Old Brown,
          Osawatomie Brown,
Raised his right hand up to Heaven, calling Heaven's
    vengeance down.

And he swore a fearful oath, by the name of the
    Almighty,
  He would hunt this ravening evil that had scathed
    and torn him so ;
He would seize it by the vitals ; he would crush it day
    and night ; he
  Would so pursue its footsteps, so return it blow
    for blow,
          That Old Brown,
          Osawatomie Brown,
Should be a name to swear by, in backwoods or in
    town !

Then his beard became more grizzled, and his wild
      blue **eye grew** wilder,
  And more sharply curved his hawk's-nose, snuffing
      battle from afar ;
And he and the two boys left, though **the Kansas strife
      waxed** milder,
  Grew more sullen, till was over the bloody Border
      War,
             And Old **Brown,**
             Osawatomie Brown,
Had gone **crazy, as they** reckoned by his fearful **glare
      and** frown.

So he **left the** plains of Kansas **and their** bitter woes
      behind **him,**
  Slipt off into Virginia, where the statesmen all are
      born,
Hired a farm by Harper's Ferry, and no one knew
      where to find **him,**
  Or whether **he 'd turned parson, or** was jacketed and
      shorn ;
             For Old Brown,
             Osawatomie **Brown,**
Mad as he was, knew texts enough to wear a parson's
      gown.

He bought no ploughs **and** harrows, spades and shov-
      els, and such trifles ;
  But quietly to **his** rancho **there** came, by every train,
Boxes **full of** pikes and pistols, and his well-beloved
      Sharp's rifles ;
  And eighteen other madmen joined their leader there
      again.

Says Old Brown,
Osawatomie Brown,
"Boys, we 've got an army large enough to march
and take the town !

"Take the town, and seize the muskets, free the ne-
groes and then arm them ;
Carry the County and the State, ay, and all the po-
tent South.
On their own heads be the slaughter, if their victims
rise to harm them —
These Virginians ! who believed not, nor would
heed the warning mouth."
Says Old Brown,
Osawatomie Brown,
"The world shall see a Republic, or my name is not
John Brown."

'T was the sixteenth of October, on the evening of a
Sunday :
"This good work," declared the captain, "shall be
on a holy night ! "
It was on a Sunday evening, and before the noon of
Monday,
With two sons, and Captain Stephens, fifteen pri-
vates — black and white,
Captain Brown,
Osawatomie Brown,
Marched across the bridged Potomac, and knocked the
sentry down ;

Took the guarded armory-building, and the muskets
and the cannon ;
Captured all the county majors and the colonels, one
by one ;

Scared to death each gallant scion of Virginia they ran
    on,
  And before the noon of Monday, I say, the deed was
    done.
            Mad Old Brown,
            Osawatomie Brown,
With his eighteen other crazy men, went in and took
    the town.

Very little noise and bluster, little smell of powder
    made he ;
  It was all done in the midnight, like the Emperor's
    coup d'état.
" Cut the wires ! Stop the rail-cars ! Hold the streets
    and bridges ! " said he,
  Then declared the new Republic, with himself for
    guiding star, —
            This Old Brown,
            Osawatomie Brown ;
And the bold two thousand citizens ran off and left the
    town.

Then was riding and railroading and expressing here
    and thither ;
  And the Martinsburg Sharpshooters and the Charles-
    town Volunteers,
And the Shepherdstown and Winchester Militia has-
    tened whither
  Old Brown was said to muster his ten thousand
    grenadiers.
            General Brown !
            Osawatomie Brown !!
Behind whose rampant banner all the North was pour-
    ing down.

But at last, 't is said, some prisoners escaped from Old
      Brown's durance,
  And the effervescent valor of the Chivalry broke
      out,
When they learned that nineteen madmen had the
      marvellous assurance —
  Only nineteen — thus to seize the place and drive
      them straight about ;
              And Old Brown,
              Osawatomie Brown,
Found an army come to take him, encamped around
      the town.

But to storm, with all the forces I have mentioned,
      was too risky ;
  So they hurried off to Richmond for the Government
      Marines,
Tore them from their weeping matrons, fired their
      souls with Bourbon whiskey,
  Till they battered down Brown's castle with their lad-
      ders and machines ;
              And Old Brown,
              Osawatomie Brown,
Received three bayonet stabs, and a cut on his brave
      old crown.

Tallyho ! the old Virginia gentry gather to the baying !
  In they rushed and killed the game, shooting lustily
      away ;
And whene'er they slew a rebel, those who came too
      late for slaying,
  Not to lose a share of glory, fired their bullets in his
      clay ;

And Old Brown,
Osawatomie Brown,
Saw his sons fall dead beside him, and between them
laid **him down.**

How the conquerors wore their laurels ; how they has-
tened on the trial ;
How Old Brown was placed, half dying, on **the**
Charlestown court-house floor ;
How he spoke **his** grand oration, in the scorn of all de-
nial ;
What the brave old madman told them, — these **are**
known the country o'er.
" Hang Old **Brown,**
Osawatomie Brown,"
Said the judge, " and all such rebels ! " with his **most**
judicial frown.

But, Virginians, don't do it ! for I tell **you that the**
flagon,
**Filled with blood of Old Brown's offspring, was first
poured by Southern hands ;**
**And each drop from Old Brown's life-veins, like the
red gore of the** dragon,
May spring **up a** vengeful Fury, hissing through your
slave-worn lands !
And Old Brown,
Osawatomie Brown,
May trouble you more than ever, when you 've nailed
his coffin down !

November, 1859.

SONNETS.

HOPE DEFERRED.

BRING no more flowers and books and precious
    things !
O speak no more of our beloved Art,
Of summer haunts, — melodious wanderings
In leafy refuge from this weary mart !
Surely such thoughts were dear unto my heart ;
Now every word a newer sadness brings !
Thus oft some forest-bird, caged far apart
From verdurous freedom, droops his careless wings,
Nor craves for more than food from day to day ;
So long bereft of wildwood joy and song,
Hopeless of all he dared to hope so long,
The music born within him dies away ;
Even the song he loved becomes a pain,
Full-freighted with a yearning all in vain.

A MOTHER'S PICTURE.

SHE seemed an angel to our infant eyes !
    Once, when the glorifying moon revealed
Her who at evening by our pillow kneeled, —
Soft-voiced and golden-haired, from holy skies
Flown to her loves on wings of Paradise, —
We looked to see the pinions half concealed.
The Tuscan vines and olives will not yield
Her back to me, who loved her in this wise,
And since have little known her, but have grown
To see another mother, tenderly
Watch over sleeping children of my own.
Perchance the years have changed her : yet alone
This picture lingers ; still she seems to me
The fair young angel of my infancy.

POEMS WRITTEN IN YOUTH.

POEMS WRITTEN IN YOUTH.

ELFIN SONG.

FROM "THE RIME OF THE ELLE-KING."

I.

FAR in the western ocean's breast
   The summer fairies have found a nest ;
The heavens ever unclouded smile
Over the breadth of their beautiful isle ;
Through it a hundred streamlets flow,
In spangled paths, to the sea below,
And woo the vales that beside them lie
With a low and tremulous minstrelsy.
The elfin brood have homes they love
In the earth below and skies above ;
But the haunt which of all they love the best
Is the palm-crowned isle, in the ocean's breast,
   That mortals call Canary ;
And many an Ariel, blithesome, airy,
And each laughing Fay and lithesome Fairy,
Know well the mystical way in the West
   To the sweet isle of Canary.

2.

With an ever-sounding choral chant,
And a clear, cerulean, wild desire
To clasp that fairy island nigher,
The sinuous waves of ocean pant ;
For here all natural things are free
To mingle in passionate harmony.
The light from their mirror turns away
With a golden splendor, in the day,
But nightly, when coroneted Even
Marshals the shining queen of heaven,
There gleams a silvery scenery,
From the rim of the great prismatic sea
    Around the isle of Canary,
To the central crags of Pisgatiri,
Where the crested eagle builds his eyry,
    Scanning the shores of sweet Canary.

3.

Lustrously sailing here and there,
Afloat in the beatific air,
Birds, of purple and blue and gold,
Pour out their music manifold ;
All day long in the leas they sing,
While the sun-kissed flowers are blossoming ;
At eve, when the dew-drop feeds the rose,
And the fragrant water-lilies close,
The marvellous-throated nightingale
With a dying music floods each vale,
Till the seaward breezes, listening, stay
To catch the harmony of his lay
    And cool the air of Canary ;
And thus the melodies ever vary,
In the vales of the ocean aviary,
    In the blissful valleys of sweet Canary.

4.

The Elle-King's palace was builded there
By elves of water and earth and air;
Lovingly worked each loyal sprite,
And it grew to life in a summer night.
Over the sheen of its limpid moat,
Wafted along, in a magic boat,
By fairy wings that fan the sails,
And eddying through enchanted vales,
Through walls of amber and crystal gates,
We come where a fairy warder waits;
And so, by many a winding way
Where sweet bells jingle and fountains play,
To the inmost, royalest room of all, —
The elfin monarch's reception-hall,
    The pearl and pride of Canary!
To guard its fastness the elves are wary,
And no weird thing, of pleasure chary,
    Can enter with evil in sweet Canary!

5.

All that saddens, and care and pain,
Are banished far from that fair domain;
There forever, by day and night,
Is naught but pleasance and love's delight;
Daily, the Genii of the flowers
Shade with beauty a hundred bowers;
Nightly, the Gnomes of precious stones
Emblazon and light a hundred thrones;
And the Elves of the field, so swift and mute,
Bring wine and honey and luscious fruit;
And the Sylphs of the air, at noontide, cool
The depths of each bower and vestibule;

And all are gay, — from the tricksome Fay
Who flutters in woodlands far away,
To the best-beloved attendant Elf,
And the royal heart of the King himself,
    Who rules in bright Canary ;
And the laboring Fairies are blithe and merry,
Who press the juice from the swollen berry
    That reddens the vines of sweet Canary.

6.

What if there be a fated day
When the Faëry Isle shall pass away,
And its beautiful groves and fountains seem
The myths of a long, delicious dream !
A century's joys shall first repay
Our hearts, for the evil of that day ;
And the Elfin-King has sworn to wed
A daughter of Earth, whose child shall be,
By cross and water hallowéd,
From the fairies' doom forever free.
What if there be a fated day !
It is far away ! it is far away !
Maiden, fair Maiden, I, who sing
Of this summer isle am the island King.
I come from its joys to make thee mine :
Half of my kingdom shall be thine ;
Our horses of air and ocean wait —
Then hasten, and share the Elle-King's state
    In the sweet isle of Canary ;
And many an Ariel, blithesome, airy,
And each laughing Fay and lithesome Fairy,
Shall rovingly hover around and over thee,
And the love of a king shall evermore cover thee,
    Nightly and daily in sweet Canary.

1850.

AMAVI.

I LOVED : and in the morning sky,
  A magic castle upward grew !
Cloud-haunted turrets pointing high
  Forever to the dreamy blue ;
  Bright fountains leaping through and through
The golden sunshine ; on the air
  Gay banners streaming ; — never drew
Painter or poet scene more fair.

And in that castle I would live,
  And in that castle I would die ;
And there, in curtained bowers, would give
  Heart-warm responses, sigh for sigh ;
  There, when but one sweet face was nigh,
The hours should lightly move along,
  And ripple, as they glided by,
Like stanzas of an antique song.

O foolish heart ! O young romance,
  That faded with the noonday sun !
Alas, for gentle dalliance,
  For life-long pleasures never won !
  O for a season dead and gone !
A wizard time, which then did seem
  Only a prelude, leading on
To sweeter portions of the dream.

She died, — nor wore my orange flowers : —
  No longer, in the morning sky,

That magic castle lifts its towers
  Which shone, awhile, so lustrously.
  Torn are the bannerols, and dry
The silver fountains in its halls ;
  But the drear sea, with endless sigh,
Moans round and over the crumbled walls.

Let the winds blow ! let the white surge
  Ever among those ruins wail !
Its moaning is a welcome dirge
  For wishes that could not avail.
  Let the winds blow ! a fiercer gale
Is wild within me ! what may quell
  That sullen tempest ?   I must sail
Whither, O whither, who can tell !

ODE TO PASTORAL ROMANCE.

" Sounds and sweet airs, that give delight and hurt not."
                               THE TEMPEST.

I.

QUEEN of the shadowy clime !
  Thou of the fairy-spell and wondrous lay :
Sweet Romance ! breathe upon my way,
Not with the breath of this degenerate time,
But of that age when life was summer play,
  When Nature wore a verdurous hue,
    And Earth kept holiday ;
When on the ground Chaldæan shepherds lay,

Gazing all night, with calm, creative view,
　　Into the overhanging blue,
And found, amid the many-twinkling stars,
　　　Warriors and maidens fair,
Heroes of marvellous deeds and direful wars,
　　　Serpents and flaming hair,
　　　The Dragon and the Bear,
A silvery Venus and a lurid Mars.

II.

　　Come at thy lover's call,
　　Thou, that, with embraces kind,
Throwing thy tendrils round the lives of all,
Something in all to beautify dost find!
　　So thine own ivy, on the Gothic wall,
　　　Or pendent from the arms
Of gnarléd oaks, where'er its clusters fall,
Clings to adorn and adds perennial charms.
　　And therefore, Romance, would I greet
　　Thee by the fairest of fair names,
　　Calling thee debonair and sweet;
For sweet thou art — inspiring Manhood's dreams,
When all aweary of the actual life;
　　And sweet thy influence seems
To Woman, shrinking from the strife,
The sordid tumult of the wrangling mart.
　　But doubly sweet thou art,
Leading the tender child by gentle streams,
Among the lilies of our flowery Youth;
　　Filling his all-believing heart
With thoughts that glorify the common truth;
Building before him, in the lustrous air,
Ethereal palaces and castles fair.

III.

With such mild innocence the Earth
Received thy blessings at her birth ;
And in the pastoral days of yore,
   To Man's enchanted gaze,
Nature was fair — O, how much more
   Than in our wiser days !
Then deities of sylvan form,
While yet the hearts of men were young and warm,
Like shepherds wandered through the arching groves,
Or sang aloud, the listening flocks among,
   Sweet legends of their loves ;
Then Cupid and fair Psyche breathed their vows, —
He with the feathered darts and bow unstrung,
   And garlands on his brows ;
She folding gently to her bosom doves
Snow-white, forever, as their mistress, young;
And, as they sighed together, peerless Joy
Enwreathed the maiden and the raptured boy !

IV.

Yes ! on romantic pilgrimage,
To the calm piety of Nature's shrine,
Through summer-paths, thou ledst our human-kind,
   With influence divine.
  In that orient, elden age,
   Ere man had learned to wage
Dispassionate war against his natural mind,
   Thy voice of mystery,
Reading aloud the Earth's extended page,
  Bade human aspirations find

In the cool fountain and the forest-tree
    A sentient imagery ;
The flowing river and the murmuring wind,
        The land — the sea —
    Were all informed by thee !

v.

Through coral grottoes wandering and singing,
The merry Nereid glided to her cave ;
Anon, with warm, luxurious motion flinging
Her sinuous form above the moonlit wave,
        To the charmed mariner gave
A glimpse of snowy arms and amber tresses,
        While on his startled ear
The sea-nymph's madrigal fell clear ;
        Then to the far recesses,
Where drowsy Neptune wears the emerald crown,
        Serenely floated down,
Leaving the mariner all amort with fear.
    In the under-opening wood,
What time the Gods had crowned the full-grown year,
The Dryad and the Hamadryad stood
        Among the fallow deer ;
Bending the languid branches of their trees,
        With every breeze,
To view their image in the fountains near : —
The fountains ! whence the white-limbed Naiads sang,
Pouring upon the air melodious trills,
And, while the echoes through the forest rang,
The white-limbed Naiads of a thousand rills
Far o'er the Arcadian vales a pæan spread.
    Led by Diana, in the dewy dawn,
        The Oread sisters chased the dappled fawn

Through all the coverts of their native hills ;
Home, with the spoils, at sultry noon they fled, —
 Home to their shaded bowers,
Where, with the ivy, and those sacred flowers
That now have faded from the weary earth,
Each laughing Oread crowned an Oread's head.
The mountains echoed back their maiden mirth,
Rousing old Pan, who, from a secret lair,
Shook the wild tangles of his frosty hair,
And laid him down again with sullen roar :
But now the frightened nymphs like statues stand,
One balancing her body half in air,
Dreading to hear again that tumult sore ;
One, with a liquid tremor in her eye,
Waving above her head a glimmering hand ;
Till suddenly, like dreams, away they fly,
 Leaving the forest stiller than before !

VI.

Such was thy power, O Pastoral Romance !
In that ambrosial age of classic fame,
 The spirit to entrance.   .
Fain would I whisper of the latter days,
 When, in thy royal name,
The mailéd knights encountered lance to lance,
All for sweet Romance and fair ladies' praise ;
 But no ! I bowed the knee
 And vowed allegiance to thee,
As I beheld thee in thy golden prime,
And now from thy demesne must haste away :
 Perchance that of the aftertime,
 Of nodding plumes and chivalrous array,
 In aftertime I sing a roundelay.

VII.

Fair Spirit of ethereal birth,
In whom such mysteries and beauties blend !
Still from thine ancient dwelling-place descend
And idealize our too material earth ;
Still to the Bard thy chaste conceptions lend,
To him thine early purity renew ;
Round every image grace majestic throw !
Till rapturously the living song shall glow
With inspiration as thy being true,
And Poesy's creations, decked by thee,
Shall wake the tuneful thrill of sensuous ecstasy.

1850.

ALICE OF MONMOUTH,

AN

IDYL OF THE GREAT WAR;

AND

OTHER POEMS.

1864.

This Volume

IS DEDICATED TO THE MEMORY

OF

C. F. S.

DIED: MAY 13, 1863.

ALICE OF MONMOUTH.

I.

1.

HENDRICK VAN GHELT of Monmouth shore,
His fame still rings the county o'er !
The stock that he raised, the stallion he rode,
The fertile acres his farmers sowed ;
The dinners he gave ; the yacht which lay
At his fishing-dock in the Lower Bay ;
The suits he waged, through many a year,
For a rood of land behind his pier, —
Of these the chronicles yet remain
From Navesink Heights to Freehold Plain.

2.

The Shrewsbury people in autumn help
Their sandy toplands with marl and kelp,
And their peach and apple orchards fill
The gurgling vats of the cross-road mill.
They tell, as each twirls his tavern-can,
Wonderful tales of that stanch old man,

And they boast, of the draught they have tasted and
      smelt,
"'T is good as the still of Hendrick Van Ghelt!"

3.

Were he alive, and at his prime,
In this, our boisterous modern time,
He would surely be, as he could not then,
A stalwart leader of mounted men, —
A ranger, shouting his battle-cry,
Who knew how to fight and dared to die;
And the fame which a county's limit spanned
Might have grown a legend throughout the land.

4.

He would have scoured the Valley through,
Doing as now our bravest do;
Would have tried rough-riding on the border,
Punishing raider and marauder;
With bearded Ashby crossing swords
As he took the Shenandoah fords;
Giving bold Stuart a bloody chase
Ere he reached again his trysting-place.
Horse and horseman of the foe
The blast of his bugle-charge should know,
And his men should water their steeds, at will,
From the banks of Southern river and rill.

5.

How many are there of us, in this
Discordant social wilderness,
Whose thriftiest scions the power gain,
Through meet conditions of sun and rain,

To yield, on the fairest blossoming shoot,
A mellow harvest of perfect fruit?
Fashioned after so rare a type,
How should his life grow full and ripe,
There, in the passionless haunts of Peace,
Through trade, and tillage, and wealth's increase?

6.

But at his manor-house he dwelt,
And royally bore the name Van Ghelt;
Nor found a larger part to play
Than such as a county magnate may:
Ruling the hustings as he would,
Lord of the rustic neighborhood;
With potent wishes and quiet words
Holding an undisputed sway.
The broadest meadows, the fattest herds,
The fleetest roadsters, the warmest cheer, —
These were old Hendrick's many a year.
Daughters unto his hearthstone came,
And a son — to keep the ancient name.

7.

Often, perchance, the old man's eye
From a seaward casement would espy,
Scanning the harborage in the bay,
A ship which idly at anchor lay;
Watching her as she rose and fell,
Up and down, with the evening swell,
Her cordage slackened, her sails unbent,
And all her proud life somnolent.
And perchance he thought — " My life, it seems,
Like her, unfreighted with aught but dreams;

Yet I feel within me a strength to dare
Some outward voyage, I know not where!"
But the forceful impulse wore away
In the common life of every day,
And for Hendrick Van Ghelt no timely hour
Ruffled the calm of that hidden power;
Yet in the prelude of my song
His storied presence may well belong,
As a Lombardy poplar, lithe and hoar,
Stands at a Monmouth farmer's door,
Set like a spire against the sky,
Marking the hours, while lover and maid
Linger long in its stately shade,
And round its summit the swallows fly.

II.

I.

NATURE a devious by-way finds: solve me her
  secret whim,
That the seed of a gnarled oak should sprout to a sap-
  ling straight and prim;
That a russet should grow on the pippin stock, on the
  garden-rose a brier;
That a stalwart race, in old Hendrick's son, should
  smother its wonted fire.

Hermann, fond of his book, and shirking the brawny
  out-door sports;
Sent to college, and choosing for life the law with her
  mouldy courts;

Proud, and of tender honor, as well became his father's
    blood,
But with cold and courtly self-restraint weighing the ill
    and good ;

Wed to a lady whose delicate veins that molten azure
    held,
Ichor of equal birth, wherewith our gentry their coup-
    lings weld ;
Viewing his father's careless modes with half a tolerant
    eye,
As one who honors, regretting not, old fashions pass-
    ing by.

After a while the moment came when, unto the son
    and heir,
A son and heir was given in turn, — a moment of joy
    and prayer ;
For the angel who guards the portals twain oped, in
    the self-same breath,
To the child the pearly gate of life, to the mother the
    gate of death.

Father, and son, and an infant plucking the daisies
    over a grave :
The swell of a boundless surge keeps on, wave follow-
    ing after wave ;
Ever the tide of life sets toward the low invisible shore :
Whence had the current its distant source ? when
    shall it flow no more ?

2.

Nature's serene renewals, that make the scion by one
    remove

Bear the ancestral blossom and thrive as the forest
    wilding throve !
Roseate stream of life, which hides the course its ducts
    pursue,
To rise, like that Sicilian fount, in far-off springs anew !

For the grandsire's vigor, rude and rare, asleep in the
    son had lain,
To waken in Hugh, the grandson's frame, with the
    ancient force again ;
And ere the boy, said the Monmouth wives, had grown
    to his seventh year,
Well could you tell whose mantling blood swelled in
    his temples clear.

Tall, and bent in the meeting brows ; swarthy of hair
    and face ;
Shoulders parting square, but set with the future hunts-
    man's grace ;
Eyes alive with a fire which yet the old man's visage
    wore
At times, like the flash of a thunder-cloud when the
    storm is almost o'er.

3.

Toward the mettled stripling, then, the heart of the old
    man yearned ;
And thus — while Hermann Van Ghelt once more,
    with a restless hunger, turned
From the grave of her who died so young, to his books
    and lawyer's gown,
And the ceaseless clangor of mind with mind in the
    close and wrangling town —

They two, the boy and the grandsire, lived at the manor-
    house, and grew,
The one to all manly arts apace, the other a youth
    anew —
Pleased with the boy's free spirit, and teaching him,
    step by step, to wield
The mastery over living things, and the craft of flood
    and field.

Apt, indeed, was the scholar; and born with a subtle
    art to gain
The love of all dumb creatures at will; now lifting
    himself, by the mane,
Over the neck of the three-year colt, for a random
    bareback ride,
Now chasing the waves on the rifted beach at the turn
    of the evening tide.

Proud, in sooth, was the master: the youngster, he oft
    and roundly swore,
Was fit for the life a gentleman led in the lusty days of
    yore !
And he took the boy wherever he drove, — to a county
    fair or race ;
Gave him the reins and watched him guide the span at
    a spanking pace ;

Taught him the sportsman's keen delight : to swallow
    the air of morn,
And start the whistling quail that hides and feeds in
    the dewy corn ;
Or in clear November underwoods to bag the squirrels,
    and flush
The brown-winged, mottled partridge a-whir from her
    nest in the tangled brush ;

Taught him the golden harvest laws, and the signs of
    sun and shower,
And the thousand beautiful secret ways of graft and
    fruit and flower ;
Set him straight in his saddle, and cheered him gallop-
    ing over the sand ;
Sailed with him to the fishing-shoals and placed the
    helm in his hand.

Often the yacht, with all sail spread, was steered by
    the fearless twain
Around the beacon of Sandy Hook, and out in the open
    main ;
Till the great sea-surges rolling in, as south-by-east
    they wore,
Lifted the bows of the dancing craft, and the buoyant
    hearts she bore.

But in dreamy hours, which young men know, Hugh
    loved with the tide to float
Far up the deep, dark-channeled creeks, alone in his
    two-oared boat ;
While a fiery woven tapestry o'erhung the waters low,
The warp of the frosted chestnut, the woof with maple
    and birch aglow ;

Picking the grapes which dangled down ; or watching
    the autumn skies,
The osprey's slow imperial swoop, the scrawny heron's
    rise ;
Nursing a longing for larger life than circled a rural
    home,
An instinct of leadership within, and of action yet to
    come.

"Often the yacht, with all sail spread."   Page 98.

4.

Curtain of shifting seasons dropt on moor and meadow
and hall,
Open your random vistas of changes that come with
time to all !
Hugh grown up to manhood ; foremost, searching the
county through,
Of the Monmouth youth, in birth and grace, and the
strength to will and do.

The father, past the prime of life, and his temples
flecked with toil,
A bookman still, and leaving to Hugh the care of stock
and soil.
Hendrick Van Ghelt, a bowed old man in a fireside-
corner chair,
Counting the porcelain Scripture tiles which frame the
chimney there, —

The shade of the stalwart gentleman the people used
to know,
Forgetful of half the present scenes, but mindful of
long-ago ;
Aroused, mayhap, by growing murmurs of Southern
feud, that came
And woke anew in his fading eyes a spark of their
ancient flame.

5.

Gazing on such a group as this, folds of the curtain
drop,
Hiding the grandsire's form ; and the wheels of the
sliding picture stop.

Gone, that stout old Hendrick, at last! and from miles
    around they came, —
Farmer, and squire, and whispering youths, recalling
    his manhood's fame.

Dead : and the Van Ghelt manor closed, and the home-
    stead acres leased ;
For their owner had moved more near the town, where
    his daily tasks increased,
Choosing a home on the blue Passaic, whence the
    Newark spires and lights
Were seen, and over the salt sea-marsh the shadows
    of Bergen Heights.

Back and forth from his city work, the lawyer, day by
    day,
With the press of eager and toiling men, followed his
    wonted way ;
And Hugh, — he dallied with life at home, tending the
    garden and grounds ;
But the mansion longed for a woman's voice to soften
    its lonely sounds.

" Hugh," said Hermann Van Ghelt, at length, " choose
    for yourself a wife,
Comely, and good, and of birth to match the mother
    who gave you life.
No words of woman have charmed my ear since last I
    heard her voice ;
And of fairest and proudest maids her son should make
    a worthy choice."

But now the young man's wandering heart from the
    great world turned away,

To long for the healthful Monmouth meads, the shores
    of the breezy bay;
And often the scenes and mates he knew in boyhood
    he sought again,
And roamed through the well-known woods, and lay in
    the grass where he once had lain.

III.

LADIES, in silks and laces,
    Lunching with lips that gleam,
Know you aught of the places
    Yielding such fruit and cream?

South from your harbor-islands
    Glisten the Monmouth hills;
There are the ocean highlands,
    Lowland meadows and rills,

Berries in field and garden,
    Trees with their fruitage low,
Maidens (asking your pardon)
    Handsome as cities show.

Know you that, night and morning,
    A beautiful water-fay,
Covered with strange adorning,
    Crosses your rippling bay?

Her sides are white and sparkling;
    She whistles to the shore;
Behind, her hair is darkling,
    And the waters part before.

Lightly the waves she measures
  Up to the wharves of the town ;
There, unlading her treasures,
  Lovingly puts them down.

Come with me, ladies ; cluster
  Here on the western pier ;
Look at **her jewels'** lustre,
  Changed with the changing year !

First of the months to woo her,
  June his strawberries flings
Over her garniture,
  Bringing her exquisite things ;

Rifling his richest casket ;
  Handing her, everywhere,
Garnets in crate and basket ;
  Knowing she soon will wear

Blackberry jet and lava,   .
  Raspberries ruby-red,
Trinkets that August gave **her,**
  Over her toilet spread.

After such gifts have faded,
  Then the peaches are seen, —
Coral and ivory braided,
  Fit for an Indian queen.

And September will send her,
  Proud of his wealth, and bold,
Melons glowing in splendor,
  Emeralds set with gold.

So she glides to **the Narrows,**
    Where the forts are astir :
Her speed is a shining arrow's !
    Guns are silent for her.

So she glides to the ringing
    Bells of the belfried town,
Kissing the wharves, and flinging
    All of her jewels down.

Whence she gathers her riches,
    Ladies, now would you see ?
Leaving your city niches,
    Wander awhile with me.

IV.

1.

THE strawberry-vines lie in the sun,
    Their myriad tendrils twined in one ;
Spread like a carpet of richest dyes,
The strawberry-field in sunshine lies.
Each timorous berry, blushing red,
Has folded the leaves above her head,
The dark, green curtains gemmed with dew ;
But **each** blushful berry, peering through,
Shows like a flock of the underthread, —
The crimson woof of a downy cloth
Where the elves may kneel and plight their troth.

2.

Run through the rustling vines, to **show**
Each picker an even space to go,

Leaders of twinkling cord divide
The field in lanes from side to side;
And here and there with patient care,
Lifting the leafage everywhere,
Rural maidens and mothers dot
The velvet of the strawberry-plot:
Fair and freckled, old and young,
With baskets at their girdles hung,
Searching the plants with no rude haste,
Lest berries should hang unpicked, and waste: —
Of the pulpy, odorous, hidden quest,
First gift of the fruity months, and best.

3.

Crates of the laden baskets cool
Under the trees at the meadow's edge,
Covered with grass and dripping sedge,
And lily-leaves from the shaded pool;
Filled, and ready to be borne
To market before the morrow morn.
Beside them, gazing at the skies,
Hour after hour a young man lies.
From the hillside, under the trees,
He looks across the field, and sees
The waves that ever beyond it climb,
Whitening the rye-slope's early prime;
At times he listens, listlessly,
To the tree-toad singing in the tree,
Or sees the catbird peck his fill
With feathers adroop and roguish bill.
But often, with a pleased unrest,
He lifts his glances to the west,
Watching the kirtles, red and blue,
Which cross the meadow in his view;

And he hears, anon, the busy throng
Sing the Strawberry-Pickers' Song :

4.

" Rifle the sweets our meadows bear,
   Ere the day has reached its nooning ;
While the skies are fair, and the morning air
   Awakens the thrush's tuning.

   " *Softly the rivulet's ripples flow ;*
   Dark is the grove that lovers know ;
   Here, where the whitest blossoms blow,
   The reddest and ripest berries grow.

" Bend to the crimson fruit, whose stain
   Is glowing on lips and fingers ;
The sun has lain in the leafy plain,
   And the dust of his pinions lingers.

   " *Softly the rivulet's ripples flow ;*
   Dark is the grove that lovers know ;
   Here, where the whitest blossoms blow,
   The reddest and ripest berries grow.

" Gather the cones which lie concealed,
   With their vines your foreheads wreathing ;
The strawberry-field its sweets shall yield
   While the western winds are breathing.

   " *Softly the rivulet's ripples flow ;*
   Dark is the grove that lovers know ;
   Here, where the whitest blossoms blow,
   The reddest and ripest berries grow."

5 *

5.

From the far hillside comes again
An echo of the pickers' strain.
Sweetly the group their cadence keep ;
Swiftly their hands the trailers sweep ;
The vines are stripped and the song is sung,
A joyous labor for old and young ;
For the blithe children, gleaning behind
The women, marvellous treasures find.

6.

From the workers a maiden parts :
The baskets at her waistband shine
With berries that look like bleeding hearts
Of a hundred lovers at her shrine ;
No Eastern girl were girdled so well
With silken belt and silver bell.
Her slender form is tall and strong ;
Her voice is the sweetest in the song ;
Her brown hair, fit to wear a crown,
Loose from its bonnet ripples down.
Toward the crates, that lie in the shade
Of the chestnut copse at the edge of the glade,
She moves from her mates, through happy rows
Of the children loving her as she goes.
Alice, our Alice ! one and all,
Striving to stay her footsteps, call
(For children with skilful choice dispense
The largesse of their innocence) ;
But on, with a sister's smile, she moves
Into the darkness of the groves,
And deftly, daintily, one by one,
Shelters her baskets from the sun,
Under the network, fresh and cool,
Of lily-leaves from the crystal pool.

7.

Turning her violet eyes, their rays
Glistened full in the young man's gaze ;
And each at each, for a moment's space,
Looked with a diffident surprise.
" Heaven ! " thought Hugh, " what artless grace
That laborer's daughter glorifies !
I never saw a fairer face,
I never heard a sweeter voice ;
And oh ! were she my father's choice,
My father's choice and mine were one
In the strawberry-field and morning sun."

V.

LOVE, from that summer morn
    Melting the souls of these two ;
Love, which some of you know
Who read this poem to-day —
Is it the same desire,
The strong, ineffable joy,
Which Jacob and Rachel felt,
When he served her father long years,
And the years were swift as days —
So great was the love he bore ?
Race, advancing with time,
Growing in thought and deed,
Mastering land and sea,
Say, does the heart advance,
Are its passions more pure and strong ?
They, like Nature, remain,
No more and no less than of yore.
Whoso conquers the earth,

Winning its riches and fame,
Comes to the evening at last,
The sunset of threescore **years**,
Confessing that Love was real,
All the rest was a dream !
The sum of his gains is dross ;
The song in his praise is mute ;
The wreath of his laurels fades :
But the kiss of his early love
Still burns on his trembling lip,
The spirit of one he **loved**
Hallows his dreams **at night.**
A little while, and the **scenes**
Of the play of Life are closed ;
Come, let us rest an hour,
And by the pleasant streams,
Under the fresh, green trees,
Let us walk hand in hand,
And think of the days that **were.**

VI.

I.

ON river and **height and** salty moors **the haze of**
autumn fell,
And the cloud of a troubled joy enwrapt the **face of**
Hugh as well, —
The spell of a secret haunt that far from home his foot-
steps drew ;
A love which over the brow of **youth the mask of**
manhood threw.

Birds of the air to the father, at length, the common
    rumor brought :
"Your son," they sang, "in the cunning toils of a rus-
    tic lass is caught ! "
"A fit betrothal," the lawyer said, "must make these
    follies cease ;
Which shall it be ? — the banker's ward ? — Edith, the
    judge's niece ? "

"Father, I pray" — said Hugh. "O yes !" out-leapt
    the other's mood,
"I hear of your wanton loiterings ; they ill become
    your blood !
If you hold our name at such light worth, forbear to
    darken the life
Of this Alice Dale" — "No, Alice Van Ghelt ! fa-
    ther, she is my wife."

2.

Worldlings, who say the eagle should mate with eagle,
    after his kind,
Nor have learned from what far and diverse cliffs the
    twain each other find,
Yours is the old, old story, of age forgetting its wiser
    youth ;
Of eyes which are keen for others' good and blind to
    an inward truth.

But the pride which closed the father's doors swelled
    in the young man's veins,
And he led his bride, in the sight of all, through the
    pleasant Monmouth lanes,
To the little farm his grandsire gave, years since, for a
    birthday gift :

Unto such havens unforeseen the barks of our fortune
    drift !

There, for a happy pastoral year, he tilled the teeming
    field,

Scattered the marl above his land, and gathered **the**
    orchard's yield ;

And Alice, **in** fair and simple guise, kissed him at even-
    fall ;

And her face was to him an angel's face, **and love was**
    all in all.

— What is this light in the southern sky, painting a
    red alarm ?

What is this trumpet call, which **sounds through peace-**
    ful village and farm, —

Jarring the sweet idyllic rest, stilling **the children's**
    throng,

Ḥushing the cricket on the hearth, **and the lovers'**
    evening song ?

VII.

I.

W AR ! war ! war !

Manning **of** forts on land and ships for sea ;

Innumerous lips that speak the righteous wrath

Of days which have **been and** again may be ;

Flashing of tender eyes disdaining tears ;

A pause of men with indrawn breath,

Knowing **it** awful **for the people's will**

Thus, thus **to** end the **mellow years**

Of harvest, growth, prosperity,

And bring the years of famine, fire, and death,

Though fear and **a nation's** shame are more awful sti⊮.

2.

War ! war ! war !
A thundercloud in the South in the early Spring, —
The launch of a thunderbolt ; and then,
With one red flare, the lightning stretched its wing,
And a rolling echo roused a million men !
   Then the ploughman left his field ;
   The smith, at his clanging forge,
   Forged him a sword to wield.
   From meadow, and mountain-gorge,
   And the Western plains, they came,
   Fronting the storm and flame.
      War ! war ! war !
      Heaven aid the right !
God nerve the hero's arm in the fearful fight !
God send the women sleep, in the long, long night,
When the breasts on whose strength they leaned shall
         heave no more !

VIII.

1.

SPAKE each mother to her son,
   Ere an ancient field was won :
" Spartan, who me your mother call,
Our country is mother of us all ;
In her you breathe, and move, and are.
In peace, for her to live — in war,
For her to die — is, gloriously,
A patriot to live and die ! "

2.

The times are now as grand as then
With dauntless women, earnest men ;

For thus the mothers whom we know
Bade their sons to battle go ;
And, with a smile, the loyal **North**
Sent her million freemen **forth.**

3.

"**What men** should stronger-hearted be
Than **we, who** dwell by the open sea,
Tilling the lands our fathers won
In battle on the Monmouth Plains ?
Ah ! a memory remains,
Telling us what they have done,
Teaching us **what we should do.**
Let us send our rightful share, —
Hard-handed yeomen, horsemen **rare,**
A hundred riders fleet and true."

4.

A hundred horsemen, led by Hugh :
"Were he still here," their captain thought,
"The brave old man who trained my youth,
What a leader he would make
Where the battle's topmost billows **break !**
The crimes which brought our land to ruth,
How in his soul they would have wrought !
God help me, no deed of mine shall shame
The honor of my grandsire's **name ;**
And my father shall see how pure and good
Runs in these veins the olden blood."

5.

Shore and inland their men have sent :
Away, to the mounted regiment,

The silver-hazed Potomac heights,
The circling raids, the hundred fights,
The booth, the bivouac, the tent.
Away, from the happy Monmouth farms,
To noontide marches, night alarms,
Death in the shadowy oaken glades,
Emptied saddles, broken blades, —
All the turmoil that soldiers know
Who gallop to meet a mortal foe,
Some to conquer, some to fall :
War hath its chances for one and all.

6.

Heroes, who render up their lives
On the country's fiery altar-stone —
They do not offer themselves alone.
What shall become of the soldiers' wives ?
They stay behind in the lonely cots,
Weeding the humble garden-plots ;
Some to speed the needle and thread,
For the soldiers' children must be fed ;
All to sigh, through the toilsome day,
And at night teach lisping lips to pray
For the fathers marching far away.

IX.

1.

CLOUD and flame on the dark frontier,
  Veiling the hosts embattled there :
Peace, and a boding stillness, here,
Where the wives at home repeat their prayer.

H

2.

The weary August days are long ;
The locusts sing a plaintive song,
The cattle miss their master's call
When they see the sunset shadows fall.
The youthful mistress, at even-tide,
Stands by the cedarn wicket's side,
With both hands pushing from the front
Her hair, as those who listen are wont ;
Gazing toward the unknown South,
While silent whispers part her mouth :

3.

" O, if a woman could only find
Other work than to wait behind,
Through midnight dew and noonday drouth, —
To wait behind, and fear, and pray !
O, if a soldier's wife could say, —
' Where thou goest, I will go ;
Kiss thee ere thou meet'st the foe ;
Where thou lodgest, worst or best,
Share and soothe thy broken rest ! '
— Alas, to stifle her pain, and wait,
This was ever a woman's fate !
But the lonely hours at least may be
Passed a little nearer thee,
And the city thou guardest with thy life
Thou 'lt guard more fondly for holding thy wife."

4.

Ah, tender heart of woman leal,
Supple as wax and strong as steel !
Thousands as faithful and as lone,
Following each some dearest one,

Found in those early months a home
Under the brightness of that dome
Whose argent arches for aye enfold
The hopes of a people in their hold, —
Irradiate, in the sight of all
Who guard the Capital's outer wall.
Lastly came one, amid the rest,
Whose form a sunburnt soldier prest,
As lovers embrace in respite lent
From unfulfilled imprisonment.
And Alice found a new content :
Dearer for perils that had been
Were short-lived meetings, far between ;
Better, for dangers yet to be,
The moments she still his face could see.
These, for the pure and loving wife,
Were the silver bars that marked her life,
That numbered the days melodiously ;
While, through all noble daring, Hugh
From a Captain to a Colonel grew,
And his praises sweetened every tongue
That reached her ear, — for old and young
Gave him the gallant leader's due.

X.

I.

FLIGHT of a meteor through the sky,
    Scattering firebrands, arrows, and death, —
A baleful year, that hurtled by
While ancient kingdoms held their breath.

2.

The Capital grew aghast with sights
Flashed from the lurid river-heights,
Full of the fearful things sent down,
By demons haunting the **middle air,**
Into the hot, beleaguered **town,** —
All woful sights and sounds, which seem
The fantasy of a sickly dream :
Crowded wickedness everywhere ;
Everywhere a stifled sense
Of the noonday-striding pestilence ;
Every church, from wall to wall,
A closely-mattressed hospital ;
And ah ! our bleeding heroes, brought
From smouldering fields so vainly fought,
Filling each place where a man could lie
To gasp a dying wish — and die ;
While the sombre sky, relentlessly,
Covered the town with a funeral-pall,
A death-damp, trickling funeral-pall.

3.

Always the dust and mire ; the sound
Of the rumbling wagon's **ceaseless** round,
The cannon jarring the trampled ground.
The sad, unvarying picture wrought
Upon the pitying woman's **heart**
Of Alice, the Colonel's wife, and **taught**
Her spirit to choose the better part. —
The labor of loving angels, sent
To men in their sore encompassment.
Daily her gentle steps were bent
Through **the** thin pathways which divide
The patient sufferers, side from side,

In dolorous wards, where Death and Life
Wage their silent, endless strife ;
And she gave to all her soothing words,
Sweet as the songs of homestead birds.
Sometimes that utterance musical
On the soldier's failing sense would fall
Seeming, almost, a prelude given
Of whispers that calm the air of Heaven ;
While her white hand, moistening his poor lips
With the draught which slakeless fever sips,
Pointed him to that fount above, —
River of water of life and love, —
Stream without price, of whose purity
Whoever thirsteth may freely buy.

4

How many — whom in their mortal pain
She tended — 't was given her to gain,
Through Him who died upon the rood,
For that divine beatitude,
Who of us all can ever know
Till the golden books their records show ?
But she saw their dying faces light,
And felt a rapture in the sight.
And many a sufferer's earthly life
Thanked for new strength the Colonel's wife ;
Many a soldier turned his head,
Watching her pass his narrow bed,
Or, haply, his feeble frame would raise,
As the dim lamp her form revealed ;
And, like the children in the field,
(For soldiers like little ones become, —
As simple in heart, as frolicsome,)
One and another breathed her name,
Blessing her as she went and came.

5.

So, through all actions pure and good,
Unknowing evil, shame, or fear,
She grew to perfect ladyhood, —
Unwittingly the mate and peer
Of the proudest of her husband's blood.

XI.

1.

LIKE an affluent, royal town, the summer camps
Of a hundred thousand men are stretched away.
At night, like multitudinous city lamps,
Their numberless watch-fires beacon, clear and still,
And a glory beams from the zenith lit
With lurid vapors that over its star-lights flit ;
But wreaths of opaline cloud o'erhang, by day,
The crystal-pointed tents, from hill to hill,
From vale to vale — until
The heavens on endless peaks their curtain lay.
A magical city ! spread to-night
On hills which slope within our sight :
To-morrow, as at the waving of a wand,
Tents, guidons, bannerols are moved afar, —
Rising elsewhere, as rises a morning-star,
Or the dream of Aladdin's palace in fairy-land.

2.

Camp after camp, like marble square on square ;
Street following street, with many a park between ;
Bright bayonet-sparkles in the tremulous air ;
Far-fading, purple smoke above their sheen ;

Green central fields with flags like flowers abloom;
And, all about, close-ordered, populous life:
But here no festering trade, no civic strife,
Only the blue-clad soldiers everywhere,
Waiting to-morrow's victory or doom, —
Men of the hour, to whom these pictures seem,
Like school-boy thoughts, half real, half a dream.

3.

Camps of the cavalry, apart,
Are pitched with nicest art
On hilly suburbs where old forests grow.
Here, by itself, one glimmers through the pines, —
One whose high-hearted chief we know:
A thousand men leap when his bugles blow;
A thousand horses curvet at his lines,
Pawing the turf; among them come and go
The jacketed troopers, changed by wind and rain,
Storm, raid, and skirmish, sunshine, midnight dew,
To bronzéd men who never ride in vain.

4.

In the great wall-tent at the head of the square,
The Colonel hangs his sword, and there
Huge logs burn high in front at the close of the day;
And the captains gather ere the long tattoo,
While the banded buglers play;
Then come the tales of home and the troopers' song.
Clear over the distant outposts float the notes,
And the lone vidette to catch them listens long;
And the officer of the guard, upon his round,
Pauses, to hear the sound
Of the chiming chorus poured from a score of throats:

5.

CAVALRY SONG.

Our good steeds snuff the evening air,
   Our pulses with their purpose tingle ;
The foeman's fires are twinkling there ;
   He leaps to hear our sabres jingle !
      HALT !
   Each carbine sends its whizzing ball :
   Now, cling ! clang ! forward all,
      Into the fight !

Dash on beneath the smoking dome,
   Through level lightnings gallop nearer !
One look to Heaven !   No thoughts of home :
   The guidons that we bear are dearer.
      CHARGE !
   Cling ! clang ! forward all !
   Heaven help those whose horses fall !
      Cut left and right !

They flee before our fierce attack !
   They fall, they spread in broken surges !
Now, comrades, bear our wounded back,
   And leave the foeman to his dirges.
      WHEEL !
   The bugles sound the swift recall :
   Cling ! clang ! backward all !
      Home, and good night !

"When April rains." Page 121.

XII.

1.

WHEN April rains and the great spring-tide
Cover the lowlands far and wide,
And eastern winds blow somewhat harsh
Over the salt and mildewed marsh,
Then the grasses take deeper root,
Sucking, athirst and resolute ;
And when the waters eddy away,
Flowing in trenches to Newark Bay,
The fibrous blades grow rank and tall,
And from their tops the reed-birds call.
Five miles in width the moor is spread ;
Two broad rivers its borders thread ;
The schooners which up their channels pass
Seem to be sailing in the grass,
Save as they rise with the moon-drawn sea,
Twice in the day, continuously.

2.

Gray with an inward struggle grown,
The brooding lawyer, Hermann Van Ghelt,
Lived at the mansion-house, alone ;
But a chilling cloud at his bosom felt,
Like the fog which crept, at morn and night,
Across the rivers in his sight,
And rising, left the moorland plain
Bare and spectral and cold again.
He saw the one tall hill, which stood
Huge with its quarry and gloaming wood,
And the creeping engines, as they hist

6

Through the dim reaches of the mist, —
Serpents, with ominous eyes aglow,
Thridding the grasses to and fro ;
And he thought how each dark, receding train
Carried its freight of joy and pain,
On toil's adventure and fortune's quest,
To the troubled city of unrest ;
And he knew that under the desolate pall
Of the bleak horizon, skirting all,
The burdened ocean heaved, and rolled
Its moaning surges manifold.

3.

Often at evening, gazing through
The eastward windows on such a view,
Its sense enwrapt him as with a shroud ;
Often at noon, in the city's crowd,
He saw, as 't were in a mystic glass,
Unbidden faces before him pass :
A soldier, with eyes unawed and mild
As the eyes of one who was his child ;
A woman's visage, like that which blest
A year of his better years the best ;
And the plea of a voice, remembered well,
Deep in his secret hearing fell.
And as week by week its records brought
Of heroes fallen as they fought,
There little by little awakenéd
In the lawyer's heart a shapeless dread,
A fear of the tidings which of all
On ear and spirit heaviest fall, —
Changeless sentence of mortal fate,
Freezing the marrow with — Too Late !

XIII.

1.

THUS, — when ended the morning tramp,
    And the regiment came back to camp,
And the Colonel, breathing hard with pain,
Was carried within the lines again, —
Thus a Color-Sergeant told
The story of that skirmish bold :

2.

" 'T was an hour past midnight, twelve hours ago, —
We were all asleep, you know,
Save the officer on his rounds,
And the guard-relief, — when sounds
The signal-gun ! once — twice —
Thrice ! and then, in a trice,
The long assembly-call rang sharp and clear,
Till ' Boots and Saddles ' made us scamper like mice.
No time to waste
In asking whether a fight was near ;
Over the horses went their traps in haste ;
Not ten minutes had past
Ere we stood in marching gear,
And the call of the roll was followed by orders fast :
' Prepare to mount ! '
' Mount ! ' — and the company ranks were made ;
Then in each rank, by fours, we took the count,
And the head of the column wheeled for the long parade.

3.

" There, on the beaten ground,
The regiment formed from right to left ;

Our Colonel, straight in his saddle, looked around,
Reining the stallion in, that felt the heft
Of his rider, and stamped his foot, and wanted to dance.
At last the order came :
'By twos : forward, march !' — and the same
From each officer in advance ;
And, as the rear-guard left the spot,
We broke into the even trot.

4.

" 'Trot, march !' — two by two,
In the dust and in the dew,
Roads and open meadows through.
Steadily we kept the tune
Underneath the stars and moon.
None, except the Colonel, knew
What our orders were to do ;
Whether on a forage-raid
We were tramping, boot and blade,
Or a close reconnoissance
Ere the army should advance ;
One thing certain, we were bound
Straight for Stuart's camping-ground.
Plunging into forest-shade,
Well we knew each glen and glade !
Sweet they smelled, the pine and oak,
And of home my comrade spoke.
Tramp, tramp, out again,
Sheer across the ragged plain,
Where the moonbeams glaze our steel
And the fresher air we feel.
Thus a triple league, and more,
Till behind us spreads the gray,
Pallid light of breaking day,

And on cloudy hills, before,
Rebel camp-fires smoke away.
Hard by yonder clump of pines
We should touch the rebel lines :
'Walk, march !' and, softly now,
Gain yon hillock's westward brow.

5.

"'Halt !' and 'Right into line !' — There on the ridge
In battle-order we let the horses breathe ;
The Colonel raised his glass and scanned the bridge,
The tents on the bank beyond, the stream beneath.
Just then the sun first broke from the redder east,
And their pickets saw five hundred of us, at least,
Stretched like a dark stockade against the sky ;
We heard their long-roll clamor loud and nigh :
In half a minute a rumbling battery whirled
To a mound in front, unlimbering with a will,
And a twelve-pound solid shot came right along,
Singing a devilish morning-song,
And touched my comrade's leg, and the poor boy
    curled
And dropt to the turf, holding his bridle still.
Well, we moved out of range, — were wheeling round,
I think, for the Colonel had taken his look at their
    ground,
(Thus he was ordered, it seems, and nothing more :
Hardly worth coming at midnight for !)
When, over the bridge, a troop of the enemy's horse
Dashed out upon our course,
Giving us hope of a tussle to warm our blood.
Then we cheered, to a man, that our early call
Had n't been sounded for nothing, after all ;
And halting, to wait their movements, the column stood.

6.

"Then into squadrons we saw their ranks enlarge,
And slow and steady they moved to the charge,
Shaking the ground as they came in carbine-range.
'Front into line! March! Halt! Front!'
Our Colonel cried; and in squadrons, to meet the brunt,
We too from the walk to the trot our paces change:
'Gallop, march!'—and, hot for the fray,
Pistols and sabres drawn, we canter away.

7.

" Twenty rods over the slippery clover
We galloped as gayly as lady and lover;
Held the reins lightly, our good weapons tightly,
Five solid squadrons all shining and sightly;
Not too fast, half the strength of our brave steeds to
        wasten,
Not too slow, for the warmth of their fire made us
        hasten,
As it came with a rattle and opened the battle,
Tumbling from saddles ten fellows of mettle.
So the distance grew shorter, their sabres shone broader;
Then the bugle's wild blare and the Colonel's loud
        order, —

" CHARGE!" and we sprang, while the far echo rang,
And their bullets, like bees, in our ears fiercely sang.
Forward we strode to pay what we owed,
Right at the head of their column we rode;
Together we dashed, and the air reeled and flashed;
Stirrups, sabres, and scabbards all shattered and crashed
As we cut in and out, right and left, all about,
Hand to hand, blow for blow, shot for shot, shout for
        shout,

Till the earth seemed to boil with the heat of our toil.
But in less than five minutes we felt them recoil,
Heard their shrill rally sound, and, like hares from the
      hound,
Each ran for himself: one and all fled the ground !
Then we goaded them up to their guns, where they
      cowered,
And the breeze cleared the field where the battle-cloud
      lowered.
Threescore of them lay, to teach them the way
Van Ghelt and his rangers their compliments pay.
But a plenty, I swear, of our saddles were bare ;
Friend and foe, horse and rider, lay sprawled every-
      where :
'T was hard hitting, you see, Sir, that gained us the
      day !

8.

" Yes, they too had their say before they fled,
And the loss of our Colonel is worse than all the rest.
One of their captains aimed at him, as he led
The foremost charge — I shot the rascal dead,
But the Colonel fell, with a bullet through his breast.
We lifted him from the mire, when the field was won,
And their captured colors shaded him from the sun
In the farmer's wagon we took for his homeward ride ;
But he never said a word, nor opened his eyes,
Till we reached the camp. 'In yon hospital tent he lies,
And his poor young wife will come to watch by his
      side.
The surgeon has n't found the bullet, as yet,
But he says it 's a mortal wound.   Where will you get
Another such man to lead us, if he dies ? "

XIV.

1.

SPRUNG was the bow at last;
    And the barbed and pointed dart,
Keen with stings of the past,
Barbed with a vain remorse,
Clove for itself a course
Straight to the father's heart;
And a lonely wanderer stood,
Mazed in a mist of thought,
On the edge of a field of blood.
— For a battle had been fought,
And the cavalry skirmish was but a wild prelude
To the broader carnage that heaped a field in vain:
A terrible battle had been fought,
Till its changeful current brought
Tumultuous, angry surges roaring back
To the lines where our army had lain.
The lawyer, driven hard by an inward pain,
Was crossing, in search of a dying son, the track
Where the deluge rose and fell, and its stranded wrack
Had sown the loathing earth with human slain.

2.

Friends and foes, — who could discover which,
As they marked the zigzag, outer ditch,
Or lay so cold and still in the bush,
Fallen and trampled down in the last wild rush?
Then the shattered forest-trees; the clearing there
Where a battery stood; dead horses, pawing the air
With horrible upright hoofs; a mangled mass
Of wounded and stifled men in the low morass;

And the long trench dug in haste for a burial-pit,
Whose yawning length and breadth all comers fit.

3.

And over the dreadful precinct, like the lights
That flit through graveyard walks in dismal nights,
Men with lanterns were groping among the dead,
Holding the flame to every hueless face,
And bearing those whose life had not wholly fled
On stretchers, that looked like biers, from the ghastly
    place.

4.

The air above seemed heavy with errant souls,
Dense with ghosts from those gory forms arisen, —
Each rudely driven from its prison,
'Mid the harsh jar of rattling musket-rolls,
And quivering throes, and unexpected force ;
In helpless waves adrift confusedly,
Freighting the sombre haze without resource.
Through all there trickled, from the pitying sky,
An infinite mist of tears upon the ground,
Muffling the groans of anguish with its sound.

5.

On the borders of such a land, on the bounds of Death,
The stranger, shuddering, moved as one who saith :
"God ! what a doleful clime, a drear domain !"
And onward, struggling with his pain,
Traversed the endless camp-fires, spark by spark,
Past sentinels that challenged from the dark,
Guided through camp and camp to one long tent
Whose ridge a flying bolt from the field had rent,
Letting the midnight mist, the battle din,
Fall on the hundred forms that writhed within.

6.

Beyond the gaunt Zouave at the nearest cot,
And the bugler shot in the arm, who lay beside
(Looking down at the wounded spot
Even then, for all the pain, with boyish pride),
And a score of men, with blankets opened wide,
Showing the gory bandages which bound
The paths of many a deadly wound,
— Over all these the stranger's glances sped
To one low stretcher, at whose head
A woman, bowed and brooding, sate,
As sit the angels of our fate,
Who, motionless, our births and deaths await.
He whom she tended moaned and tost,
Restless, as some laborious vessel, lost
Close to the port for which we saw it sail,
Groans in the long perpetual gale ;
But she, that watched the storm, forbore to weep.
Sometimes the stranger saw her move
To others, who also with their anguish strove ;
But ever again her constant footsteps turned
To one who made sad mutterings in his sleep ;
Ever she listened to his breathings deep,
Or trimmed the midnight lamp that feebly burned.

XV.

LEANING her face on her hand
   She sat by the side of Hugh,
Silently watching him breathe,
As a lily curves its grace
Over the broken form

Of the twin which stood by its side.
A glory upon her head
Trailed from the light above,
Gilding her tranquil hair.
There, as she sat in a trance,
Her soul flowed through the past,
As a river, day and night,
Passes through changeful shores, —
Sees, on the twofold bank,
Meadow and mossy grange,
Castles on hoary crags,
Forests, and fortressed towns,
And shrinks from the widening bay,
And the darkness which overhangs
The unknown, limitless sea.
Was it a troubled dream,
All that the stream of her life
Had mirrored along its course?
All — from that summer morn
When she seemed to meet in the field
One whom she vowed to love,
And with whom she wandered thence,
Leaving the home of her youth?
Were they visions indeed, —
The pillars of smoke and flame,
The sound of a hundred fights,
The grandeur, and ah ! the gloom,
The shadows which circled her now,
And the wraith of the one she loved
Gliding away from her grasp,
Vanishing swiftly and sure?
Yes, it was all a dream ;
And the strange, sad man, who moved
To the other side of the couch,

Bending over it long,
Pressing his hand on his heart,
And gazing, anon, in her eyes, —
He, with his scanty hair,
And pallid, repentant face,
He, too, was a voiceless dream,
A vision like all the rest ;
He with the rest would fade
When the day should dawn again,
When the spectral mist of night,
Fused with the golden morn,
Should melt in the eastern sky.

XVI.

I.

"**S**TEADY ! forward the squadron !" cries
The dying soldier, and strives amain
To rise from the pillow and his pain.
Wild and wandering are his eyes,
Painting once more, on **the empty air,**
The wrathful battle's wavering glare.
"Hugh !" said Alice, and checked her fear
"Speak to me, Hugh ; your father is here."
"Father ! what of my father ? he
Is anything but a father to me ;
What need I of a father, when
I have the hearts of a thousand men ?"
" — Alas, Sir, he knows not me nor you !"
And with caressing words, the twain —
The man with all remorsefulness,
The woman with loving tenderness —

Soothed the soldier to rest anew,
And, as the madness left his brain,
Silently watched his sleep again.

2.

And again the father and the wife,
Counting the precious sands of life,
Looked each askance, with those subtle eyes,
That probe through human mysteries
And hidden motives fathom well ;
But the mild regard of Alice fell,
Meeting the other's contrite glance,
On his meek and furrowed countenance,
Scathed, as it seemed, with troubled thought :
" Surely, good angels have with him wrought,"
She murmured, and halted, even across
The sorrowful threshold of her loss,
To pity his thin and changing hair,
And her heart forgave him, unaware.

3.

And he, — who saw how she still represt
A drear foreboding within her breast,
And, by her wifehood's nearest right,
Ever more closely through the night
Clave unto him whose quickened breath
Came like a waft from the realm of Death, —
He felt what a secret, powerful tie
Bound them in one, mysteriously.
He studied her features, as she stood
Lighting the shades of that woful place
With the presence of her womanhood,
And thought — as the dying son had thought
When her beauty first his vision caught —

"I never saw a fairer face;
I never heard a sweeter voice!"
And a sad remembrance travelled fast
Through all the labyrinth of the past,
Till he said, as the scales fell off at last,
"How could I blame him for his choice?"
Then he looked upon the sword, which lay
At the headboard, under the night-lamp's ray;
He saw the coat, the stains, the dust,
The gilded eagles worn with rust,
The swarthy forehead and matted hair
Of the strong, brave hero lying there;
And he felt how gently Hugh held command, —
The life how gallant, **the** death how grand;
And with trembling lips, and the words that choke,
And the tears which burn the cheek, he spoke:
"Where is the father who would not joy
In the manhood of such a noble boy?
This life, which had being through my own,
Was a better life than I have known;
O that its fairness should be earth,
Ere I could prize it at its worth!"
"Too late! too late!" — he made his moan —
"I find a daughter, and her alone.
He deemed you worthy to bear his name,
His spotless honor, his lasting fame:
I, who have wronged you, bid you live
To comfort the lonely — and forgive."

4.

Dim and silvery from the east
The infant light of another morn
Over the stirring camps was borne;
But the soldier's pulse had almost ceased,

And there crept upon his brow the change —
Ah, how sudden ! alas, how strange !
Yet again his eyelids opened wide,
And his glances moved to either side,
This time with a clear intelligence
Which took all objects in its sense,
A power to comprehend the whole
Of the scene that girded his passing soul.
The father, who saw it, slowly drew
Nearer to her that wept anew,
And gathered her tenderly in his hold, —
As mortals their precious things enfold,
Grasping them late and sure ; and Hugh
Gazed on the two a space, and smiled
With the look he wore when a little child, —
A smile of pride and peace, that meant
A free forgiveness, a full content ;
Then his clouding sight an instant clung
To the flag whose stars above him hung,
And his blunted senses seemed to hear
The long reveillée sounding near ;
But the ringing clarion could not vie
With the richer notes which filled his ear,
Nor the breaking morn with that brighter sky.

XVII.

1.

WEAR no armor, timid heart ;
    Fear no keen misfortune's dart,
Want, nor scorn, nor secret blow
Dealt thee by thy mortal foe.

2.

Let the Fates their weapons wield,
For a wondrous woven shield
Shall be given thee, erelong.
Mesh of gold were not so strong;
Not so soft were silken shred;
Not so fine the spider's thread
Barring the enchanted door
In that tale of ancient lore,
Guarding, silently and well,
All within the mystic cell.
Such a shield, where'er thou art,
Shall be thine, O wounded heart!
From the ills that compass thee
Thou behind it shalt be free;
Envy, slander, malice, all
Shall withdraw them from thy — Pall.

3.

Build no house with patient care,
Fair to view, and strong as fair;
Walled with noble deeds' renown;
Shining over field and town,
Seen from land and sea afar,
Proud in peace, secure in war.
For the moments never sleep,
Building thee a castle-keep, —
Proof alike 'gainst heat and cold,
Earthly sorrows manifold,
Sickness, failure of thine ends,
And the falling off of friends.
Treason, want, dishonor, wrong,
None of these shall harm thee long.

Every day a beam is made;
Hour by hour a stone is laid.
Back the cruellest shall fall
From the warder at the wall;
Foemen shall not dare to tread
On the ramparts o'er thy head;
Dark, triumphant flags shall wave
From the fastness of thy — Grave.

XVIII.

1.

THERE's an hour, at the fall of night, when the
 blissful souls
Of those who were dear in life seem close at hand;
There's a holy midnight hour, when we speak their
 names
In pauses between our songs on the trellised porch;
And we sing the hymns which they loved, and almost
 know
Their phantoms are somewhere with us, filling the
 gaps,
The sorrowful chasms left when they passed away;
And we seem, in the hush of our yearning voices, to
 hear
Their warm, familiar breathing somewhere near.

2.

At such an hour, — when again the autumn haze
Silvered the moors, and the new moon peered from the
 west
Over the blue Passaic, and the mansion shone

Clear and white on the ridge which skirts the stream, —
At the twilight hour a man and a woman sat
On the open porch, in the garb of those who mourn.
Father and daughter they seemed ; and with thoughtful
 eyes,
Silent, and full of the past, they watched the skies.

XIX.

SILENT they were, not sad; for the sod that covers
 the grave
Of those we have given to fame smells not of the hate-
 ful mould,
But of roses and fragrant ferns, while marvellous im-
 mortelles
Twine in glory above, and their graces give us joy.
Silent, but oh ! not sad : for the babe on the couch
 within
Drank at the mother's breast, till the current of life,
 outdrawn,
Opened inflowing currents of faith and sweet content ;
And the gray-haired man, repenting in tears the foolish
 past,
Had seen in the light from those inscrutable infant
 eyes,
Fresh from the unknown world, the glimpses which,
 long ago,
Gladdened his golden youth, and had found his soul at
 peace.

XX.

1.

LASTLY the moon went down ; like burnished steel
  The infinite ether wrapt the crispy air.
Then, arm in arm on the terrace-walk, the pair
Moved in that still communion where we feel
No need of audible questions and replies,
But mutual pulses all our thoughts reveal ;
And, as they turned to leave the outer night,
Far in the cloudless North a radiant sight
Stayed their steps for a while and held their eyes.

2.

There, through the icy mail of the boreal heaven,
Two-edged and burning swords by unseen hands
Were thrust, till a climbing throng its path had riven
Straight from the Pole, and, over seas and lands,
Pushed for the zenith, while from East to West
Flamed many a towering helm and gorgeous crest ;
And then, a rarer pageant than the rest,
An angrier light glared from the southern sky,
As if the austral trumpets made reply,
And the wrath of a challenged realm had swiftly tost
On the empyrean the flags of another host, —
Pennons with or and scarlet blazing high,
Crimson and orange banners proudly crost ;
While through the environed space, that lay between
Their adverse fronts, the ether seemed to tremble,
Shuddering to view such ruthless foes assemble,
And one by one the stars withdrew their sheen.

3.

The two, enrapt with such a vision, saw
Its ominous surges, dense, prismatic, vast,
Heaved from the round horizon ; and in awe,
Musing awhile, were silent. Till at last
The younger, fair in widow's garments, spoke :
"See, father, how, from either pole,
The deep, innumerous columns roll ;
As if the angelic tribes their concord broke,
And the fierce war that scathes our land had spread
Above, and the very skies with ire were red ! "

4.

Even as she spoke, there shone
High in the topmost zenith a central spark,
A luminous cloud that glowed against the dark ;
Its halo, widening toward either zone,
Took on the semblance of a mystic hand
Stretched from an unknown height ; and lo ! a band
Of scintillant jewels twined around the wrist,
Sapphire and ruby, opal, amethyst,
Turquoise, and diamond, linked with flashing joints.
Its wide and puissant reach began to clasp,
In countless folds, the interclashing points
Of outshot light, gathering their angry hues —
North, south, east, west — with noiseless grasp,
By some divine, resistless law,
Till everywhere the wondering watchers saw
A thousand colors blend and interfuse,
In aureate wave on wave ascending higher, —
Immeasurable, white, a spotless fire ;
And, glory circling glory there, behold
Gleams of the heavenly city walled with gold !

5.

" Daughter," the man replied, (his face was bright
With the effulgent reflex of that light,)
" The time shall come, by merciful Heaven willed,
When these celestial omens shall be fulfilled,
Our strife be closed and the nation purged of sin,
And a pure and holier union shall begin ;
And a jarring race be drawn, throughout the land,
Into new brotherhood by some strong hand ;
And the baneful glow and splendor of war shall fade
In the whiter light of love, that, from sea to sea,
Shall soften the rage of hosts in arms arrayed,
And melt into share and shaft each battle-blade,
And brighten the hopes of a people great and free.
But, in the story told of a nation's woes,
Of the sacrifices made for a century's fault,
The fames of fallen heroes shall ever shine,
Serene, and high, and crystalline as those
Fair stars, which reappear in yonder vault ;
In the country's heart their written names shall be,
Like that of a single one in mine and thine.

MISCELLANEOUS POEMS.

MISCELLANEOUS POEMS.

ALECTRYÔN.

GREAT Arês, whose tempestuous godhood found
   Delight in those thick-tangled solitudes
Of Hebrus, watered tracts of rugged Thrace, —
Great Arês, scouring the Odrysian wilds,
There met Alectryôn, a Thracian boy,
Stalwart beyond his years, and swift of foot
To hunt from morn till eve the white-toothed boar.
"What hero," said the war-God, "joined his blood
With that of Hæmian nymph, to make thy form
So fair, thy soul so daring, and thy thews
So lusty for the contest on the plains
Wherein the fleet Odrysæ tame their steeds?"

From that time forth the twain together chased
The boar, or made their coursers cleave the breadth
Of yellow Hebrus, and, through vales beyond,
Drove the hot leopard foaming to his lair.
And day by day Alectryôn dearer grew

To the God's restless spirit, till from Thrace
He bore him, even to Olympos; there
Before him set immortal food and wine,
That fairer youth and lustier strength might serve
His henchman ; bade him bear his arms, and cleanse
The crimsoned burnish of his brazen car :
So dwelt the Thracian youth among the Gods.

There came a day when Arês left at rest
His spear, and smoothed his harmful, unhelmed brow,
Calling Alectryôn to his side, and said :
" The shadow of Olympos longer falls
Through misty valleys of the lower world ;
The Earth shall be at peace a summer's night ;
Men shall have calm, and the unconquered host
Peopling the walls of Troas, and the tribes
Of Greece, shall sleep sweet sleep upon their arms ;
For Aphroditê, queen of light and love,
Awaits me, blooming in the House of Fire,
Girt with the cestus, infinite in grace,
Dearer than battle and the joy of war :
She, for whose charms I would renounce the sword
Forever, even godhood, would she wreathe
My brows with myrtle, dwelling far from Heaven.
Hêphæstos, the lame cuckold, unto whose
Misshapen squalor Zeus hath given my queen,
To-night seeks Lemnos, and his sooty vault
Roofed by the roaring surge ; wherein, betimes,
He and his Cyclops pound the ringing iron,
Forging great bolts for Zeus, and welding mail,
White-hot, in shapes for Heroes and the Gods.
Do thou, Alectryôn, faithful to my trust,
Hie with me to the mystic House of Fire.
Therein, with wine and fruitage of her isle,

Sweet odors, and all rarest sights and sounds,
My Paphian mistress shall regale us twain.
But when the feast is over, and thou seest
Arês and Aphroditê pass beyond
The portals of that chamber whence all winds
Of love flow ever toward the fourfold Earth,
Watch by the entrance, sleepless, while we sleep ;
And warn us ere the glimpses of the Dawn ;
Lest Hêlios, the spy, may peer within
Our windows, and to Lemnos speed apace,
In envy clamoring to the hobbling smith,
Hêphæstos, of the wrong I do his bed."

Thus Arês ; and the Thracian boy, well pleased,
Swore to be faithful to his trust, and liege
To her, the perfect queen of light and love.
So saying, they reached the fiery, brazen gates,
Encolumned high by Heaven's artisan,
Hêphæstos, rough, begrimed, and halt of foot, —
Yet unto whom was Aphroditê given
By Zeus, because from his misshapen hands
All shapely things found being ; but the gift
Brought him no joyance, nor made pure his fame,
Like those devices which he wrought himself,
Grim, patient, unbeloved.

There passed they in
At portals of the high, celestial House,
And on beyond the starry-golden court,
Through amorous hidden ways, and winding paths
Set round with splendors, to the spangled hall
Of secret audience for noble guests.
Here Charis labored, so Hêphæstos bade,
Moulding the room's adornments ; here she built

Low couches, framed in ivory, overlain
With skins of pard and panther, and the fleece
Of sheep which graze the low Hesperian isles ;
And in the midst a cedarn table spread,
Whereon the loves of all the elder Gods
Were wrought in gold and silver ; and the light
Of quenchless rubies sparkled over all.
Thus far came Arês and Alectryôn,
First leaving shield and falchion at the door,
That naught of violence should haunt that air
Serene, but laughter-loving peace, and joys
The meed of Gods, once given men to know.

Then, from her daïs in the utmost hall,
Shone toward them Aphroditê, not by firm,
Imperial footfalls, but in measureless
Procession, even as, wafted by her doves,
She kissed the faces of the yearning waves
From Cyprus to the high Thessalian mount,
Claiming her throne in Heaven ; so light she stept,
Untended by her Graces ; only he,
Erôs, th' eternal child, with welcomings
Sprang forward to Arês, like a beam of light
Flashed from a coming brightness, ere it comes ;
And the ambrosial mother to his glee
Joined her own joy, coy as she glided near
Arês, till Arês closed her in his arms
An instant, with the perfect love of Gods.
And the wide chamber gleamed with their delight,
And infinite tinkling laughters rippled through
Far halls, wherefrom no boding echoes came.

But when the passion of their meeting fell
To dalliance, the mighty lovers, sunk

Within those ivory couches golden-fleeced,
Made wassail at the wondrous board, and held
Sweet stolen converse till the middle night.
And soulless servitors came gliding in,
Handmaidens, wrought of gold, the marvellous work
Of lame Hêphæstos ; having neither will,
Nor voice, yet bearing on their golden trays
Lush fruits and Cyprian wine, and, intermixt,
Olympian food and nectar, earth with heaven.
These Erôs and Alectryôn took therefrom,
And placed before the lovers ; and, meanwhile,
Melodious breathings from unfingered lutes.
Warblings from unseen nightingales, and songs
From lips uncrimsoned, scattered music round.
So fled the light-shod moments, hour by hour,
While the grim husband clanged upon his forge
In lurid caverns of the distant isle,
Unboding, and unheeded in his home,
Save with a scornful jest.   Till now the crown
Of Artemis shone at her topmost height :
Then rose the impassioned lovers, with rapt eyes
Fixed each on each, and passed beyond the hall,
Through curtains of that chamber whence all winds
Of love flow ever toward the fourfold Earth ;
At whose dim vestibule Alectryôn
Disposed him, mindful of his master's word ;
But Erôs, heavy-eyed, long since had slept,
Deep-muffled in the softness of his plumes.
And all was silence in the House of Fire.

Only Alectryôn, through brazen bars,
Watched the blue East for Eôs, she whose torch
Should warn him of the coming of the Sun.
Even thus he kept his vigils ; but, ere half

Her silvery downward path the Huntress knew,
His senses by that rich immortal food
Grew numbed with languor.   Then the shadowy hall's
Deep columns glimmered, interblent with dreams, —
Thick forests, running waters, darkling caves
Of Thrace ; and half in thought he grasped the bow ;
Hunted once more within his native wilds,
Cheering the hounds ; until before his eyes
The drapery of all nearer pictures fell,
And his limbs drooped.   Whereat the imp of Sleep,
Hypnos, who hid him at the outer gate,
Slid in with silken-sandalled feet, and laid
A subtle finger on his lids.   And so,
Crouched at the warder-post, Alectryôn slept.

   Meanwhile the God and Goddess, recking nought
Of evil, trusting to the faithful boy,
Sank satiate in the calm of trancéd rest.
And past the sleeping warder, deep within
The portals of that chamber whence all winds
Of love flow ever toward the fourfold Earth,
Hypnos kept on, walking, yet half afloat
In the sweet air ; and fluttering with cool wings
Above their couch fanned the reposeful pair
To slumber.   Thus, a careless twilight hour,
Unknowing Eôs and her torch, they slept.

   Ill-fated rest !   Awake, ye fleet-winged Loves,
Your mistress !   Eôs, rouse the sleeping God,
And warn him of the coming of the Day !
Alectryôn, wake !   In vain : Eôs swept by,
Radiant, a blushing finger on her lips.
In vain !   Close on her flight, from furthest East,
The peering Hélios drove his lambent car,

Casting the tell-tale beams on earth and sky,
Until Olympos laughed within his light,
And all the House of Fire grew roofed with gold ;
And through its brazen windows Hêlios gazed
Upon the sleeping lovers : thence away
To Lemnos flashed, across the rearward sea,
A messenger, from whom the vengeful smith,
Hêphæstos, learned the story of his wrongs ;
Whence afterward rude scandal spread through Heaven.

But they, the lovers, startled from sweet sleep
By garish Day, stood timorous and mute,
Even as a regal pair, the hart and hind,
When first the keynote of the clarion horn
Pierces their covert, and the deep-mouthed hound
Bays, following on the trail ; then, with small pause
For amorous partings, sped in diverse ways.
She, Aphroditê, clothed in pearly cloud,
Dropt from Olympos to the eastern shore ;
Thence floated, half in shame, half laughter-pleased,
Southward across the blue Ægæan sea,
That had a thousand little dimpling smiles
At her discomfort, and a thousand eyes
To shoot irreverent glances.   But her conch
Passed the Eubœan coasts, and softly on
By rugged Dêlos, and the gentler slope
Of Naxos, to Icarian waves serene ;
Thence sailed betwixt fair Rhodos, on the left,
And windy Carpathos, until it touched
Cyprus ; and soon the conscious Goddess found
Her bower in the hollow of the isle ;
And wondering nymphs in their white arms received
Their white-armed mistress, bathing her fair limbs
In fragrant dews, twining her lucent hair

With roses, and with kisses soothing her ;
Till, glowing in fresh **loveliness, she** sank
To stillness, tended in the sacred isle,
And hid herself awhile from all her peers.

But angry Arês faced the treacherous Morn,
Spurning the palace tower ; nor looked behind,
Disdainful of himself and secret joys
That stript him **to the laughter** of the **Gods.**
Toward the **East he made, and** overhung
The broad Thermaic gulf ; then, shunning well
The crags **of** Lemnos, by **Mount** Athôs stayed
A moment, mute ; thence hurtled **sheer away,**
Across the murmuring **Northern sea, whose waves**
Are swollen in billows ruffled with the cuffs
Of endless winds ; so reached the shores of Thrace,
And spleen pursued him **in** the tangled wilds.

Hither at eventide remorseful came
Alectryôn ; but the indignant God,
With harsh revilings, changed him to the Cock,
That evermore, remembering his fault,
Heralds with warning voice the coming Day.

THE TEST.

SEVEN women loved **him.** When the wrinkled pall
    Enwrapt him from their unfulfilled desire
(Death, pale, triumphant rival, conquering all,)

They came, for that last look, around his pyre.
   One strewed white roses, on whose leaves were
      hung
Her tears, like dew ; and in discreet attire

Warbled her tuneful sorrow. Next among
   The group, a fair-haired virgin moved serenely,
Whose saintly heart no vain repinings wrung,

Reached the calm dust, and there, composed and
      queenly,
   Gazed, but the missal trembled in her hand :
"That's with the past," she said, " nor may I meanly

Give way to tears !" and passed into the land.
   The third hung feebly on the portals, moaning,
With whitened lips, and feet that stood in sand,

So weak they seemed, — and all her passion owning.
   The fourth, a ripe, luxurious maiden, came,
Half for such homage to the dead atoning

By smiles on one who fanned a later flame
   In her slight soul, her fickle steps attended.
The fifth and sixth were sisters ; at the same

Wild moment both above the image bended,
   And with immortal hatred each on each
Glared, and therewith her exultation blended,

To know the dead had 'scaped the other's reach !
   Meanwhile, through all the words of anguish spoken,
One lowly form had given no sound of speech,

     7 *

Through all the signs of woe, no sign nor token ;
  But when they came to bear him to his rest,
They found her beauty paled, — her heart was broken :

And in the Silent Land his shade confest
That she, of all the seven, loved him best.

THE OLD LOVE AND THE NEW.

ONCE more on the fallow hillside, as of old, I lie
    at rest
For an hour, while the sunshine trembles through the
    walnut-tree to the west, —
Shakes on the rocks and fragrant ferns, and the berry-
    bushes around ;
And I watch, as of old, the cattle graze in the lower
    pasture-ground.

Of the Saxon months of blossom, when the merle and
    mavis sing,
And a dust of gold falls everywhere from the soft mid-
    summer's wing,
I only know from my poets, or from pictures that hither
    come,
Sweet with the smile of the hawthorn-hedge and the
    scent of the harvest-home.

But July in our own New England — I bask myself in
    its prime,
As one in the light of a face he loves, and has not seen
    for a time !

"Once more on the fallow hillside." Page 154.

Again the perfect blue of the sky; the fresh green
    woods; the call
Of the crested jay; the tangled vines that cover the
    frost-thrown wall:

Sounds and shadows remembered well! the ground-
    bee's droning hum;
The distant musical tree-tops; the locust beating his
    drum;
And the ripened July warmth, that seems akin to a fire
    which stole,
Long summers since, through the thews of youth, to
    soften and harden my soul.

Here it was that I loved her — as only a stripling can,
Who doats on a girl that others know no mate for the
    future man;
It was well, perhaps, that at last my pride and honor
    outgrew her art,
That there came an hour, when from broken chains I
    fled — with a broken heart.

'T was well: but the fire would still flash up in sharp,
    heat-lightning gleams,
And ever at night the false, fair face shone into passion-
    ate dreams;
The false, fair form, through many a year, was some-
    where close at my side,
And crept, as by right, to my very arms and the place
    of my patient bride.

Bride and vision have passed away, and I am again
    alone;
Changed by years; not wiser, I think, but only differ-
    ent grown:

Not so much nearer wisdom is a man than a boy, forsooth,
Though, in scorn of what has come and gone, he hates
  the ways of his youth.

In seven years, I have heard it said, a soul shall change
  its frame ;
Atom for atom, the man shall be the same, yet not the
  same ;
The last of the ancient ichor shall pass away from his
  veins,
And a new-born light shall fill the eyes whose earlier
  lustre wanes.

In seven years, it is written, a man shall shift his
  mood ;
Good shall seem what was evil, and evil the thing that
  was good :
Ye that welcome the coming and speed the parting
  guest,
Tell me, O winds of summer ! am I not half-confest ?

For along the tide of this mellow month new fancies
  guide my helm,
Another form has entered my heart as rightful queen
  of the realm ;
From under their long black lashes new eyes — half-
  blue, half-gray —
Pierce through my soul, to drive the ghost of the old love
  quite away.

Shadow of years ! at last it sinks in the sepulchre of
  the past, —
A gentle image and fair to see ; but was my passion so
  vast ?

" For you," I said, " be you. false or true, are ever life
    of my life ! "
Was it myself or another who spoke, and asked her to
    be his wife ?

For here, on the dear old hillside, I lie at rest again,
And think with a quiet self-content of all the passion
    and pain,
Of the strong resolve and the after-strife ; but the vistas
    round me seem
So little changed that I hardly know if the past is not
    a dream.

Can I have sailed, for seven years, far out in the open
    world ;
Have tacked and drifted here and there, by eddying
    currents whirled ;
Have gained and lost, and found again ; and now, for a
    respite, come
Once more to the happy scenes of old, and the haven I
    voyaged from ?

Blended, infinite murmurs of True Love's earliest song,
Where are you slumbering out of the heart that gave
    you echoes so long ?
But chords that have ceased to vibrate the swell of an
    ancient strain
May thrill with a soulful music when rightly touched
    again.

Rock and forest and meadow, — landscape perfect and
    true !
O, if ourselves were tender and all unchangeful as
    you,

I should not now be dreaming of seven years that have
        been,
Nor bidding old love good by forever, and letting the
        new love in !

ESTELLE.

"How came he mad?" — HAMLET.

OF all the beautiful demons who fasten on human
        hearts
To fetter the bodies and souls of men with exquisite,
        mocking arts,
The cruellest, and subtlest, and fairest to mortal sight,
Is surely a woman called Estelle, who tortures me day
        and night.

The first time that I saw her she passed with sweet lips
        mute,
As if in scorn of the vacant praise of those who made
        her suit ;
A hundred lustres flashed and shone as she rustled
        through the crowd,
And a passion seized me for her there, — so passionless
        and proud.

The second time that I saw her she met me face to
        face ;
Her bending beauty answered my bow in a tremulous
        moment's space ;
With an upward glance that instantly fell she read me
        through and through,
And found in me something worth her while to idle
        with and subdue ;

Something, I know not what : perhaps the spirit of
    eager youth,
That named her a queen of queens at once, and loved
    her in very truth ;
That threw its pearl of pearls at her feet, and offered
    her, in a breath,
The costliest gift a man can give from his cradle to his
    death.

The third time that I saw her — this woman called
    Estelle —
She passed her milk-white arm through mine and daz-
    zled me with her spell ;
A blissful fever thrilled my veins, and there, in the
    moon-beams white,
I yielded my soul to the fierce control of that madden-
    ing delight !

And at many a trysting afterwards she wove my heart-
    strings round
Her delicate fingers, twisting them, and chanting low
    as she wound ;
The rune she sang rang sweet and clear like the chime
    of a witch's bell ;
Its echo haunts me even now, with the word, Estelle !
    Estelle !

Ah, then, as a dozen before me had, I lay at last at her
    feet,
And she turned me off with a calm surprise when her
    triumph was all complete :
It made me wild, the stroke which smiled so pitiless
    out of her eyes,
Like lightning fallen, in clear noonday, from cloudless
    and bluest skies !

The whirlwind followed upon my brain and beat my
    thoughts to **rack** :
Who knows the many a month I lay ere memory floated
    back ?
Even now, I tell you, I wonder whether this woman
    called Estelle
Is flesh and blood, or a beautiful lie, **sent up from the**
    depths of hell.

For at night she stands where the pallid moon streams
    into **this** grated cell,
And only gives me that mocking glance when I speak
    her name — *Estelle !*
With the old **resistless** longing often I strive to clasp
    her there,
But she vanishes from my open arms **and hides I know**
    not where.

And I hold that if she were **human** she could not fly
    like the wind,
But her heart would flutter against my own, **in spite**
    of her scornful mind :
Yet, oh ! she is not a phantom, since devils are not so
    bad
As to haunt and torture a man long after their tricks
    have made him mad !

EDGED TOOLS.

WELL, Helen, quite two years have flown
    Since that enchanted, dreamy night,
When **you** and I were left alone,
    And wondered whether they were right

Who said that each the other loved;
  And thus debating, yes and no,
And half in earnest, as it proved,
  We bargained to pretend 't was so.

Two sceptic children of the world,
  Each with a heart engraven o'er
With broken love-knots, quaintly curled,
  Of hot flirtations held before; .
Yet, somehow, either seemed to find,
  This time, a something more akin
To that young, natural love, — the kind
  Which comes but once, and breaks us in.

What sweetly stolen hours we knew,
  And frolics perilous as gay!
Though lit in sport, Love's taper grew
  More bright and burning day by day.
We knew each heart was only lent,
  The other's ancient scars to heal:
The very thought a pathos blent
  With all the mirth we tried to feel.

How bravely, when the time to part
  Came with the wanton season's close,
Though nature with our mutual art
  Had mingled more than either chose,
We smothered Love, upon the verge
  Of folly, in one last embrace,
And buried him without a dirge,
  And turned, and left his resting-place.

Yet often (tell me what it means!)
  His spirit steals upon me here,

K

Far, far away from all the scenes
　　His little lifetime held so dear;
He comes: I hear a mystic strain
　　In which some tender memory lies;
I dally with your hair again;
　　I catch the gleam of violet eyes.

Ah, Helen! how have matters been
　　Since those rude obsequies, with you?
Say, is my partner in the sin
　　A sharer of the penance too?
Again the vision 's at my side:
　　I drop my head upon my breast,
And wonder if he really died,
　　And why his spirit will not rest.

THE SWALLOW.

HAD I, my love declared, the tireless wing
　　That wafts the swallow to her northern skies,
I would not, sheer within the rich surprise
Of full-blown Summer, like the swallow, fling
My coyer being; but would follow Spring,
Melodious consort, as she daily flies,
Apace with suns, that o'er new woodlands rise
Each morn — with rains her gentler stages bring.
My pinions should beat music with her own;
Her smiles and odors should delight me ever,
Gliding, with measured progress, from the zone
Where golden seas receive the mighty river,
Unto yon lichened cliffs, whose ridges sever
Our Norseland from the arctic surge's moan.

REFUGE IN NATURE.

WHEN the rude world's relentless war has pressed
    Fiercely upon them, and the hot campaign
Closes with battles lost, some yield their lives,
Or linger in the ruins of the fight —
Unwise, and comprehending not their fate,
Nor gathering that affluent recompense
Which the all-pitying Earth has yet in store.
Surely such men have never known the love
Of Nature ; nor had recourse to her fount
Of calm delights, whose influences heal
The wounded spirits of her vanquished sons ;
Nor ever — in those fruitful earlier days,
Wherein her manifest forms do most enrich
Our senses void of subtler cognizance —
Wandered in summer fields, climbed the free hills,
Pursued the murmuring music of her streams,
And found the borders of her sounding sea.

    But thou — when, in the multitudinous lists
Of traffic, all thine own is forfeited
At some wild hazard, or by weakening drains
Poured from thee ; or when, striving for the meed
Of place, thou failest, and the lesser man
By each ignoble method wins thy due ;
When the injustice of the social world
Environs thee ; when ruthless public scorn,
Black slander, and the meannesses of friends
Have made the bustling practice of the world
To thee a discord and a mockery ;
Or even if that last extremest pang

Be thine, and, added to such other woes,
The loss of that forever faithful love
Which else had balanced all : the putting out,
Untimely, of the light in dearest eyes ; —
At such a time thou well may'st count the days
Evil, and for a season quit the field ;
Yet not surrendering all human hopes,
Nor the rich physical life which still remains
God's boon and thy sustainer.   It were base
To join alliance with the hosts of Fate
Against thyself, crowning their victory
By loose despair, or seeking rest in death.

More wise, betake thee to those sylvan haunts
Thou knewest when young, and, once again a child,
Let their perennial loveliness renew
Thy natural faith and childhood's heart serene.
Forgetting all the toilsome pilgrimage,
Awake from strife and shame, as from a dream
Dreamed by a boy, when under waving trees
He sleeps and dreams a languid afternoon.
Once more from these harmonious beauties gain
Repose and ransom, and a power to feel
The immortal gladness of inanimate things.

There is the mighty Mother, ever young
And garlanded, and welcoming her sons.
There are her thousand charms to soothe thy pain,
And merge thy little, individual woe
In the broad health and happy fruitfulness
Of all that smiles around thee.   For thy sake
The woven arches of her forests breathe
Perpetual anthems, and the blue skies smile
Between, to heal thee with their infinite hope.

There are her crystal waters : lave thy brows,
Hot with long turmoil, in their purity ;
Wash off the battle-dust from those poor limbs
Blood-stained and weary.   Holy sleep shall come
Upon thee ; waking, thou shalt find in bloom
The lilies, fresh as in the olden days ;
And once again, when Night unveils her stars,
Thou shalt have sight of their high radiance,
And feel the old, mysterious awe subdue
The phantoms of thy pain.

                       And from that height
A voice shall whisper of the faith, through which
A man may act his part until the end.
Anon thy ancient yearning for the fight
May come once more, tempered by poise of chance,
And guided well with all experience.
Invisible hands may gird thy armor on,
And Nature put new weapons in thy hands,
Sending thee out to try the world again, —
Perchance to conquer, being cased in mail
Of double memories ; knowing smaller griefs
Can add no sorrow to the woful past ;
And that, howbeit thou mayest stand or fall,
Earth proffers men her refuge everywhere,
And Heaven's promise is for aye the same.

MONTAGU.

QUEEN Katherine of Arragon
    In gray Kimbolton dwelt,
A joyous bride, ere bluff King Hal
    At Bullen's footstool knelt.

Still in her haughty Spanish eyes
    Their childhood's lustre shone,
That lit with love two royal hearts,
    And won the English throne.

From gray Kimbolton's castle-gate
    She rode, each summer's day,
And blithely led the greenwood chase
    With hawk and hound away.

And ever handsome Montagu,
    Her Master of the Horse,
To guard his mistress kept her pace
    O'er heather, turf, and gorse.

O, who so brave as Montagu
    To leap the hedges clear !
And who so fleet as he to find
    The coverts of the deer !

And who so wild as Montagu,
    To seek his sovereign's love !
More hopeless than a child, who craves
.   The brightest star above.

Day after day her presence fed
    The fever at his heart ;
Yet loyally the young knight scorned
    To play a traitor's part.

Only, when at her palfrey's side
    He bowed him by command,
Lightening her footfall to the earth,
    He pressed her dainty hand ;

A tender touch, as light as love,
    Soft as his heart's desire;
But aye, in Katherine's artless blood,
    It woke no answering fire.

King Hal to gray Kimbolton came
    Erelong, and true love's sign,
Unused in colder Arragon,
    She prayed him to divine:

"Canst tell me, Sire," she said, "what mean
    The gentry of your land,
When softly, thus, and thus, they take
    And press a lady's hand?"

"Ha! ha!" laughed Hal, "but tell me, Chick,
    Each answering in course,
Do any press your hand?" "O yes,
    My Master of the Horse."

Off to the wars her gallant went,
    And pushed the foremost dikes,
And gashed his fair young form against
    A score of Flemish pikes.

Heart's blood ebbed fast; but Montagu,
    Dipping a finger, wove
These red words in his shield: "Dear Queen,
    I perish of your love!"

Kimbolton, after many a year,
    Again met Katherine's view:
The banished wife, with half a sigh,
    Remembered Montagu.

WILD WINDS WHISTLE.

1.

S IR ULRIC a Southern dame has **wed**;
  Wild winds whistle and snow is come;
He has brought her home to his bower **and bed.**
  Hither and thither the birds fly home.

Her hair is darker than thick of night;
  Wild winds whistle, &c.
Her hands are fair, **and her step is light.**
  Hither and thither, &c.

From out his castel in the North
Sir Ulric to hunt rode lightly forth.

Three things he left her for good or ill,—
A bonny bird that should sing **at will,**

With carol sweeter than silver bell,
Day and night in the old castel;

A lithe little page to gather flowers;
And a crystal dial to mark the hours.

2.

Lady Margaret watched Sir **U**lric speed
Away to the chase on his faithful steed.

From morning till night, the first day long,
She sat and listened the bonny bird's song.

The second day long, with fingers fair,
She curled and combed her page's hair.

The third day's sun rose up on high ;
By the dial she was seated nigh :

She loathed the bird and the page's face,
And counted the shadow's creeping **pace.**

3.

The strange knight drew his bridle-rein ;
He looked at the sky and he looked at the plain.

"O lady!" he said, "'t was a sin and **shame**
To leave for the chase so fair a dame.

"O lady!" he said, "we two will flee
To the blithesome land of Italie ;

"There the orange grows, and the fruitful vine,
And a bower of myrtle shall be thine."

He has taken her hand and kissed her mouth :
Now Ho! sing Ho! for the sunny South.

He has kissed her mouth and clasped her waist :
Now, good gray steed, make haste, make haste !

4.

Sir Ulric back from the chase has come,
And sounds the horn at his castel-home.

Or ever he drew his bridle-rein,
He saw the dial split in twain ;

8

The bonny blithe bird was stark and dead,
And the lithe little page hung down his head.

The lithe little page hung down his head ;
  Wild winds whistle and snow is come;
"O where, Sir Page, has my lady fled ?"
  Hither and thither the birds fly home.

PETER STUYVESANT'S NEW YEAR'S CALL.

I JAN. A. C. 1661.

WHERE nowadays the Battery lies,
    New York had just begun,
A new-born babe, to rub its eyes,
  In Sixteen Sixty-One.
They christened it Nieuw Amsterdam,
  Those burghers grave and stately,
And so, with schnapps and smoke and psalm,
  Lived out their lives sedately.

Two windmills topped their wooden wall,
  On Stadthuys gazing down,
On fort, and cabbage-plots, and all
  The quaintly gabled town ;
These flapped their wings and shifted backs,
  As ancient scrolls determine,
To scare the savage Hackensacks,
  Paumanks, and other vermin.

At night the loyal settlers lay
  Betwixt their feather-beds ;

In hose and breeches walked by day,
   And smoked, and wagged their heads.
No changeful fashions came from France,
   The freulen to bewilder,
And cost the burgher's purse, perchance,
   Its every other guilder.

In petticoats of linsey-red,
   And jackets neatly kept,
The vrouws their knitting-needles sped
   And deftly spun and swept.
Few modern-school flirtations there
   Set wheels of scandal trundling,
But youths and maidens did their share
   Of staid, old-fashioned bundling.

— The New Year opened clear and cold ;
   The snow, a Flemish ell
In depth, lay over Beeckman's Wold
   And Wolfert's frozen well.
Each burgher shook his kitchen-doors,
   Drew on his Holland leather,
Then stamped through drifts to do the chores,
   Beshrewing all such weather.

But — after herring, ham, and kraut —
   To all the gathered town
The Dominie preached the morning out,
   In Calvinistic gown ;
While tough old Peter Stuyvesant
   Sat pewed in foremost station, —
The potent, sage, and valiant
   Third Governor of the nation.

Prayer over, at his mansion hall,
　With cake and courtly smile
He met the people, one and all,
　In gubernatorial style ;
Yet missed, though now the day was old,
　An ancient fellow-feaster, —
Heer Govert Loockermans, that bold
　Brewer and burgomeester ;

Who, in his farm-house, close without
　The picket's eastern end,
Sat growling at the twinge of gout
　That kept **him** from **his** friend.
But Peter strapped his wooden peg,
　When tea and cake were ended
(Meanwhile **the sound** remaining **leg**
　Its high jack-boot defended),

A woolsey cloak about him **threw,**
　And swore, by wind and limb,
Since Govert kept from Peter's **view,**
　Peter would visit him ;
Then sallied forth, through snow **and blast,**
　While many a humble greeter
Stood wondering whereaway so fast
　Strode bluff Hardkoppig Pieter.

Past quay and cowpath, through a lane
　Of vats and mounded tans,
He puffed along, with might and **main,**
　To Govert Loockermans ;
Once there, his right of entry took,
　And hailed his ancient crony:
"Myn G6d ! in dese Manhattoes, **Loock,**
　Ve gets more snow as money ! "

To which, and after whiffs profound,
  With doubtful wink and nod,
There came at last responsive sound:
  " Yah, Peter ; yah, Myn Gód ! "
Then goedevrouw Marie sat her guest
  Beneath the chimney-gable,
And courtesied, bustling at her best
  To spread the New Year's table.

She brought the pure and genial schnapps,
  That years before had come —
In the " Nieuw Nederlandts," perhaps —
  To cheer the settlers' home ;
The long-stemmed pipes ; the fragrant roll
  Of pressed and crispy Spanish ;
Then placed the earthen mugs and bowl,
  Nor long delayed to vanish.

Thereat, with cheery nod and wink,
  And honors of the day,
The trader mixed the Governor's drink
  As evening sped away.
That ancient room ! I see it now :
  The carven nutwood dresser ;
The drawers, that many a burgher's vrouw
  Begrudged their rich possessor ;

The brace of high-backed leathern chairs,
  Brass-nailed at every seam ;
Six others, ranged in equal pairs ;
  The bacon hung abeam ;
The chimney-front, with porcelain shelft ;
  The hearty wooden fire ;
The picture, on the steaming delft,
  Of David and Goliah.

I see the two old Dutchmen sit
  Like Magog and his mate,
And hear them, when their pipes are lit,
  Discuss affairs of state :
The clique that would their sway demean ;
  The pestilent importation
Of wooden nutmegs, from the lean
  And losel Yankee nation.

But when the subtle juniper
  Assumed its sure command,
They drank the buxom loves that were, —
  They drank the Motherland ;
They drank the famous Swedish wars,
  Stout Peter's special glory,
While Govert proudly showed the scars
  Of Indian contests gory.

Erelong, the berry's power awoke
  Some music in their brains,
And, trumpet-like, through rolling smoke,
  Rang long-forgotten strains, —
Old Flemish snatches, full of blood,
  Of phantom ships and battle ;
And Peter, with his leg of wood,
  Made floor and casement rattle.

Then round and round the dresser pranced,
  The chairs began to wheel,
And on the board the punch-bowl danced
  A Netherlandish reel ;
Till midnight o'er the farm-house spread
  Her New-Year's skirts of sable,
And, inch by inch, each puzzled head
  Dropt down upon the table.

But still to Peter, as he dreamed,
   That table spread and turned;
The chimney-log blazed high, and seemed
   To circle as it burned;
The town into the vision grew
   From ending to beginning;
Fort, wall, and windmill met his view,
   All widening and spinning.

The cowpaths, leading to the docks,
   Grew broader, whirling past,
And checkered into shining blocks, —
   A city fair and vast;
Stores, churches, mansions, overspread
   The metamorphosed island,
While not a beaver showed his head
   From Swamp to Kalchook highland.

Eftsoons the picture passed away;
   Hours after, Peter woke
To see a spectral streak of day
   Gleam in through fading smoke;
Still slept old Govert, snoring on
   In most melodious numbers;
No dreams of Eighteen Sixty-One
   Commingled with his slumbers.

But Peter, from the farm-house door,
   Gazed doubtfully around,
Rejoiced to find himself once more
   On sure and solid ground.
The sky was somewhat dark ahead,
   Wind east, and morning lowery;
And on he pushed, a two-miles' tread,
   To breakfast at his Bouwery.

TRANSLATION.

8 *   L

TRANSLATION.

———◆———

JEAN PROUVAIRE'S SONG AT THE BARRICADE.

"While the men were making cartridges and the women lint; while a large frying-pan, full of melted pewter and lead, destined for the bullet-mould, was smoking over a burning furnace; while the videttes were watching the barricades with arms in their hands; while Enjolras, whom nothing could distract, was watching the videttes, — Combeferre, Courfeyrac, Jean Prouvaire, Feuilly Bossuet, Joly, Bahorel, a few others besides, sought each other and got together, as in the most peaceful days of their student-chats, and in a corner of this wine-shop changed into a casemate, within two steps of the redoubt which they had thrown up, their carbines, primed and loaded, resting on the backs of their chairs, these gallant young men, so near their last hour, began to sing love-rhymes. . . . . The hour, the place, these memories of youth recalled, the few stars which began to shine in the sky, the funereal repose of these deserted streets, the imminence of the inexorable event, gave a pathetic charm to these rhymes, murmured in a low tone in the twilight by Jean Prouvaire, who, as we have said, was a sweet poet." — *Les Misérables: Saint Denis,* Book XII. Chapter VI.

DO you remember our charming times,
    When we were both at the age which knows,
Of all the pleasures of Paris, none
    Like making love in one's Sunday clo'es;

When all your birthdays, added to mine,
    A total of forty would not bring,

And when, in our humble and cosey roost,
    All, even the Winter, to us was Spring?

Rare days! then prudish Manuel stalked,
    Paris feasted each saintsday in;
Foy thundered away; and — ah, your waist
    Pricked me well with a truant pin!

Every one ogled you. At Prado's,
    Where you and your briefless barrister dined,
You were so fair that the roses, I thought,
    Turned to look at you from behind.

They seemed to whisper: "How handsome she is!
    What wavy tresses! what sweet perfume!
Under her mantle she hides her wings;
    Her flower of a bonnet is just in bloom!"

I roamed with you, pressing your dainty arm,
    And the passers thought that Love, in play,
Had mated, in unison so sweet,
    The gallant April with gentle May.

We lived so coseyly, all by ourselves,
    On love, — that choice forbidden fruit, —
And never a word my lips could speak
    But your heart already had followed suit.

The Sarbonne was that bucolic place
    Where night till day my passion throve:
'T is thus that an ardent youngster makes
    The Student's Quarter a Realm of Love.

O Place Maubert! O Place Dauphine!
    Sky-parlor reaching heavenward far,

In whose depths, when you drew your stocking on,
  I saw a twinkling morning-star.

Hard-learned Plato I 've long forgot :
  Neither Malebranche nor Lamennais
Could teach me such faith in Providence
  As the flower which in your bosom lay.

You were my servant and I your slave :
  O golden attic ! O joy, to lace
Your corset ; to watch you showing, at morn,
  The ancient mirror your youthful face !

Ah ! who indeed could ever forget
  That sky and dawn commingling still ;
That ribbony, flowery, gauzy glory,
  And Love's sweet nonsense talked at will ?

Our garden a pot of tulips was ;
  Your petticoat curtained the window-pane ;
I took the earthen bowl of my pipe
  And gave you a cup of porcelain.

What huge disasters to make us fun !
  Your muff afire ; your tippet lost ;
And that cherished portrait of Shakespeare, sold,
  One hungry evening, at half its cost.

I was a beggar and you were kind :
  A kiss from your fair round arms I 'd steal,
While the folio-Dante we gayly spread
  With a hundred chestnuts, our frugal meal.

And oh ! when first my favored mouth
  A kiss to your burning lips had given,

You were dishevelled and all aglow ;
  I, pale with rapture, believed in Heaven.

Do you remember our countless joys,
  Those neckerchiefs rumpled every day?
Alas, what sighs from our boding hearts
  The infinite skies have borne away !

THE BLAMELESS PRINCE

AND OTHER POEMS.

1869.

Affectionately Enscribed

TO

RICHARD HENRY STODDARD.

THE BLAMELESS PRINCE.

PRELUDE.

POET, wherefore hither bring
Old romance, while others **sing**
  Sweeter idyls of to-day?
  Why not picture in your lay
Western woods and waters grand,
Clouds and skies of this fair land?
  Are there fairer far away?

I **have many** another song
Of those regions where belong,
  First of all, my heart and **home.**
  If for once my fancy roam,
Trust me, in the land I view
Falls the sunshine, falls the dew,
  And the Spring and Summer come.

Why from yonder stubble glean
Ancient names of King and Queen,
  Knightly men and maidens fair?
  Are there in our time no rare
Beauteous women, heroes brave?

Is there naught this side the grave
  Worth the dust you gather there?

Nay, but these were human too,
Strong or wayward, false or true.
    Art will seek through every clime
    For her picture or her rhyme;
Yes, nor looking far around,
But to-day I sought and found
    These who lived in that old time.

Why should we again be told
Dross will mingle with all gold?
    That which time nor test can stain
    Was not smelted quite in vain.
What of Albert's blameless heart,
Arthur's old heroic part,
    Saxon Alfred's glorious reign?

Yes, my Prince was such as they,
Part of gold, and part of clay,
    Though his metal shone as bright,
    And his dross was hid from sight.
He who brightest is, and best,
Still may fear the secret test
    That shall try his heart aright.

Let me, then, of what befell
Hearts that loved, my story tell.
    Turn the leaf that lies between
    You who listen and the scene!
Your pity for the Lady, since
She died of sorrow; spare my Prince;
    Love to the last my gentle Queen!

"The open sea bore commerce to her marts." Page 189.

THE BLAMELESS PRINCE.

L ONG since, there was a Princess of the blood,
 Sole heiress to the crown her father wore, —
Plucked from a dying stem, that one fair bud
 Put forth, and withered ere it others bore ;
And scarce the King her blossomed youth had seen,
When he, too, slept the sleep, and she was Queen.

Hers was a goodly realm, not stretched afar
 In desert wilds by wolf and savage scoured,
But locked in generous limits, strong in war,
 Serene in peace, with mountains walled and towered,
Fed by the tilth of many a fertile plain,
And veined with streams that proudly sought the main.

The open sea bore commerce to her marts,
 Tumbling half round her borders with its tide ;
Her vessels shot the surge ; all noble arts
 Of use and beauty in her towns were plied ;
Her court was regal ; lords and ladies lit
The palace with their graces and their wit.

Wise councillors devised each apt decree
 That gained the potent sanction of her hand ;
Great captains led her arms on shore and sea ;
 She was the darling of a loyal land ;
Poets sang her praises, and in hut and hall
Her excellence was the discourse of all.

Her pride was suited to her high estate,
 Her gentleness was equal with her youth,
Her wisdom in her goodness found its mate ;
 Her beauty was not that which brings to ruth
Men's lives, yet pure and luminous ; — and fair
Her locks, and over all a sovereign air.

Without, she bore herself as rulers should,
 Queenly in walk and gesture and attire ;
Within, she nursed her flower of maidenhood,
 Sweet girlish thoughts and virginal desire :
No woman's head so keen to work its will
But that the woman's heart is mistress still.

Three years she ruled a nation well content
 To have a maiden queen ; then came a day
When those on whom her councils chiefly leant
 Began to speak of marriage, and to pray
Their sovereign not to hold herself alone,
Nor trust the tenure of an heirless throne ;

And then the people took the cry, nor lack
 Was there of courtly suitors far or near, —
Kings, dukes, crown-princes, — swift upon the track,
 Like huntsmen closing round a royal deer.
These she regarded not, but still, among
Her maids and missals, to her freedom clung.

And with the rest there came a puissant king,
 Whose country pressed against her own domain, —
In strength its equal, but continuing
 Its dearest foe through many a martial reign.
He sued to join his hand and realm with hers,
And end these wars ; then all her ministers

Pleaded his suit ; but, asking yet for grace,
   And that her hand might wait upon her heart,
She halted, till the proud king turned his face
   Homeward ; and still the people, for their part,
Waited her choice, nor grudged her sex's share
Of coyness to a queen so young and fair.

There was a little State that nestled close
   Beside her boundaries, as wont to claim,
Though free, protection there from outer foes,
   A Principality — at least in name —
Whose ruler was her father's life-long friend
And firm ally, a statesman skilled to lend

Shrewd counsel, and who made, in days gone by,
   A visit to this court, and with him led
His son, a gentle Prince, of years anigh
   Her own, — twelve summers shone from either head ;
And while their elders moved from place to place, —
The field-review, the audience, the chase, —

The Princess and the Prince, together thrown,
   With their companions held a mimic court,
And with that sweet equality, the crown
   Of Childhood, — which discovers in its sport
No barriers of rank or wealth or power, —
He named himself her consort.   From that hour

The mindful Princess never quite forgot
   Those joyous days, nor him, the fair-haired Prince ;
And though she well had learned her greater lot,
   And haply from his thought had passed long since
Her girlish image, chance, that moves between
Two courts, had brought his portrait to the Queen.

This from her cabinet she took one morn,
   When they still urged the suit of that old king,
And said, half jesting, with a pretty scorn,
   " Why mate your wilful **Queen with** mouldering
And crabbed **Age ?   Now were he shaped like this,**
With such a face, he were not so amiss.

" Queens are but women ; 't is a sickly year
   That couples frost and thaw, our minstrels sing."—
" **Ho !"** thought the graybeards, " sets the wind so
      near ? "
   And thought again : " Why not ? the schemeful king
Perchance would rule us where he should be ruled ;
A humbler consort will be sooner schooled."

Forewarned are those whom Fortune's gifts await.
   Ere waned a moon the elder prince **had** learned —
From half the weathercocks which gilt the state,
   Spying the wind and shifting **where** it turned —
That for love's simple sake his **son** could gain
The world's chief prize, which kings had sought in vain.

How could he choose but clutch **it ?   Yet the son**
   Seemed worthy, for his parts were of that mould
Oft-failing Nature **strives** to join in **one,**
   And shape a hero, — pure and wise and bold :
In arts and arms the wonder **of** his peers,
The flower of princes, prince of cavaliers ;

Tall, lithe of form, and of **a** Northern mien,
   Gentle in speech and thought, — while thus he shone,
A rising star, though chosen of a queen,
   Why seek the skies less tranquil than his own ?
Why should he climb beside her perilous height,
And in that noonday blaze eclipse his light ?

Ah, why ? — one's own life may be bravely led,
  But not another's.   Yet, as to and fro
The buzzing private embassies were sped,
  And when the Queen's own pages, bowing low,
Told in his ear a sweet and secret story,
The Prince, long trained to seek his house's glory,

Let every gracious sentence seem a plume
  Of love and beckoning beauty for his helm.
So passed a season ; then the cannon's boom
  And belfry's peal delivered to the realm
The Queen's betrothal, and the councils met,
And for the nuptial rites a day was set.

NOW when the time grew ripe, the favored Prince
  Rides forth, and through the little towns that mourn
His loss, and past the boundaries ; and, since
  To ape the pomp to which he was not born
Seemed in his soul a foolish thing and vain,
A few near comrades, only, made his train.

Nor pressed the populace along the ways ;
  But — for he wished it so — unheralded
He rode from post to post through many days,
  Yet gained a greatness as the distance fled,
As some dim comet, drawing near its bound,
Takes lustre from the orb it courses round.

And league by league his fantasies outran
  His progress, brooding on his mistress' power,
Until his own estate the while began
  To seem of lesser worth each passing hour;
And with misdoubt this fortune weighed him down,
As though a splendid mantle had been thrown

About him, which he knew not well to wear,
  And might not forfeit.   Yet he spurred apace,
And reached a country-seat that bordered near
  The Capital.   Here, for a little space,
He was to rest from travel, and await
His day of entrance at the city's gate.

Upon these grounds a gray-haired noble dwelt,
  A ribboned courtier of the former reign;
A tedious proper man, who glibly knelt
  To royalty, — this ancient chamberlain, —
Yoked with a girlish wife, and, for the rest,
Proud of the charge that made a prince his guest.

The highway ran beside a greenwood keep
  That reached, herefrom, quite to the city's edge;
Across, the fields with golden corn were deep;
  The level sunset pierced the wayside hedge;
The banks were all abloom; a pheasant whirred
Far in the bush; anon, some tuneful bird

Broke into song, or, from a covert dark,
  A bounding deer its dappled haunches showed
As though it heard the stag-hound's distant bark.
  The wistful Prince with loitering purpose bode,
And thought how good it were to spend one's life
Far off from men, nor jostled with their strife.

Even as he mused he saw his host ahead,
 Speeding to welcome him, in lordly wont,
And all the household in a line bestead ;
 And lightly with that escort, at the front,
A peerless woman rode across the green ;
Then the Prince thought, " It surely is the Queen,

Who comes to meet me of her loving grace ! "
 And his blood mounted ; but he knew how fair
The royal locks, and, when she neared his place,
 He saw the lady's prodigal dark hair
And wondrous loveliness were wide apart
From the sweet, tranquil picture next his heart.

And when the chamberlain, with halted suit,
 Made reverence, and was answered courteous-wise,
The lady to her knightly guest's salute
 Turned her face full, so that he marked her eyes, —
How dewy gray beneath each long, black lid,
And danger somewhere in their light lay hid.

There are some natures housed so chaste within
 Their placid dwellings that their heads control
The tumult of their hearts ; and thus they win
 A quittance from this pleading of the soul
For Love, whose service does so wound and heal ;
How should they crave for what they cannot feel ?

From passion and from pain enfranchised quite,
 Alike from gain and never-stanched Regret,
Calm as the blind who have not seen the light,
 The dumb who hear no precious voice ; and yet
The sun forever pours his lambent fire
And the high winds are vocal with desire.

And there are those whose fervent souls are wed
   To glorious bodies, panoplied for love,
Born to hear sweetest words that can be said,
   To give and gather kisses, and to move
All men with longing after them, — to know
What flowers of paradise for lovers grow.

The Vestal, with her silvery content,
   The Lesbian, with the passion and the pain, —
Which creature hath their one Creator lent
   More light of heaven ?   Who would dare restrain
The beams of either ? who the radiance mar
Of the white planet or the burning star ?

If in its innocence a life is bound
   With cords that thrall its birthright and design,
Let those whose hands the evil meshes wound
   Pray that it cast no look beyond their line ;
That no strong voice too late may enter in
Its prison-range, to teach what might have been.

Was there no conscious spirit thus to plead
   For this bright lady, as the wondering guest
Closed with his welcomers, and each took heed
   Of each, and horse to horse they rode abreast,
Nearing a fair and spacious house that stood,
Half hidden, in the edges of the wood ?

And while, the last court-tidings running o'er,
   Their talk on this and that at random fell,
And the trains joined behind, the lady bore
   Her beauteous head askance, yet wist full well
How the Prince looked and spoke ; unwittingly,
With the strange female sense and secret eye,

Made of him there her subtile estimate,
  Forecast his lot, and thought how all things flow
To those who have a surfeit. Could the great,
  The perfect Queen, she marvelled, truly know
And love him at his value? In his turn,
He read her face as 't were a marble urn

Embossed with **Truth and blushful** Innocence,
  Yet with the wild Loves carven in repose;
And as he looked he felt, and knew not whence,
  A thought like this come as the wind that blows:
" A face to lose one's life for; ay, and more,
To live for ! " — So they reached the sculptured door

And casements gilded with the dying light.
  That eve the host spread **out a stately board,**
And with his household far into the night
  Feasted the Prince. The lady, next her lord,
Drooped like a musk-rose trained beside a tomb.
Loath was the guest that night to seek his room.

.

AH ! wherefore tell again an oft-told **tale,** —
  That of the sleeping knight who lost his wage
In the enchanted land, though cased with mail,
  And bore the sacred shrine an empty gage ?
How this thing went it were not worth to view
But for the triple coil which thence outgrew;

How, with the morn, the ancient chamberlain
  Made off, and on the marriage business moved;
How day by day those young hearts fed amain
  Upon the food of lovers, till — they loved.
Beneath the mists of duty and degree
A warmth of passion crept deliciously

About the twain ; and there, within the gleam
  Of those gray languid eyes, his nearing fate
Seemed to the one a far, unquiet dream.
  So when the heralds said, "All things await
Your princely coming," the glad summons broke
Upon him like a harsh bell's jangling stroke,

And waked him, and he knew he must be gone
  And put that honeyed chalice quite away ;
Yet once more met the lady, and alone,
  It chanced, within the grounds.   The two, that day,
Lured by a falling water's sound, went deep
Beyond the sunlight, in the forest-keep.

Here from a range of wooded uplands leapt
  A mountain brook and far-off meadows sought ;
Now under firs and tasselled chestnuts crept,
  Then on through jagged rocks a passage fought,
Until it clove this shadowy gorge and cool
In one white cataract, — with a dark, broad pool

Beneath, the home of mottled trout.   One side
  Rose the cliff's hollowed height, and overhung
An open sward across that basin wide.
  The liberal sun through slanting larches flung
Rich spots of gold upon the tufted ground,
And the great royal forest gloomed around.

The Prince, divided from the world so far,
  Sat with the lady on a fallen tree ;
They looked like lovers, yet a prison-bar
  Between them had not made the two less free.
Only their eyes told what they could not say,
For still their lips spoke alien words that day.

She told a legend of an early king
  Who knew the fairy of this wildwood glen,
And often sought her haunt, far off to fling
  His grandeur, and be loved like common men.
He died long since, the lady said ; but she,
Who could not die, how weary she must be !

They talked of the strange beauty of the spot,
  The light that glinted through the ancient trees,
Their own young lives, the Prince's future lot ;
  Then jested with false laughs.   Like tangled bees,
Each other and themselves they sweetly stung ;
They sung fond songs, and mocked the words they sung.

At last he hung his picture by a chain
  About her neck, and on it graved the date.
Her merry eyes grew soft with tender pain ;
  She heard him sigh, " Alas, by what rude fate
Our lives, like ships at sea, an instant meet,
Then part forever on their courses fleet ! "

And in sheer pity of herself she dropped
  Her lovely head ; and, though with self she strove,
One hot tear fell.   The shadow, which had stopped
  On her life's dial, moved again, and Love
Went sobbing by, and only left his wraith ;
For both were loyal to their given faith.

Farewells they breathed and self-reproaches found,
  Half gliding with the current to the fall,
Yet struggling for the shore. Was she not bound?
  Did not his plighted future, like a wall,
Jut 'cross the stream? They feared themselves, and rose,
And through the forest gained the mansion-close

Unmissed, and parted thus, nor met anew;
  For on the morrow, when the Prince took horse,
The lady feigned an illness, or 't was true, —
  Yet maybe from her oriel marked his course,
Watching his plume, that into distance past,
Like some dear sail which sinks from sight at last.

He rode beneath their arch, where pennons flared
  And standards with his colors blazoned in.
Then thousands shouted welcome; trumpets blared;
  He felt the glories of his life begin!
Far, far behind, that eddy in its stream
Now seemed; its vanished shores, in turn, a dream.

Enough; he passed the ways and reached the Queen.
  With pomp and pageantry the vows were said
Leave to the chroniclers the storied scene,
  The church, the court, the masks and jousts that sped;
Not theirs, but ours, to follow Love apart,
Where first the bridegroom held his bride to heart,

And saw her purity and regnant worth
  Thus kept for him and yielded to his care.
What marvel that of all who dwelt on earth
  He seemed most fortunate and she most fair
That self-same hour? And "By God's grace," he thought,
"May I to some ignoble end be brought,

"Unless I so reward her for her choice,
  And shape my future conduct in this land
By her deserving, that the world's great voice
  Proclaim me not unworthy! Let my hand
Henceforward make her tasks its own ; my life
Be merged in this fair ruler, precious wife,

"The paragon and glory of her kind!"
  Who reads his own heart will not think it strange
He put that yester romance from his mind
  So readily.   Men's lives, like oceans, change
In shifting tides, and ebb from either shore
Till the strong planet draws them on once more.

AND as a pilgrim, shielded by the wings
  Of some bright angel, crosses perilous ground,
Through unknown ways, and, while she leads and sings,
  Forgets the past, nor sees what pits surround
His footsteps, so the young Prince cast away
That self-distrust, and with his sovereign May

The gladness joined, and with her sat in state,
  Beneath the ancient scutcheons of her throne,
And welcome gave, and led the revels late ;
  But when the still and midnight heavens shone
They fled the masquers, and the city's hum
Was silent, and the palace halls grew dumb,

9 *

And Love and Sleep in that serene eclipse
 Moved, making prince and clown of one degree,
Then was she all his own ; then from her lips
 He learned with what a sweet humility
She, whose least word a spacious kingdom ruled,
In Love's free vassalage would fain be schooled.

How poor, she said, her sovereignty seemed,
 Unless it made her richer in his eye !
And poor his life, until her sunlight beamed
 Upon it, said the Prince.   So months went by ;
They were a gracious pair ; the Queen was glad ;
Peace smiled, and the wide land contentment had.

And for a time the courteous welcome paid
 The chosen consort, and the people's joy
In the Queen's joy, kept silent those who weighed
 The Prince's make, and sought to find alloy
In his fine gold ; but, when the freshness fled
From these things told, some took new thought and said :

" Look at the Queen : her heart is wholly set
 Upon the Prince ! what if he warp her mind
To errant policies, and rule us yet
 By proxy ?"   " What and if he prove the kind
Of trifling gallant," others said, " to slight
Our mistress, for each new and base delight ?

" Ay, we will watch him, lest he do her wrong !"
 And his due station, even from the first,
The peers of haughty rank and lineage long,
 Jealous of one whose blossom at a burst
Outflamed their own, begrudged him ; till their pique
Grew plain, and sent proud color to his cheek.

So now he fared as some new actor fares,
　Who through dark arras gains the open boards,
Facing the lights, and feels a thousand stares
　Come full upon him ; and the great throng hoards
Its plaudits ; and, as he begins his tale,
His rivals wait to mock him if he fail.

But here a brave simplicity of soul
　And careless vigilance, by honor bred,
Stayed him, and o'er his actions held control.
　A host of generous virtues stood in stead,
To help him on ; with patient manliness
He kept his rank, no greater and no less ;

His life was as a limpid rivulet ;
　His thoughts, like golden sands, were through it seen,
Not on himself in poor ambition set,
　But on his chosen country and the Queen ;
And with such gentle tact he bore a sense
Of conduct due, nor took nor gave offence,

That, as time went, he earned their trust, who first
　Withheld it him, and brought them, one by one,
To seek him for a comrade ; but he nursed
　His friendships with such equal care that none
Could claim him as their own ; nor was his word
Of counsel dulled by being often heard ;

Nor would he sully his fresh youth among
　The roisterers and pretty wanton dames
Who strove to win him ; nor with ribald tongue
　Joined in the talk that round a palace flames ;
Nor came and went alone, save — 't was his wont
In his own land — he haply left the hunt

On forest days, and, plunging down the wood,
    There in the brakes and copses half forgot
The part he bore, and caught anew the mood
    Of youth, and felt a heart for **any lot ;**
Then, loitering cityward behind the train,
With fresher courage took his place again.

His pure life made the wits about the court
    Find in its very blamelessness a fault
That lacked the generous failings of their sort.
    "With so much sweet," they swore, "a grain of salt
Were welcome ! lighter tongue and freer mood
Were something more of man, if less of prude ! "

And others to his praises would oppose
    Suspicion of his prowess, and they said,
"Our rose of princes is a thornless **rose,**
    A woman's toy !" and, when the months were sped,
And the glad Queen was childed with a son,
Light jests upon his mission well begun

They bandied ; yet the Prince, who felt the sting,
    Bided his time.   Till on the land there brake
A sudden warfare ; for that haughty king,
    Gathering a mighty armament to take
Revenge for his lost suit, with sword and flame
Against the borders on short pretext came.

Then with hot haste the Queen's whole forces poured
    To meet him.   With the call to horse and blade
The Prince, deep-chafed in spirit, placed his sword
    At orders of the General, and prayed
A humble station, but, as due his rank,
Next in command was made, and led the flank.

And so with doubtful poise a fierce war raged,
  Till on a day encountered face to face
The two chief hosts, and dreadful battle waged
  To close the issue. In its opening space
Death smote the General, and in tumult sore
The line sank back; but swiftly, at the fore

Placing himself, the Prince right onward hurled
  The strife once more, and with his battle-shout
Woke victory; again his forces whirled
  The hostile troops, and drove them on in rout.
The strength of ten battalions seemed to yield
Before his arm; and so he won that field,

And slew with his own hand the vengeful king,
  And with that death-stroke brought the war to end,
Conquering the common foe, and conquering
  The hate, from which he would not else defend
His clear renown than with such manful deeds
As fall to faith and valor at their needs.

Again — this time the chaplet was his own —
  The people wreathed their laurels for his brow;
His horses trod on flowers; the city shone
  With flags of victory; and none but now —
As with no vaunting mien he wore his bays —
Confessed him brave as good, and gave their praise.

PEACE smiled anew ; the kingdom was at rest.
 Ah, happy Queen ! whom every matron's tongue
Ran envious of, with such a consort blest
 As wins the heart of women, old and young ;
So gallant, yet so good, the gentlest maid
By this fair standard her own suitor weighed.

I hold the perfect mating of two souls,
 Through wedded love, to be the sum of bliss.
When Earth, this fruit that ripens as it rolls
 In sunlight, grows more prime, lives will not miss
Their counterparts, and each shall find its own ;
But now with what blind chance the lots are thrown !

And because Love sets with a rising tide
 Along the drift where much has gone before
One holds of worth, — we lavish first, beside,
 Heart, honors, regal gifts, and love the more
When yielding most, — for this the Queen's love knew
No slack, but still its current deeper grew.

And because Love is free, and follows not
 On gratitude, nor comes from what is given
So much as on the giving ; and, I wot,
 Partly because it irks one to have thriven
At hands which seem the weaker, and should thrive
While those of him they cling to lift and strive ;

And partly that his marriage seemed a height
 Which raised him from the passions of our kind,
Nor with his own intent ; and that, despite
 Its clear repose, he somehow longed to find
The lower world, starve, hunger, and be fed
With joy and sorrow, sweet and bitter bread, —

For all these things the Prince loved not the Queen
  With that sufficience which alone can take
A rapture in itself and rest serene ;
  Yet knew not what his life lacked that should make
It worth to live, — our custom has such art
To dull the craving of the famished heart, —

Perchance had never known it, but a light
  Flashed in his path and lit a fiery train
About him ; else, day following day, and night
  By night, through years his soul had felt no pain,
No triumph, but had shared the common lull,
Been all it seemed, as blameless, true, and dull.

And yet in one fair woman beauty, youth,
  And passion were united, and her love
Was framed about his likeness.   Some, forsooth,
  May shift their changeful worship as they rove,
Or clowns or princes ; but her fancy slept,
Dreaming upon that picture which she kept,

A secret pain and pleasance.   With what strife
  Men sought her love she wist not, for the prize
Was not for them.   She lived a duteous life.
  'T was something thus to let her constant eyes
Feed on his face, to hear his name, — to know
He lived, had walked those paths, had loved her so.

There is a painting of a youthful monk
  Who sits within a walled and cloistered nook,
His breviary closed, and listens, sunk
  In day-dreams, to a viol, — with a look
Of strange regret fixed on two pairing doves,
Who find their fate and simple natural loves.

Yet bonds of gold, linked hands, and chancel vows,
   Even spousal beds, do not a marriage make.
When such things chain the soul that never knows
   Love's mating, little vantage shall it take,
Wandering with alien feet throughout the wide,
Hushed temple, over those who pine outside !

So this young wife forecast her horoscope
   And found its wedded lines of little worth,
Yet owned not to herself what hopeless hope
   Or dumb intent made green her spot of earth.
So passed three changeless years, as such years be ;
At last the old lord died, and left her free,

The mistress of his rank and broad estate,
   In honor of her constancy.   Then life
Rushed back ; she saw her beauty grown more great,
   Ripened as if a summer field were rife
With grain, the harvester neglectful, since
Hers was no mean desire that sought a prince,

Eager to make his birth and bloom her own,
   Or reign a wanton favorite.   But she thought,
" I might have loved and clung to him alone,
   Am fairer than he knew me ; yet, if aught
Of rarity make sweet my hair and lips,
What sweetness hath the honey that none sips ? "

After her time of mourning she grew bold,
   And said, " Once let me look upon his face !
The Queen will take no harm if I behold
   What all the world can see."   She left her place,
And with a kinsman, at a palace rout,
Followed the long line passing in and out

Before the dais.   The Prince's eyes and hers
  Met like the clouds that lighten.   In a breath
Swift memory flamed between them, as, when stirs
  No wind, and the dark sky is still as death,
One lance of living fire is hurled across ;
Then comes the whirlwind, and the forests toss !

Yet as she bent her beauteous shoulders down,
  And heard the kindly greeting of the Queen,
He spoke such words as one who wears a crown
  Speaks, and no more ; and with a low, proud mien
She murmured answer, from the presence past
Lightly, nor any look behind her cast.

In that first glimpse each read the other's heart ;
  But not without a summoning of himself
To judgment did the Prince forever part
  From truth and fealty.   As he pondered, still
With stronger voice Love claimed a debt unpaid,
And youth's hot pulses would not be gainsaid.

She with a fierce, full gladness saw again
  Their broken threads of love begin to spin
In one red strand, and let it guide her then,
  Whether it led to danger or to sin ;
And shortly, on the morrow, took the road,
And gained her country-seat, and there abode.

The Prince, a bright near morning, mounted horse,
  Garbed for the hunt, and left the town, and through
The deep-pathed wood rode on a wayward course,
  With a set purpose in him, — though he knew
It not, and let his steed go where it might ;
For this sole thought pursued him since that night : —

N

" What recompense for me who have not sown
   The seed and reaped the harvest of my days ?
Youth passes like a bird ; but love alone
   Makes wealth of riches, power of rank, men's praise
A goodly sound.   Of such things have I aught ?
There is a foil to make their substance naught.

" What were his gifts who made each lovely thing,
   Yet lacked the gift of love ? or what the fame
Of some dwarfed poet, whose numbers still we sing,
   If no fair woman trembled where he came ?
The beggar dying in ditch is not accurst
If love once crowned him !   Fate may do her worst.

" For Age that erst has drawn the wine of love
   And filled its birth-cup to the jewelled brim,
And, while it sparkled, held it high above,
   And drained it slowly, swiftly, — then, though dim
Grow the blurred eyes, and comfort and desire
Are but the ashes of their ancient fire,

" Yet will it bide its exit in content,
   Remembering the past, nor grudge, with hoar
And ravenous look, the youth we have not spent.
   No earthly sting has power to harm it more ;
It lived and loved, was young, and now is old,
And life is rounded like a ring of gold."

Thereat with sudden rein the Prince wheeled horse,
   And sought a pathway that he long had known
Yet shunned till now.   Beside a water-course
   It led him for a winding league and lone ;
Then made a rugged circuit, — where the brook
Down a steep ledge of rock its plunges took, —

And ended at an open sward, the same
   Against whose edge the leaping cataract fell
From those high cliffs. Five years ago he came
   To bury youth and love within that dell,
And, as again he reached the spot he sought,
Truth, fame, his child, the Queen, were all as naught.

Dismounting then, he pushed afoot, between
   The alder saplings, to the outer wood,
The grounds, the garden-walks, and found, unseen,
   A private door, nor tarried till he stood
Within the threshold of my Lady's room, —
A shadowed nook, all stillness and perfume.

Jasmine and briony the lattice climbed,
   The rose and honeysuckle trailed above ;
'T was such an hour as poets oft have rhymed,
   And such a chamber as all lovers love.
He found her there, and at her footstool knelt.
Each in the other's fancies had so dwelt,

That, as one sees for days a sweet strange face,
   Until at night in dreams he does caress
Its owner, and next morning in some place
   Meets her, and wonders if she too can guess
How near and known he thinks her, — in this wise
They read one story in each other's eyes.

Her thick hair falling from its lilies hid
   Their first long kiss of passion and content.
He heard her soft, glad murmur, as she slid
   Within his hold, and 'gainst his bosom leant,
Whispering : " At last ! at last ! the years were sore."
" Their spite," he said, " shall do us wrong no more ! "

What else, when mingled longings swell full-tide,
  And the heart's surges leap their bounds for aye,
And fell the landmarks ?   What but fate defied,
  Time clutched, and any future held at bay ?
They recked not of the thorn, but seized the flower ;
For all the sin, their joy was great that hour.

And since, for all the joy, theirs was a sin
  That baned them with one bane ; since many men
Had sought her love, but one alone could win
  That largess, with his blameless life till then
Inviolate, — they bargained for love's sake
No severance of their covert league to make.

Yet, since nobility compelled them still,
  They pledged themselves for honor's sake to hold
This hidden unto death ; at either's will
  To meet and part in secret ; to infold
In their own hearts their trespass and delight,
Nor look their love, but guard it day or night.

S O fell the blameless Prince.   That day more late
    Than wont he reached the presence of the Queen,
Deep in a palace chamber, where she sate
  Fondling his child.   The sunset lit her mien,
And made a saintly glory in her hair ;
An awe came on him as he saw her there.

And, because perfect love suspecteth not,
　　She found no blot upon his brow.　'T was good
To take a pleasure in her wedded lot,
　　And watch the infant creeping where he stood ;
And, as he bent his head, she little wist
What kisses burned upon the lips she kissed.

And he, still kind and wise in his decline,
　　Seeing her trustful calm, had little heart
To shake it.　So his conduct gave no sign
　　Of broken faith ; no slurring of his part
Betrayed him to the courtiers or the wife.
Perhaps a second spring-time in his life

Waxed green, and fresh-bloomed love renewed again
　　The joys that light our youth and leave our prime,
And women found him tenderer, and men
　　A blither, heartier comrade ; but, meantime,
What hidden gladness made his visage bright
They could not guess ; nor with what craft and sleight

The paramours, in fealty to that Love
　　Who laughs at locks and walks in hooded guise,
Met here and there, yet made no careless move
　　Nor bared their strategy to cunning eyes.
And though, a portion of the winter year,
The Queen's own summons brought her rival near

The Prince, among the ladies of her train,
　　Then, meeting face to face at morn and night,
They were as strangers.　If it was a pain
　　To pass so coldly on, in love's despite,
It was a joy to hear each other's tone,
And keep the life-long secret still their own.

Once having dipped their palms they drank full draught,
  And, like the desert-parched, alone at first
Felt the delight of drinking, while they quaffed
  As if the waters could not slake their thirst;
That nicer sense unreached, when down we fling,
And view the oasis around the spring.

And, in that first bewilderment, perchance
  The Prince's lapse had caught some peering eye,
But that his long repute, and maintenance
  Against each test, had put suspicion by.
Now no one watched or doubted him. So long
His inner strength had made his outwork strong,

So long had smoothed his face, 't was light to take,
  From what had been his blamelessness, a mask.
And still, for honor's and the country's sake,
  He set his hands to every noble task;
Held firmly yet his place among the great,
Won by the sword and saviour of the state;

And as in war, so now in civic peace,
  He led the people on to higher things,
And fostered Art and Song, and brought increase
  Of Knowledge, gave to Commerce broader wings,
And with his action strengthened fourfold more
The weight his precept in their councils bore.

Then as the mellow years their fruitage brought,
  And fair strong children made secure the throne,
He reared them wisely, heedfully; and sought
  Their good, the Queen's desire, and these alone.
Himself so pure, that fathers bade their sons,
"Observe the Prince, who every license shuns;

"Who, being most brave, is purest!" Wedded wives,
   Happy themselves, the Queen still happiest found,
And plighted maids still wished their lovers' lives
   Conformed to his. Such manhood wrapt him round,
So winsome were his grace and knightly look,
The dames at court their lesser spoil forsook,

And wove a net to snare him, and their mood
   Grew warmer for his coldness ; and the hearts
Of those most heartless beat with quicker blood,
   Foiled of his love ; yet, heedless of their arts,
Courteous to all, he went his way content,
Nor ever from his princely station bent.

"What is this charm," they asked, "that makes him
       chaste
   Beyond all men?" and wist not what they said.
The common folk, — because the Prince had cased
   His limbs in silver mail, and on his head
Worn snowy plumes, and, covered thus in white,
Shone in the fiercest turmoil of the fight ;

And mostly for the whiteness of his soul,
   Which seemed so virginal and all unblurred, —
They called him the White Prince, and through the whole
   True land the name became a household word.
"God save the Queen!" the loyal people sung,
"And the White Prince!" came back from every
       tongue.

So passed the stages of a glorious reign.
   The Queen in tranquil goodness reached her noon ;
The Prince wore year by year his double chain ;
   His mistress kept her secret like the moon,
That hides one half its splendor and its shade ;
And newer times and men their entrance made.

But did these two, who took their secret fill
    Of stolen waters, find the greater bliss
They sought?   At first, to meet and part at will
    Was, for the peril's sake, a happiness ;
Ay, even the sense of guilt made such delights
More worth, as one we call the wisest writes.

But with the later years Time brought-about
    His famed revenges.   Not that love grew cold,
The lady never found a cause to doubt
    That with the Prince his passion kept its hold ;
And while their loved are loyal to them yet,
'T is not the wont of women to regret.

Yet 't was her lot to live as one whose wealth
    Is in another's name ; to sigh at fate
That hedged her from possession, save by stealth
    And trespass on the guileless Queen's estate ;
To see her lover farthest when most near,
Nor dare before the world to make him dear.

To see her perfect beauty but a lure,
    That made men list to follow where she went,
And kneel to woo the hand they deemed so pure,
    And hunger for her pitying mouth's consent ;
Calling her hard, who was so gently made,
Nor found delight in all their homage paid.

Nor ever yet was woman's life complete
    Till at her breast the child of him she loved
Made life and love one name.   Though love be sweet,
    And passing sweet, till then its growth has proved
In woman's paradise a sterile tree,
Fruitless, though fair its leaves and blossoms be.

Meanwhile the Prince put on his own disguise,
   Holding it naught for what it kept secure,
Nor wore it only in his comrades' eyes ;
   Beneath this cloak and seeming to be pure
He felt the thing he seemed. For some brief space
His conscience took the reflex of his face.

But lastly through his heart there crept a sense
   Of falseness, like a worm about the core,
Until he grew to loathe the long pretence
   Of blamelessness, and would the mask he wore
By some swift judgment from his face were torn,
So might the outer quell the inner scorn.

Such self-contempt befell him, when the feast
   Rang with his praise, he blushed from nape to crown,
And ground his teeth in silence, yet had ceased
   To bear it, crying, " Crush me not quite down,
Who ask your scorn, as viler than you deem
Your vilest, and am nothing that I seem ! "

With such a cry his conscience riotous
   Had thrown, perchance, the burden on it laid,
But love and pity held his voice ; and thus
   The paramours their constant penance made ;
False to themselves, before the world a lie,
Yet each for each had cast the whole world by.

In those transcendent moments, when the fire
   Leapt up between them rapturous and bright,
One incompleteness bred a wild desire
   To let the rest have token of its light ;
So natural seemed their love, — so hapless, too,
They might not make it glorious to view,

And speak their joy.   'T was all as they had come,
　They two, in some far wildwood wandering mazed,
Upon a mighty cataract, whose foom　　　·
　And splendor ere that time had never dazed
Men's eyes, nor any hearing save their own
Could listen to its immemorial moan,

And felt amid their triumph bitter pain
　That only for themselves was spread that sight.
Oft, when his comrades sang a tender strain,
　And music, talk, and wine, outlasted night,
Rose in the Prince's throat this sudden tide,
" And I, — I also know where Love doth hide ! "

Yet still the seals were ever on his mouth ;
　No heart, save one, his joy and dole might share.
Passed on the winter's rain and summer's drouth ;
　Friends more and more, and lovers true, the pair,
Though life its passion and its youth had spent,
Still kept their faith as seasons came and went.

ONE final hour, with stammering voice and halt,
　　The Prince said : " Dear, for you, — whose only
　　　gain
Was in your love that made such long default
　To self, — Heaven deems you sinless ! but a pain
Is on my soul, and shadow of guilt threefold :
First, in your fair life, fettered by my hold ;

" Then in the ceaseless wrong I do the Queen,
  Who worships me, unknowing ; worse than all,
To wear before the world this painted mien !
  See to it : on my head some bolt will fall !
We have sweet memories of the good years past,
Now let this secret league no longer last."

So of her love and pure unselfishness
  She yielded at his word, yet fain would pray
For one more tryst, one day of tenderness,
  Where first their lives were mated.   Such a day
Found them entwined together, met to part,
Lips pressed to lips, and voiceless grief at heart.

And last the Prince drew off his signet-stone,
  And gave it to his mistress, — as he rose
To shut the book of happy moments gone,
  For so all earthly pleasures find a close, —
Yet promised, at her time of utmost need
And summons by that token, to take heed

And do her will.   " And from this hour," he said,
  " No woman's kiss save one my lips shall know."
So left her pale and trembling there, and fled,
  Nor looked again, resolved it must be so ;
But somewhere gained his horse, and through the wood
Moved homeward with his thoughts, a phantom brood

That turned the long past over in his mind,
  Poising its good and evil, while a haze
Gathered around him, of that sombre kind
  Which follows from a place where many days
Have seen us go and come ; and even if sore
Has been our sojourn there, we feel the more

That parting is a sorrow, — though we part
  With those who loved us not, or go forlorn
From pain that ate its canker in the heart;
  But when we leave the paths where Love has borne
His garlands to us, Pleasure poured her wine,
Where life was wholly precious and divine,

Then go we forth as exiles.   In such wise
  The loath, wan Prince his homeward journey made,
Brooding, and marked not with his downcast eyes
  The shadow that within the coppice shade
Sank darker still; but at the horse's gait
Kept slowly on, and rode to meet his fate.

For from the west a silent gathering drew,
  And hid the summer sky, and brought swift night
Across that shire, and went devouring through
  The strong old forest, stronger in its might.
With the first sudden crash the Prince's steed
Took the long stride, and galloped at good need.

The wild pace tallied with the rider's mood,
  And on he spurred, and even now had reached
The storm that charged the borders of the wood,
  When one great whirlwind seized an oak which
    bleached
Across his path, and felled it; and its fall
Bore down the Prince beneath it, horse and all.

There lay he as he fell; but the mad horse
  Plunged out in fright, and reared upon his feet,
And for the city struck a headlong course,
  With clatter of hoof along the central street,
Nor halted till, thus masterless and late,
Bleeding and torn, he reached the palace-gate.

Then rose a clamor and the tidings spread,
    And servitors and burghers thronged about,
Crying, " The Prince's horse ! the Prince is dead ! "
    Till on the courser's track they sallied out,
And came upon the fallen oak, and found
The Prince sore maimed and senseless on the ground.

Then wattling boughs, they raised him in their hold,
    And after that rough litter, and before,
The people went in silence ; but there rolled
    A fiery vapor from the lights they bore,
Like some red serpent huge along the road.
Even thus they brought him back to his abode.

There the pale Queen fell on him at the porch,
    Dabbling her robes in blood, and made ado,
And over all his henchman held a torch,
    Until with reverent steps they took him through ;
And the doors closed, and midnight from the domes
Was sounded, and the people sought their homes.

But on the morrow, like a dreadful bird,
    Flew swift the tidings of this sudden woe,
And reached the Prince's paramour, who heard
    Aghast, as one who crieth loud, " The blow
Is fallen ! I am the cause ! " — as one who saith,
" Now let me die, whose hands have given death ! "

So gat her to the town remorsefully,
    White with a mortal tremor and the sin
Which sealed her mouth, and waited what might be,
    And watched the doors she dared not pass within.
Alas, poor lady ! that lone week of fears
Outlived the length of all her former years.

Some days the Prince, upon the skirts of death,
  Spake not a word nor heard the Queen's one prayer,
Nor turned his face, nor felt her loving breath,
  Nor saw his children when they gathered there,
But rested dumb and motionless ; and so
The Queen grew weak with watching and her woe,

Till from his bed they bore her to her own
  A little.   In the middle-tide of night,
Thereafter, he awoke with moan on moan,
  And saw his death anigh, and said outright,
" I had all things, but love was worth them all ! "
Then sped they for the Queen, yet ere the call

Reached her, he cried once more, " Too late ! too late ! "
  And at those words, before they led her in,
Came the sure dart of him that lay in wait.
  The Prince was dead : what goodness and what sin
Died with him were untold.   At sunrise fell
Across the capital his solemn knell.

All respite it forbade, and joyance thence,
  To one for whom his passion till the last
Wrought in the dying Prince.   Her wan suspense
  Thus ended, a great fear upon her passed.
" I was the cause ! " she moaned from day to day,
" Now let me bear the penance as I may ! "

So with her whole estate she sought and gained
  A refuge in a nunnery close at view,
And there for months withdrew her, and remained
  In tears and prayers.   Anon a sickness grew
Upon her, and her face the ghost became
Of what it was, the same and not the same.

SO died the blameless Prince. The spacious land
  Was smitten in his death, and such a wail
Arose, as when the midnight angel's hand
  Was laid on Egypt. Gossips ceased their tale,
Or whispered of his goodness, and were mute ;
No sound was heard of viol or of lute ;

The streets were hung with black ; the artisan
  Forsook his forge ; the artist dropped his brush ;
The tradesmen closed their windows. Man with man
  Struck hands together in the first deep hush
Of grief ; or, where the dead Prince lay in state,
Spoke of his life, so blameless, pure, and great.

But when, within the dark cathedral vault,
  They joined his ashes to the dust of kings,
No royal pomp was shown ; for Death made halt
  Above the palace yet, on dusky wings,
Waiting to gain the Queen, who still was prone
Along the couch where haply she had thrown,

At knowledge of the end, her stricken frame.
  With visage pale as in a mortal swound
She stayed, nor slept, nor wept, till, weeping, came
  The crown-prince and besought her to look round
And speak unto her children. Then she said:
" Hereto no grief has fallen on our head ;

" Now all our earthly portion in one mass
  Is loosed against us with this single stroke !
Yet we are Queen, and still must live, — alas ! —
  As he would have us." Even as she spoke
She wept, and mended thence, yet bore the face
Of one whose fate delays but for a space.

Thenceforth she worked and waited till the call
   Of Heaven should close the labor and the pause.
Months, seasons passed, yet evermore a pall
   Hung round the court.   The sorrow and the cause
Were always with her ; after things were tame
Beside the shadow of his deeds and fame.

Her palaces and parks seemed desolate ;
   No joy was left in sky or street or field ;
No age, she thought, would see the Prince's mate :
   What matchless hand his knightly sword could wield ?
The world had lost, this royal widow said,
Its one bright jewel when the Prince was dead.

So that his fame might be enduring there
   For many a reign, and sacred through the land,
She gathered bronze and lazuli, and rare
   Swart marbles, while her cunning artists planned
A stately cenotaph, — and bade them place
Above its front the Prince's form and face,

Sculptured, as if in life.   But the pale Queen,
   Watching the work herself, would somewhat lure
Her heart from plaining ; till, behind a screen,
   The tomb was finished, glorious and pure,
Even like the Prince : and they proclaimed a day
When the Queen's hand should draw its veil away.

It chanced, the noon before, she bade them fetch
   Her equipage, and with her children rode
Beyond the city walls, across a stretch
   Of the green open country, where abode
Her subjects, happy in the field and grange,
And with their griefs, that took a meaner range,

Content.   But as her joyless vision dwelt
   On beauty that so failed her wound to heal,
She marked the Abbey's ancient pile, and felt
   A longing at its chapel-shrine to kneel,
To pray, and think awhile on Heaven, — her one
Sole passion, now the Prince had thither gone.

She reached the gate, and through the vestibule
   The nuns, with reverence for the royal sorrow,
Led to the shrine, and left her there to school
   Her heart for that sad pageant of the morrow.
O, what deep sighs, what piteous tearful prayers,
What golden grief-blanched hair strewn unawares !

Anon her coming through the place was sped,
   And when from that lone ecstasy she rose
The saintly Abbess held her steps, and said :
   " God rests those, daughter, who in others' woes
Forget their own !   In yonder corridor
A sister-sufferer lies, and will no more

" Pass through her door to catch the morning's breath,—
   A worldling once, the chamberlain's young wife,
But now a pious novice, meet for death ;
   She prays to see your face once more in life."
" She, too, is widowed," thought the Queen.   Aloud
She answered, " I will visit her," and bowed

Her head, and, following, reached the room where lay
   One that had wronged her so ; and shrank to see
That beauteous pallid face, so pined away,
   And the starved lips that murmured painfully,
" I have a secret none but she may hear."
At the Queen's sign, they two were left anear.

10 *   O

With that the dying rushed upon her speech,
　　As one condemned, who gulps the poisoned wine
Nor pauses, lest to see it stand at reach
　　Were crueller still.   " Madam, I sought a sign,"
She cried, " to know if God would have me make
Confession, and to you ! now let me take

" This meeting as the sign, and speak, and die ! "
　　" Child," said the Queen, " your years are yet too few.
See how I live, — and yet what sorrows lie
　　About my heart."—" I know,—the world spake true !
You too have loved him ; ay, he seems to stand
Between us !   Queen, you had the Prince's hand,

" But not his love ! "   Across the good Queen's brow
　　A flame of anger reddened, as when one
Meets unprepared a swift and ruthless blow,
　　But instant paled to pity, as she thought,
" She wanders : 't is the fever at her brain ! "
And looked her thought.   The other cried again :

" Yes !   I am ill of body and soul indeed,
　　Yet this was as I say.   O, not for me
Pity, from you who wear the widow's weed,
　　Unknowing ! " — " Woman, whose could that love be,
If not all mine ? "   The other, with a moan,
Rose in her bed ; the pillow, backward thrown,

Was darkened with the torrent of her hair.
　　" 'T was hers," she wailed, — " 't was hers who loved
　　　　him best."
Then tore apart her night-robe, and laid bare
　　Her flesh, and lo ! against her poor white breast
Close round her gloomed a shift of blackest serge,
Fearful, concealed ! — " I might not sing his dirge,"

She said, " nor moan aloud and bring him shame,
   Nor haunt his tomb and cling about the grate,
But this I fashioned when the tidings came
   That he was dead and I must expiate,
Being left, our double sin ! " — In the Queen's heart,
The tiger — that is prisoned at life's start

In mortals, though perchance it never wakes
   From its mute sleep — began to rouse and crawl.
Her lips grew white, and on her nostrils flakes
   Of wrath and loathing stood. " What, now, is all
This wicked drivel ? " she cried ; " how dare they bring
The Queen to listen to so foul a thing ? "

" Queen ! I speak truth, — the truth, I say ! He fed
   Upon these lips, — this hair he loved to praise !
I held within these arms his bright fair head
   Pressed close, ah, close ! — Our lifetimes were the days
We met, — the rest a void ! " — " Thou spectral Sin,
Be silent ! or, if such a thing hath been, —

" If this be not thy frenzy, — quick, the proof,
   Before I score the lie thy lips amid ! "
She spoke so dread the other crouched aloof,
   Panting, but with gaunt hands somewhere undid
A knot within her hair, and thence she took
The signet-ring and passed it. The Queen's look

Fell on it, and that moment the strong stay,
   Which held her from the instinct of her wrong,
Broke, and therewith the whole device gave way,
   The grand ideal she had watched so long :
As if a tower should fall, and on the plain
Only a scathed and broken pile remain.

But in its stead she would not measure yet
　　The counter-chance, nor deem this sole attaint
Made the Prince less than one in whom 't was set
　　To prove him man. " I held him as a saint,"
She thought, " no other : — of all men alone
My blameless one ! Too high my faith had flown :

" So be it ! " With a sudden bitter scorn
　　She said : " You were his plaything, then ! the food
Wherewith he dulled what appetite is born,
　　Of the gross kind, in men. His nobler mood
You knew not ! How, shall I, — the fountain life
Of yonder children, — his embosomed wife

" Through all these years, — shall I, his Queen, for this
　　Sin-smitten harlot's gage of an hour's shame,
Misdoubt him ? " — " Yes, I was his harlot, — yes,
　　God help me ! and had worn the loathly name
Before the world, to have him in that guise ! "
" Thou strumpet ! wilt thou have me of his prize

" Rob Satan ? " cried the Queen, and one step moved.
　　" Queen, if you loved him, save me from your bane,
As something that was dear to him you loved ! "
　　Then from beneath her serge she took the chain
Which, long ago in that lone wood, the Prince
Hung round her, — she had never loosed it since, —

And gave therewith the face which, in its years
　　Of youthful, sunniest grace, a limner drew ;
And unsigned letters, darkened with her tears,
　　Writ in the hand that hapless sovereign knew
Too well ; — then told the whole, strange, secret tale,
As if with Heaven that penance could avail,

Or with the Queen, who heard as idols list
   The mad priest's cry, nor changed her place nor
      moaned,
But, clutching those mute tokens of each tryst,
   Hid them about her.   But the other groaned:
" The picture, — let me see it ere I die, —
Then take them all **! once, only** ! " — At that cry

The Queen strode forward with an awful stride,
   And seized the dying one, and bore her down,
And rose her height, and said, " Thou shouldst have died
   Ere telling **this, nor** I have **worn a crown**
To hear it told.   I am of God accurst !
Of all his hated, may he smite thee first ! "

With that wild speech she fled, nor looked behind,
   Hasting to get her from **that fearful room,**
Past the meek nuns in wait.   These did not find
   The sick one's eyes — yet **staring** through the gloom,
While her hands fumbled **at** her heart, and Death
Made her limbs quake, and combated her breath —

More dreadful than the Queen's look, as she thence
   Made through the court, and reached her own array
She knew not how, and clamored, " Bear me hence ! "
   And, even as her chariot moved away,
High **o'er** the Abbey heard the minster toll
Its doleful bell, as for a passing soul.

Though midst her guardsmen, as they speeded back,
   The wont of royalty maintained her still,
Where grief.had been were ruin now and rack !
   The firm earth reeled about, nor could her will
Make it seem stable. while her soul went through
Her wedded years in desperate review.

The air seemed full of lies; the realm, unsound;
  Her courtiers, knaves; her maidens, good and fair,
Most shameless bawds; her children clung around
  Like asps, to sting her; from the kingdom's heir,
Shuddering, she turned her face, — his features took
A shining horror from his father's look.

Along her city streets the thrifty crowd,
  As the Queen passed, their loving reverence made.
"'T is false! they love me not!" she cried aloud;
  So flung her from her chariot, and forbade
All words, but waved her ladies back, and gained
Her inmost room, and by herself remained.

"We have been alone these years, and knew it not,"
  She said; " now let us on the knowledge thrive!"
So closed the doors, and all things else forgot
  Than her own misery.   "I cannot live
And bear this death," she said, "nor die, the more
To meet him, — and that woman gone before!"

Thus with herself she writhed, while midnight gloomed,
  As lone as any outcast of us all;
And once, without a purpose, as the doomed
  Stare round and count the shadows on the wall,
Unclasped a poet's book which near her lay,
And turned its pages in that witless way,

And read the song, some wise, sad man had made,
  With bitter frost about his doubting heart.
"What is this life," it plained, " what masquerade
  Of which ye all are witnesses and part?
'T is but a foolish, smiling face to wear
Above your mortal sorrow, chill despair;

" To mock your comrades and yourselves with mirth
   That feeds the care ye cannot drive away ;
To vaunt of health, yet hide beneath the girth
   Impuissance, fell sickness, slow decay ;
To cloak defeat, and with the rich, the great,
Applaud their fairer fortunes as their mate ;

" To brave the sudden woe, the secret loss,
   Though but to-morrow brings the open shame ;
To pay the tribute of your caste, and toss
   Your last to him that 's richer save in name ;
To judge your peers, and give the doleful meed
To crime that 's white beside your hidden deed ;

" To whisper love, where of true love is none, —
   Desire, where lust is dead ; to live unchaste,
And wear the priestly cincture ; — last, to own,
   When the morn's dream is gone and noontide waste,
Some fate still kept ye from your purpose sweet,
Down strange, circuitous paths it drew your feet ! "

Thus far she read, and, " Let me read no more,"
   She clamored, " since the scales have left mine eyes
And freed the dreadful gift I lacked before !
   We are but puppets, in whatever guise
They clothe us, to whatever tune we move ;
Albeit we prate of duty, dream of love.

" Let me, too, play the common part, and wean
   My life from hope, and look beneath the mask
To read the masker ! I, who was a Queen,
   And like a hireling thought to 'scape my task !
For some few seasons left this heart is schooled :
Yet, — had it been a little longer fooled, —

"O God!"   And from her seat she bowed her down.
  The gentle sovereign of that spacious land
Lay prone beneath the bauble of her crown,
  Nor heard all night her whispering ladies stand
Outside the portal.   Greatly, in the morn,
They marvelled at her visage wan and worn.

BUT when the sun was high, the populace
  By every gateway filled the roads, and sought
The martial plain, within whose central space
  That wonder of the Prince's tomb was wrought.
Thereto from out the nearer land there passed
The mingled folk, an eager throng and vast ;

Knights, commons, men and women, young and old,
  The present and the promise of the realm.
Anon the coming of the Queen was told,
  And mounted guards, with sable plumes at helm,
Made through the middle, like a reaper's swath,
A straight, wide roadway for the sovereign's path.

Then rose the murmurous sound of her advance,
  And, with the crown-prince, and her other brood
Led close behind, she came.   Her countenance
  Moved not to right nor left, until she stood
Before the tomb ; yet those, who took the breath
That clothed her progress, felt a waft of death.

O noble martyr! queenliest intent!
   Strong human soul, that holds to pride through all!
Ah me! with what fierce heavings in them pent
   The brave complete their work, whate'er befall!
Upon her front the people only read
Pale grief that clung forever to the dead.

How should they know she trod the royal stand,
   And took within her hold the silken line,
As, while the headsman waits, one lays her hand
   Upon the scarf that slays her by a sign?
With one great pang she drew the veil, and lo!
The work was dazzling in the noonday glow.

There shone the Prince's image, golden, high,
   Installed forever in the people's sight.
"Alas!" they cried, "too good, too fair to die!"
   But at the foot the Queen had bid them write
Her consort's goodness, and his glory-roll,
Yet knew not they had carved upon the scroll

That last assurance of his stainless heart, —
   For such they deemed his words who heard them fall,—
"*Of all great things this Prince achieved his part,*
   Yet wedded Love to him was worth them all."
Thus read the Queen : till now, her injured soul
Of its forlornness had not felt the whole.

Now all her heart was broken. There she fell,
   And to the skies her lofty spirit fled.
The wrong of those mute words had smitten well.
   A cry went up : "The Queen! the Queen is dead!
O regal heart that would not reign alone!
O fatal sorrow! O the empty throne!"

· Her people made her beauteous relics room
　Within the chamber where her consort slept.
There rest they side by side.　Around the tomb
　A thousand matrons solemn vigil kept.
Long ages told the story of her reign,
And sang the nuptial love that had no stain.

MISCELLANEOUS POEMS.

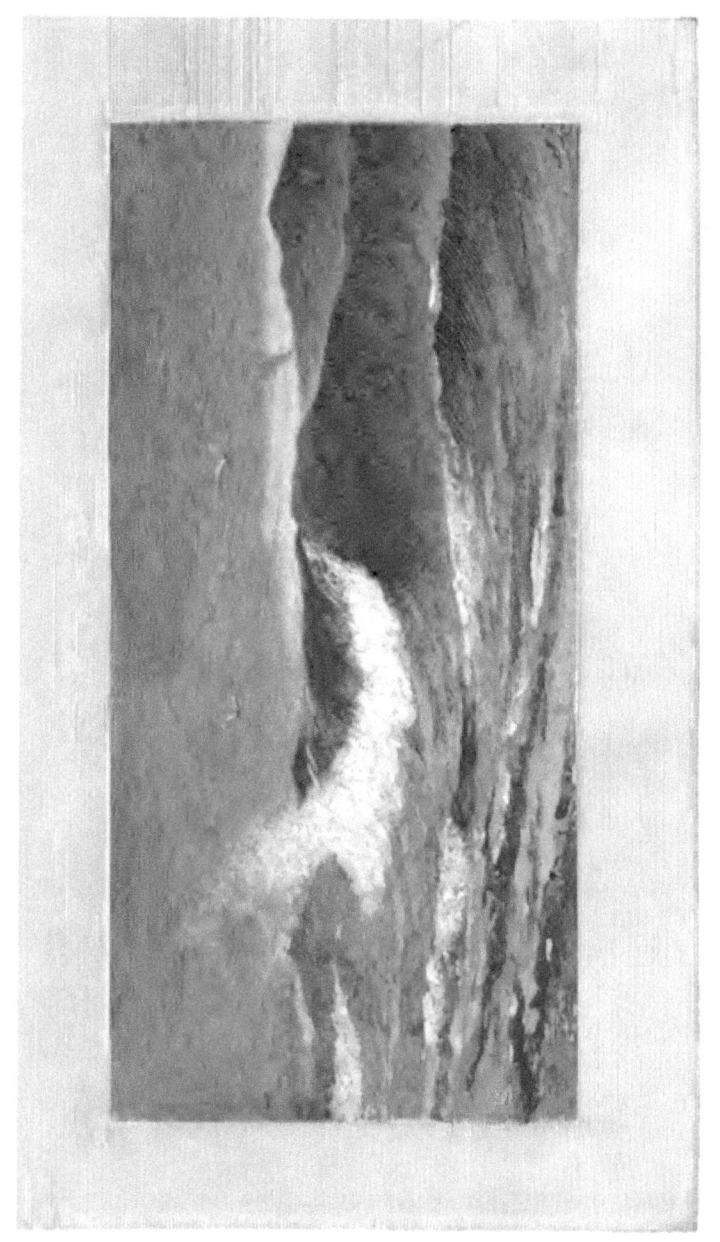

" Blue rollers breaking in surf where we stand."   Page 237.

I.

SONGS AND STUDIES.

SURF.

SPLENDORS of morning the billow-crests brighten,
  Lighting and luring them on to the land, —
Far-away waves where the wan vessels whiten,
  Blue rollers breaking in surf where we stand.
Curved like the necks of a legion of horses,
  Each with his froth-gilded mane flowing free,
Hither they speed in perpetual courses,
  Bearing thy riches, O beautiful sea !

Strong with the striving of yesterday's surges,
  Lashed by the wanton winds leagues from the shore,
Each, driven fast by its follower, urges
  Fearlessly those that are fleeting before ;
How they leap over the ridges we walk on,
  Flinging us gifts from the depths of the sea, —
Silvery fish for the foam-haunting falcon,
  Palm-weed and pearls for my darling and me !

Light falls her foot where the rift follows after,
  Finer her hair than your feathery spray,
Sweeter her voice than your infinite laughter, —
  Hist ! ye wild couriers, list to my lay !
Deep in the chambers of grottos auroral
  Morn laves her jewels and bends her red knee :
Thence to my dear one your amber and coral
  Bring for her dowry, O beautiful sea !

TOUJOURS AMOUR.

PRITHEE tell me, Dimple-Chin,
  At what age does Love begin ?
Your blue eyes have scarcely seen
Summers three, my fairy queen,
  But a miracle of sweets,
  Soft approaches, sly retreats,
  Show the little archer there,
  Hidden in your pretty hair ;
When didst learn a heart to win ?
Prithee tell me, Dimple-Chin !

  "Oh !" the rosy lips reply,
  "I can't tell you if I try.
'T is so long I can't remember :
  Ask some younger lass than I !"

Tell, O tell me, Grizzled-Face,
Do your heart and head keep pace ?
When does hoary Love expire,
When do frosts put out the fire ?
Can its embers burn below
All that chill December snow ?

Care you still soft hands to press,
Bonny heads to smooth and bless?
When does Love give up the chase?
Tell, O tell me, Grizzled-Face!

" Ah !" the wise old lips reply,
" Youth may pass and strength may die ;
But of Love I can't foretoken :
Ask some older sage than I !"

LAURA, MY DARLING.

LAURA, my darling, the roses have blushed
At the kiss of the dew, and our chamber is hushed ;
Our murmuring babe to your bosom has clung,
And hears in his slumber the song that you sung ;
I watch you asleep with your arms round him thrown,
Your links of dark tresses wound in with his own,
And the wife is as dear as the gentle young bride
Of the hour when you first, darling, came to my side.

Laura, my darling, our sail down the stream
Of Youth's summers and winters has been like a dream ;
Years have but rounded your womanly grace,
And added their spell to the light of your face ;
Your soul is the same as though part were not given
To the two, like yourself, sent to bless me from heaven, —
Dear lives, springing forth from the life of my life,
To make you more near, darling, mother and wife!

Laura, my darling, there 's hazel-eyed Fred,
Asleep in his own tiny cot by the bed,

And little King Arthur, whose curls have the art
Of winding their tendrils so close round my heart;
Yet fairer than either, and dearer than both,
Is the true one who gave me in girlhood her troth:
For we, when we mated for evil and good, —
What were we, darling, but babes in the wood?

Laura, my darling, the years which have flown
Brought few of the prizes I pledged to my own.
I said that no sorrow should roughen her way, —
Her life should be cloudless, a long summer's day.
Shadow and sunshine, thistles and flowers,
Which of the two, darling, most have been ours?
Yet to-night, by the smile on your lips, I can see
You are dreaming of me, darling, dreaming of me.

Laura, my darling, the stars, that we knew
In our youth, are still shining as tender and true;
The midnight is sounding its slumberous bell,
And I come to the one who has loved me so well.
Wake, darling, wake, for my vigil is done:
What shall dissever our lives which are one?
Say, while the rose listens under her breath,
"Naught until death, darling, naught until death!"

THE TRYST.

SLEEPING, I dreamed that thou wast mine,
   In some ambrosial lovers' shrine.
My lips against thy lips were pressed,
And all our passion was confessed;
So near and dear my darling seemed,
I knew not that I only dreamed.

Waking, this mid and moonlit night,
I clasp thee close by lover's right.
Thou fearest not my warm embrace,
And yet, so like the dream thy face
And kisses, I but half partake
The joy, and know not if I wake.

VIOLET EYES.

ONE can never quite forget
    Eyes like yours, May Margaret,
Eyes of dewy violet !
Nothing like them, Margaret,
Save the blossoms newly born
Of the May and of the Morn.

Oft my memory wanders back
To those burning eyes and black,
Whose heat-lightnings once could move
Me to passion, not to love ;
Longer in my heart of hearts
Linger those disguiséd arts,
Which, betimes, a hazel pair
Used upon me unaware ;
And the wise and tender gray —
Eyes wherewith a saint might pray —
Speak of pledges that endure
And of faith and vigils pure ;
But for him who fain would know
All the fire the first can show,
All the art, or friendship fast,
Of the second and the last, —

11   P

And would gain a subtler worth,
Part of Heaven, part of Earth, —
He these mingled rays can find
In but one immortal kind :
In those eyes of violet,
In *your* eyes, May Margaret !

THE DOORSTEP.

THE conference-meeting through at last,
We boys around the vestry waited
To see the girls come tripping past
Like snow-birds willing to be mated.

Not braver he that leaps the wall
By level musket-flashes litten,
Than I, that stepped before them all
Who longed to see me get the mitten.

But no, she blushed and took my arm !
We let the old folks have the highway,
And started toward the Maple Farm
Along a **kind of** lovers' by-way.

I can't remember what we said,
'T was nothing worth a song or story ;
Yet that rude path by which we sped
Seemed all transformed and in a glory.

The snow was crisp beneath our feet,
The moon was full, the fields were gleaming ;
By hood and tippet sheltered sweet,
Her face with youth and health was beaming.

The little hand outside her muff, —
  O sculptor, if you could but mould it ! —
So lightly touched my jacket-cuff,
  To keep it warm I had to hold it.

To have her with me there alone, —
  'T was love and fear and triumph blended.
At last we reached the foot-worn stone
  Where that delicious journey ended.

The old folks, too, were almost home ;
  Her dimpled hand the latches fingered,
We heard the voices nearer come,
  Yet on the doorstep still we lingered.

She shook her ringlets from her hood
  And with a " Thank you, Ned," dissembled,
But yet I knew she understood
  With what a daring wish I trembled.

A cloud passed kindly overhead,
  The moon was slyly peeping through it,
Yet hid its face, as if it said,
  " Come, now or never ! do it ! *do it !*"

My lips till then had only known
  The kiss of mother and of sister,
But somehow, full upon her own
  Sweet, rosy, darling mouth, — I kissed her !

Perhaps 't was boyish love, yet still,
  · O listless woman, weary lover !
To feel once more that fresh, wild thrill
  I 'd give — but who can live youth over ?

FUIT ILIUM.

ONE by one they died, —
 Last of all their race ;
Nothing left but pride,
  Lace, and buckled hose.
Their quietus made,
 On their dwelling-place
Ruthless hands are laid :
  Down the old house goes !

See the ancient manse
 Meet its fate at last !
Time, in his advance,
  Age nor honor knows ;
Axe and broadaxe fall,
 Lopping off the Past :
Hit with bar and maul,
  Down the old house goes !

Sevenscore years it stood :
 Yes, they built it well,
Though they built of wood,
  When that house arose.
For its cross-beams square
 Oak and walnut fell ;
Little worse for wear,
  Down the old house goes !

Rending board and plank,
 Men with crowbars ply,
Opening fissures dank,
  Striking deadly blows.

From the gabled **roof**
 How the shingles fly !
Keep you here aloof, —
  Down the old house goes !

Holding still its place,
 There the chimney stands,
Stanch from top to base,
  Frowning on its foes.
Heave apart the stones,
 Burst its iron bands !
How it shakes and groans !
  Down the old house goes !

Round the mantel-piece
 Glisten Scripture tiles ;
Henceforth they shall cease
  Painting Egypt's woes,
Painting David's **fight,**
 Fair Bathsheba's smiles,
Blinded Samson's might, —
  Down the old house goes !

On these oaken floors
 High-shoed ladies trod ;
Through those panelled **doors**
  Trailed their furbelows :
Long their day has ceased ;
 Now, beneath the sod,
With the worms they feast, —
  Down the old house **goes** !

Many a bride has stood
 In yon spacious room ;

Here her hand was wooed
   Underneath the rose ;
O'er that sill the dead
   Reached the family tomb :
All, that were, have fled, —
   Down the old house goes !

Once, in yonder hall,
   Washington, they say,
Led the New-Year's ball,
   Stateliest of beaux.
O that minuet,
   Maids and matrons gay !
Are there such sights yet ?
   Down the old house goes !

British troopers came
   Ere another year,
With their coats aflame,
   Mincing on their toes ;
Daughters of the house
   Gave them haughty cheer,
Laughed to scorn their vows, —
   Down the old house goes !

Doorway high the box
   In the grass-plot spreads ;
It has borne its locks
   Through a thousand snows ;
In an evil day,
   From those garden-beds
Now 't is hacked away, —
   Down the old house goes !

Lo ! the sycamores,
  Scathed and scrawny mates,
At the mansion doors
    Shiver, full of woes ;
With its life they grew,
  Guarded well its gates ;
Now their task is through, —
    Down the old house goes !

On this honored site
  Modern trade will build, —
What unseemly fright
    Heaven only knows !
Something peaked and high,
  Smacking of the guild :
Let us heave a sigh, —
    Down the old house goes !

COUNTRY SLEIGHING.

A NEW SONG TO AN OLD TUNE.

IN January, when down the dairy
  The cream and clabber freeze,
When snow-drifts cover the fences over,
  We farmers take our ease.
At night we rig the team,
  And bring the cutter out ;
Then fill it, fill it, fill it, fill it,
  And heap the furs about.

Here friends and cousins dash up by dozens,
  And sleighs at least a score ;
There John and Molly, behind, are jolly, —
  Nell rides with me, before.
All down the village street
  We range us in a row :
Now jingle, jingle, jingle, jingle,
  And over the crispy snow !

The windows glisten, the old folks listen
  To hear the sleigh-bells pass ;
The fields grow whiter, the stars are brighter,
  The road is smooth as glass.
Our muffled faces burn,
  The clear north-wind blows cold,
The girls all nestle, nestle, nestle,
  Each in her lover's hold.

Through bridge and gateway we 're shooting straightway,
  Their tollman was too slow !
He 'll listen after our song and laughter
  As over the hill we go.
The girls cry, " Fie ! for shame ! "
  Their cheeks and lips are red,
And so, with kisses, kisses, kisses,
  They take the toll instead.

Still follow, follow ! across the hollow
  The tavern fronts the road.
Whoa, now ! all steady ! the host is ready, —
  He knows the country mode !
The irons are in the fire,
  The hissing flip is got ;
So pour and sip it, sip it, sip it,
  And sip it while 't is hot.

Push back the tables, and from the stables
  Bring Tom, the fiddler, in ;
All take your places, and make your graces,
  And let the dance begin.
The girls are beating time
  To hear the music sound ;
Now foot it, foot it, foot it, foot it,
  And swing your partners round.

Last couple toward the left ! all forward !
  Cotillons through, let 's wheel :
First tune the fiddle, then down the middle
  In old Virginia Reel.
Play Money Musk to close,
  Then take the " long chassé,"
While in to supper, supper, supper,
  The landlord leads the way.

The bells are ringing, the ostlers bringing
  The cutters up anew ;
The beasts are neighing ; too long we 're staying,
  The night is half-way through.
Wrap close the buffalo-robes,
  We 're all aboard once more ;
Now jingle, jingle, jingle, jingle,
  Away from the tavern-door

So follow, follow, by hill and hollow,
  And swiftly homeward glide.
What midnight splendor ! how warm and tender
  The maiden by your side !
The sleighs drop far apart,
  Her words are soft and low ;
Now, if you love her, love her, love her,
  'T is safe to tell her so.

·

PAN IN WALL STREET.

A. D. 1867.

JUST where the Treasury's marble front
  Looks over Wall Street's mingled nations ;
Where Jews and Gentiles most are wont
  To throng for trade and last quotations ;
Where, hour by hour, the rates of gold
  Outrival, in the ears of people,
The quarter-chimes, serenely tolled
  From Trinity's undaunted steeple, —

Even there I heard a strange, wild strain
  Sound high above the modern clamor,
Above the cries of greed and gain,
  The curbstone war, the auction's hammer ;
And swift, on Music's misty ways,
  It led, from all this strife for millions,
To ancient, sweet-do-nothing days
  Among the kirtle-robed Sicilians.

And as it stilled the multitude,
  And yet more joyous rose, and shriller,
I saw the minstrel, where he stood
  At ease against a Doric pillar :
One hand a droning organ played,
  The other held a Pan's-pipe (fashioned
Like those of old) to lips that made
  The reeds give out that strain impassioned.

'T was Pan himself had wandered here
  A-strolling through this sordid city,
And piping to the civic ear
  The prelude of some pastoral ditty!
The demigod had crossed the seas, —
  From haunts of shepherd, nymph, and satyr,
And Syracusan times, — to these
  Far shores and twenty centuries later.

A ragged cap was on his head;
  But — hidden thus — there was no doubting
That, all with crispy locks o'erspread,
  His gnarléd horns were somewhere sprouting;
His club-feet, cased in rusty shoes,
  Were crossed, as on some frieze you see them,
And trousers, patched of divers hues,
  Concealed his crooked shanks beneath them.

He filled the quivering reeds with sound,
  And o'er his mouth their changes shifted,
And with his goat's-eyes looked around
  Where'er the passing current drifted;
And soon, as on Trinacrian hills
  The nymphs and herdsmen ran to hear him,
Even now the tradesmen from their tills,
  With clerks and porters, crowded near him.

The bulls and bears together drew
  From Jauncey Court and New Street Alley,
As erst, if pastorals be true,
  Came beasts from every wooded valley;
The random passers stayed to list, —
  A boxer Ægon, rough and merry,
A Broadway Daphnis, on his tryst
  With Naïs at the Brooklyn Ferry.

A one-eyed Cyclops halted long
  In tattered cloak of army pattern,
And Galatea joined the throng, —
  A blowsy, apple-vending slattern ;
While old Silenus staggered out
  From some new-fangled lunch-house handy,
And bade the piper, with a shout,
  To strike up Yankee Doodle Dandy !

A newsboy and a peanut-girl
  Like little Fauns began to caper:
His hair was all in tangled curl,
  Her tawny legs were bare and taper ;
And still the gathering larger grew,
  And gave its pence and crowded nigher,
While aye the shepherd-minstrel blew
  His pipe, and struck the gamut higher.

O heart of Nature, beating still!
  With throbs her vernal passion taught her, —
Even here, as on the vine-clad hill,
  Or by the Arethusan water !
New forms may fold the speech, new lands
  Arise within these ocean-portals,
But Music waves eternal wands, —
  Enchantress of the souls of mortals !

So thought I, — but among us trod
  A man in blue, with legal baton,
And scoffed the vagrant demigod,
  And pushed him from the step I sat on.
Doubting I mused upon the cry,
  "Great Pan is dead !"— and all the people
Went on their ways : — and clear and high
  The quarter sounded from the steeple.

ANONYMA.

HER CONFESSION.

IF I had been a rich man's girl,
   With my tawny hair, and this wanton art
Of lifting my eyes in the evening whirl
   And looking into another's heart;
Had love been mine at birth, and friends
   Caressing and guarding me night and day,
With doctors to watch my finger-ends,
   And a parson to teach me how to pray;

If I had been reared as others have, —
   With but a tithe of these looks, which came
From my reckless mother, now in her grave,
   And the father who grudged me even his name, —
Why, I should have station and tender care,
   Should ruin men in the high-bred way,
Passionless, smiling at their despair,
   And marrying where my vantage lay.

As it is, I must have love and dress,
   Jewelled trinkets, and costly food,
For I was born for plenteousness,
   Music and flowers, and all things good.
To that same father I owe some thanks,
   Seeing, at least, that blood will tell,
And keep me ever above the ranks
   Of those who wallow where they fell.

True, there are weary, weary days
  In the great hotel where I make my lair,
Where I meet the men with their brutal praise,
  Or answer the women, stare for stare.
'T is an even fight, and I 'll carry it through, —
  Pit them against me, great and small :
I grant no quarter, nor would I sue
  For grace to the softest of them all.

I cannot remember half the men
  Whose sin has tangled them in my toils, —
All are alike before me then,
  Part of my easily conquered spoils :
Tall or short, and dark or fair,
  Rich or famous, haughty or fond,
There are few, I find, who will not forswear
  The lover's oath and the wedding bond.

Fools ! what is it that drives them on
  With their perjured lips on poison fed ;
Vain of themselves, and cruel as stone,
  How should they be so cheaply led ?
Surely they know me as I am, —
  Only a cuckoo, at the best,
Watching, careless of hate and shame,
  To crouch myself in another's nest.

But the women, — how they flutter and flout,
  The stupid, terribly virtuous wives,
If I but chance to move about
  Or enter within their bustling hives !
Buz ! buz ! in the scandalous gatherings,
  When a strange queen lights amid their throng,
And their tongues have a thousand angry stings
  To send her travelling, right or wrong.

Well, the earth is wide and open to all,
  And money and men are everywhere,
And, as I roam, 't will ill befall
  If I do not gain my lawful share:
One drops off, but another will come
  With as light a head and heavy a purse;
So long as I have the world for a home,
  I' ll take my fortune, better or worse!

SPOKEN AT SEA.

THE LOG-BOOK OF THE STEAMSHIP VIRGINIA.

TWELVE hundred miles and more
  From the stormy English shore,
   All aright, the seventh night,
On her course our vessel bore.
Her lantern shone ahead,
And the green lamp and the red
  To starboard and to larboard
    Shot their light.

Close on the midnight call
What a mist began to fall,
  And to hide the ocean wide,
And to wrap us in a pall!
Beneath its folds we past:
Hidden were shroud and mast,
  And faces, in near places
    Side by side.

Sudden there also fell
A summons like a knell :
 Every ear the words could hear, —
Whence spoken, who could tell ?
"What ship is this ? where bound ?"
Gods, what a dismal sound !
 A stranger, and in danger,
  Sailing near.

" The Virginia, on her route
From the Mersey, seven days out ;
 Fore and aft, our trusty craft
Carries a thousand souls, about."
"All these souls may travel still,
Westward bound, if so they will ;
 Bodies rather, I would gather !"
  Loud he laughed.

" Who is 't that hails so rude,
And for what this idle mood ?
 Words like these, on midnight seas,
Bode no friend nor fortune good ! "
" Care not to know my name,
But whence I lastly came,
 At leisure, for my pleasure,
  Ask the breeze.

" To the people of your port
Bear a message of this sort :
 Say, I haste unto the West,
A sharer of their sport.
Let them sweep the houses clean :
Their fathers did, I ween,
 When hearing of my nearing
  As a guest !

"As by Halifax ye sail
And the steamship England hail,
   Of me, then, bespeak her men ;
She took my latest mail, —
'T was somewhere near this spot :
Doubtless they 've not forgot.
    Remind them (if you find them !)
      Once again.

"Yet that you all may know
Who is 't that hailed you so,
   (Slow he saith, and under breath,)
I leave my sign below ! "
Then from our crowded hold
A dreadful cry uprolled,
    Unbroken, and the token, —
      It was Death.

THE DUKE'S EXEQUY.

ARRAS, A. D. 1404.

CLOTHED in sable, crowned with gold,
   All his wars and councils ended,
Philip lay, surnamed The Bold :
Passing-bell his quittance tolled,
And the chant of priests ascended.

Mailéd knights and archers stand,
Thronging in the church of Arras ;
   Nevermore at his command
   Shall they scour the Netherland,
Nevermore the outlaws harass ;

Q

Naught is left of his array
Save a barren territory;
  Forty years of generous sway
  Sped his princely hoards away,
Bartered all his gold for glory.

  Forth steps Flemish Margaret then,
Striding toward the silent ashes;
  And the eyes of arméd men
  Fill with startled wonder, when
On the bier her girdle clashes!

  Swift she drew it from her waist,
And the purse and keys it carried
  On the ducal coffin placed;
  Then with proud demeanor faced
Sword and shield of him she married.

  "No encumbrance of the dead
Must the living clog forever;
  From thy debts and dues," she said,
  "From the liens of thy bed,
We this day our line dissever.

  "From thy hand we gain release,
Know all present by this token!
  Let the dead repose in peace,
  Let the claims upon us cease
When the ties that bound are broken.

  "Philip, we have loved thee long,
But, in years of future splendor,
  Burgundy shall count among
  Bravest deeds of tale and song
This, our widowhood's surrender."

Back the stately Duchess turned,
While the priests and friars chanted,
And the swinging incense burned :
Thus by feudal rite was earned
Greatness for a race undaunted.

THE HILLSIDE DOOR.

SOMETIMES within my hand
     A Spirit puts the silver key
          Of Fairyland :
From the dark, barren heath he beckons me,
     Till by that hidden hillside door,
          Where bards have passed before,
               I seem to stand.

The portal opens wide :
     In, through the wondrous, lighted halls,
          Voiceless I glide
Where tinkling music magically falls,
     And fair in fountained gardens move
          The heroes, blest with love
               And glorified.

Then by the meadows green,
     Down winding walks of elf and fay,
          I pass unseen :
There rest the valiant chieftains wreathed with bay ;
     Here maidens to their lovers cling,
          And happy minstrels sing,
               Praising their queen.

For where yon pillars are,
And birds with tuneful voices call,
There shines a star, —
The crown she wears, the Fairy Queen of all!
Led to that inmost, wooded haunt
By maidens ministrant,
I halt afar.

O joy! she sees me stand
Doubting, and calls me near her throne,
And waves her wand,
As in my dreams, and smiles on me alone.
O royal beauty, proud and sweet!
I bow me at her feet
To kiss that hand:

Ah woe! ah, fate malign!
By what a rude, revengeful gust,
From that fair shrine
Which holds my sovran mistress I am thrust!
Then comes a mocking voice's taunt,
Crying, *Thou fool, avaunt!*
She is not thine!

And I am backward borne
By unseen awful hands, and cast,
In utter scorn,
Forth from that brightness to the midnight blast:
Not mine the minstrel-lover's wreath,
But the dark, barren heath,
And heart forlorn.

AT TWILIGHT.

THE sunset darkens in the west,
  The sea-gulls haunt the bay,
And far and high the swallows fly
  To watch the dying day.
Now where is she that once with me
  The rippling waves would list?
And O for the song I loved so long,
  And the darling lips I kist!

Yon twinkling sail may whiter gleam
  Than falcon's snowy wing,
Her lances far the evening-star
  Beyond the waves may fling;
Float on, ah float, enchanted boat,
  Bear true hearts o'er the main,
But I shall guide thy helm no more,
  Nor whisper love again!

II.

POEMS OF NATURE.

WOODS AND WATERS.

"O ye valleys! O ye mountains!
O ye groves and crystal fountains!
How I love at liberty,
By turns, to come and visit ye!"

COME, let us burst the cerements and the shroud,
 And with the livelong year renew our breath,
Far from the darkness of the city's cloud
 Which hangs above us like the pall of Death.
Haste, let us leave the shadow of his wings!
 Off from our cares, a stolen, happy time!
  Come where the skies are blue, the uplands green;
   For hark! the robin sings
 Even here, blithe herald, his auroral rhyme,
  Foretelling joy, and June his sovereign queen.

See, in our pavéd courts her missal scroll
 Is dropped astealth, and every verdant line,
Emblazoned round with Summer's aureole,
 Pictures to eager eyes, like thine and mine,

Her trees new-leaved and hillsides far away.
　　Ransom has come : out from this vaulted town,
　　　Poor prisoners of a giant old and blind,
　　　　Into the breezy day,
　　Fleeing the sights and sounds that wear us down,
　　And in the fields our ancient solace find !

Again I hunger for the living wood,
　　The laurelled crags, the hemlocks hanging wide,
The rushing stream that will not be withstood,
　Bound forward to wed him with the river's tide :
O what wild leaps through many a fettered pass,
　　Through knotted ambuscade of root and rock,
　　　How white the plunge, how dark the cloven pool !
　　　　Then to rich meadow-grass,
　　And pastures fed by tinkling herd and flock,
　　Till the wide stream receives its waters cool.

Again I long for lakes that lie between
　　High mountains, fringed about with virgin firs,
Where hand of man has never rudely been,
　Nor plashing wheel the limpid water stirs ;
There let us twain begin the world again
　　Like those of old ; while tree, and trout, and deer
　　　Unto their kindred beings draw our own,
　　　　Till more than haunts of men,
　　Than place and pelf, more welcome these appear,
　　And better worth sheer life than we had known.

Thither, ay, thither flee, O dearest friend,
　　From walls wherein we grow so wan and old !
The liberal Earth will still her lovers lend
　　Water of life and storied sands of gold.
Though of her perfect form thou hast secured

Thy will, some charm shall aye thine hold defy,
And day by day thy passion yet shall grow,
Even as a bridegroom, lured
By the unravished secret of her eye,
Reads the bride's soul, yet never all can know.

And when from her embrace again thou 'rt torn,
(Though well for her the world were thrown away !)
At thine old tasks thou 'lt not be quite forlorn,
Remembering where is peace ; and thou shalt say,
" I know where beauty has not felt the curse, —
Where, though I age, all round me is so young
That in its youth my soul's youth mirrored seems ;
Yes, in their rippling verse,
For all our toil, they have not falsely sung
Who said there still was rest beyond our dreams.

TO BAYARD TAYLOR.

WITH A COPY OF THE ILIAD.

BAYARD, awaken not this music strong,
While round thy home the indolent sweet breeze
Floats lightly as the summer breath of seas
O'er which Ulysses heard the Sirens' song.
Dreams of low-lying isles to June belong,
And Circe holds us in her haunts of ease ;
But later, when these high ancestral trees
Are sere, and such melodious languors wrong
The reddening strength of the autumnal year,
Yield to heroic words thy ear and eye ; —

12

Intent on these broad pages thou shalt hear
The trumpets' blare, the Argive battle-cry,
And see Achilles hurl his hurtling spear,
And mark the Trojan arrows make reply !

THE MOUNTAIN.

TWO thousand feet in air it stands
 Betwixt the bright and **shaded lands,**
Above the regions it divides
And borders with its furrowed sides.
The seaward valley laughs with light
Till **the round** sun o'erhangs this height ;
But then the shadow of the crest
No more the plains **that** lengthen **west**
Enshrouds, yet slowly, surely creeps
Eastward, until the coolness steeps
A darkling league of tilth and wold,
And chills the flocks **that** seek their fold.

Not like those ancient summits lone,
Mont Blanc, on his eternal throne, —
The city-gemmed Peruvian peak, —
The sunset-portals landsmen seek,
Whose train, to reach the Golden Land,
Crawls slow and pathless through the sand, —
Or that, whose ice-lit beacon guides
The mariner on tropic **tides,**
And flames across the Gulf afar,
A torch by day, by night a star, —

"Two thousand feet in air it stands."   Page 266.

Not thus, to cleave the outer skies,
Does my serener mountain rise,
Nor aye forget its gentle birth
Upon the dewy, pastoral earth.

But ever, in the noonday light,
Are scenes whereof I love the sight, —
Broad pictures of the lower world
Beneath my gladdened eyes unfurled.
Irradiate distances reveal
Fair nature wed to human weal;
The rolling valley made a plain;
Its checkered squares of grass and grain;
The silvery rye, the golden wheat,
The flowery elders where they meet, —
Ay, even the springing corn I see,
And garden haunts of bird and bee;
And where, in daisied meadows, shines
The wandering river through its vines,
Move specks at random, which I know
Are herds a-grazing to and fro.

Yet still a goodly height it seems
From which the mountain pours his streams,
Or hinders, with caressing hands,
The sunlight seeking other lands.
Like some great giant, strong and proud,
He fronts the lowering thunder-cloud,
And wrests its treasures, to bestow
A guerdon on the realm below;
Or, by the deluge roused from sleep
Within his bristling forest-keep,
Shakes all his pines, and far and wide
Sends down a rich, imperious tide.

At night the whistling tempests meet
In tryst upon his topmost seat,
And all the phantoms of the sky
Frolic and gibber, storming by.

By day I see the ocean-mists
Float with the current where it lists,
And from my summit I can hail
Cloud-vessels passing on the gale, —
The stately argosies of air, —
And parley with the helmsmen there;
Can probe their dim, mysterious source,
Ask of their cargo and their course, —
Whence come? where bound? — and wait reply,
As, all sails spread, they hasten by.

If, foiled in what I fain would know,
Again I turn my eyes below
And eastward, past the hither mead
Where all day long the cattle feed,
A crescent gleam my sight allures
And clings about the hazy moors, —
The great, encircling, radiant sea,
Alone in its immensity.

Even there, a queen upon its shore,
I know the city evermore
Her palaces and temples rears,
And wooes the nations to her piers;
Yet the proud city seems a mole
To this horizon-bounded whole;
And, from my station on the mount,
The whole is little worth account
Beneath the overhanging sky,

That seems so far and yet so nigh.
Here breathe I inspiration rare,
Unburdened by the grosser air
That hugs the lower land, and feel
Through all my finer senses steal
The life of what that life may be,
Freed from this dull earth's density,
When we, with many a soul-felt thrill,
Shall thrid the ether at our will,
Through widening corridors of morn
And starry archways swiftly borne.

Here, in the process of the night,
The stars themselves a purer light
Give out, than reaches those who gaze
Enshrouded with the valley's haze.
October, entering Heaven's fane,
Assumes her lucent, annual reign :
Then what a dark and dismal clod,
Forsaken by the Sons of God,
Seems this sad world, to those which march
Across the high, illumined arch,
And with their brightness draw me forth
To scan the splendors of the North !
I see the Dragon, as he toils
With Ursa in his shining coils,
And mark the Huntsman lift his shield,
Confronting on the ancient field
The Bull, while in a mystic row
The jewels of his girdle glow ;
Or, haply, I may ponder long
On that remoter, sparkling throng,
The orient sisterhood, around
Whose chief our Galaxy is wound ;

Thus, half enwrapt in classic dreams,
And brooding over Learning's gleams,
I leave to gloom the under-land,
And from my watch-tower, close at hand,
Like him who led the favored race,
I look on glory face to face !

So, on the mountain-top, alone,
I dwell, as one who holds a throne ;
Or prince, or peasant, him I count
My peer, who stands upon a mount,
Sees farther than the tribes below,
And knows the joys they cannot know ;
And, though beyond the sound of speech
They reign, my soul goes out to reach,
Far on their noble heights elsewhere,
My brother-monarchs of the air.

HOLYOKE VALLEY.

" Something sweet
Followed youth, with flying feet,
And will never come again."

HOW many years have made their flights,
   Northampton, over thee and me,
Since last I scaled those purple heights
   That guard the pathway to the sea ;

Or climbed, as now, the topmost crown
   Of western ridges, whence again
I see, for miles beyond the town,
   That sunlit stream divide the plain ?

There still the giant warders stand
  And watch the current's downward flow,
And northward still, with threatening hand,
  The river bends his ancient bow.

I see the hazy lowlands meet
  The sky, and count each shining spire,
From those which sparkle at my feet
  To distant steeples tipt with fire.

For still, old town, thou art the same :
  The redbreasts sing their choral tune,
Within thy mantling elms aflame,
  As in that other, dearer June,

When here my footsteps entered first,
  And summer perfect beauty wore,
And all thy charms upon me burst,
  While Life's whole journey lay before.

Here every fragrant walk remains,
  Where happy maidens come and go,
And students saunter in the lanes
  And hum the songs I used to know.

I gaze, yet find myself alone,
  And walk with solitary feet :
How strange these wonted ways have grown !
  Where are the friends I used to meet ?

In yonder shaded Academe
  The rippling metres flow to-day,
But other boys at sunset dream
  Of love, and laurels far away ;

And ah ! from yonder trellised home,
  Less sweet the faces are that peer
Than those of old, and voices come
  Less musically to my ear.

Sigh not, ye breezy elms, but give
  The murmur of my sweetheart's vows,
When Life was something worth to live,
  And Love was young beneath your boughs !

Fade beauty, smiling everywhere,
  That can from year to year outlast
Those charms a thousand times more fair,
  And, O, our joys so quickly past !

Or smile to gladden fresher hearts
  Henceforth : but they shall yet be led,
Revisiting these ancient parts,
  Like me to mourn their glory fled.

THE FEAST OF HARVEST.

THE fair Earth smiled and turned herself and woke,
  And to the Sun with nuptial greeting said :
" I had a dream, wherein it seemed men broke
  A sovran league, and long years fought and bled,
Till down my sweet sides ran my children's gore,
  And all my beautiful garments were made red,
  And all my fertile fields were thicket-grown,
  Nor could thy dear light reach me through the air ;
At last a voice cried, ' Let them strive no more ! '
  Then music breathed, and lo ! from my despair
    I wake to joy, — yet would not joy alone !

" For, hark ! I hear a murmur on the meads, —
   Where as of old my children seek my face, —
The low of kine, the peaceful tramp of steeds,
   Blithe shouts of men in many a pastoral place,
The noise of tilth through all my goodliest land,
   And happy laughter of a dusky race
     Whose brethren lift them from their ancient toil,
   Saying : " The year of jubilee has come ;
Gather the gifts of Earth with equal hand ;
     Henceforth ye too may share the birthright soil,
   The corn, the wine, and all the harvest-home."

" O my dear lord, my radiant bridegroom, look !
   Behold their joy who sorrowed in my dreams, —
The sword a share, the spear a pruning-hook ;
   Lo, I awake, and turn me toward thy beams
Even as a bride again !   O, shed thy light
   Upon my fruitful places in full streams !
     Let there be yield for every living thing ;
   The land is fallow, — let there be increase
After the darkness of the sterile night ;
   Ay, let us twain a festival of Peace
     Prepare, and hither all my nations bring !"

The fair Earth spake : the glad Sun speeded forth,
   Hearing her matron words, and backward drave
To frozen caves the icy Wind of the North, —
   And bade the South Wind from the tropic wave
Bring watery vapors over river and plain, —
   And bade the East Wind cross her path, and lave
     The lowlands, emptying there her laden mist, —
   And bade the Wind of the West, the best wind, blow
After the early and the latter rain, —
     And beamed himself, and oft the sweet Earth kissed,
   While her swift servitors sped to and fro.

12 *   R

Forthwith the troop that, at the beck of **Earth,**
  Foster her children, brought a glorious **store**
Of viands, food of immemorial worth,
  Her earliest gifts, her tenderest evermore.
First came the Silvery Spirit, whose marshalled files
  Climb up the glades in billowy breakers hoar,
    Nodding their crests ; and at his side there sped
  The Golden Spirit, whose yellow harvests trail
Across the continents and fringe the isles,
  And freight men's argosies where'er they sail :
    O, **what** a wealth of sheaves he there outspread !

Came the dear Spirit whom **Earth** doth love the best,
  Fragrant of clover-bloom and new-mown hay,
Beneath whose mantle weary ones finds rest,
  On whose green skirts the little children play :
She bore the food our patient cattle crave.
  Next, robed in silk, with tassels scattering spray,
    Followed the generous Spirit of the Maize ;
  And many a kindred shape of high renown
Bore in the clustering grape, the fruits that wave
    On orchard branches or in gardens blaze,
  And those the wind-shook forest hurtles down.

Even thus they laid a great and marvellous feast,
  And Earth her children summoned joyously,
Throughout that goodliest land wherein had ceased
  The vision of battle, and with glad hands free
These took their fill, and plenteous measures poured,
  Beside, for those who dwelt beyond the sea ;
    Praise, like an incense, upward rose to Heaven
  For that full harvest ; and the autumnal Sun
Stayed long above ; and ever at the board,
    Peace, white-robed angel, held the high seat given,
  And **War** far off withdrew his visage **dun.**

AUTUMN SONG.

NO clouds are in the morning sky,
 The vapors hug the stream, —
Who says that life and love can die
 In all this northern gleam ?
At every turn the maples burn,
 The quail is whistling free,
The partridge whirs, and the frosted burs
 Are dropping for you and me.
  Ho! hilly ho! heigh O!
   Hilly ho!
In the clear October morning.

Along our path the woods are bold,
 And glow with ripe desire ;
The yellow chestnut showers its gold,
 The sumachs spread their fire ;
The breezes feel as crisp as steel,
 The buckwheat tops are red :
Then down the lane, love, scurry again,
 And over the stubble tread !
  Ho! hilly ho! heigh O!
   Hilly ho!
In the clear October morning.

WHAT THE WINDS BRING.

WHICH is the Wind that brings the cold ?
 The North-Wind, Freddy, and all the snow ;
And the sheep will scamper into the fold
 When the North begins to blow.

Which is the Wind that brings the heat?
  The South-Wind, Katy; and corn will grow,
And peaches redden for you to eat,
  When the South begins to blow.

Which is the Wind that brings the rain?
  The East-Wind, Arty; and farmers know
That cows come shivering up the lane
  When the East begins to blow.

Which is the Wind that brings the flowers?
  The West-Wind, Bessy; and soft and low
The birdies sing in the summer hours
  When the West begins to blow.

BETROTHED ANEW.

THE sunlight fills the trembling air,
  And balmy days their guerdons bring;
The Earth again is young and fair,
  And amorous with musky Spring.

The golden nurslings of the May
  In splendor strew the spangled green,
And hues of tender beauty play,
  Entangled where the willows lean.

Mark how the rippled currents flow:
  What lustres on the meadows lie!
And hark, the songsters come and go,
  And trill between the earth and sky.

"The sunlight fills the trembling air." Page 276.

BETROTHED ANEW.

Who told us that the years had fled,
  Or borne afar our blissful youth?
Such joys are all about us spread,
  We know the whisper was not truth.

The birds, that break from grass and grove,
  Sing every carol that they sung
When first our veins were rich with love,
  And May her mantle round us flung.

O fresh-lit dawn! immortal life!
  O Earth's betrothal, sweet and true,
With whose delights our souls are rife
  And aye their vernal vows renew!

Then, darling, walk with me this morn:
  Let your brown tresses drink its sheen;
These violets, within them worn,
  Of floral fays shall make you queen.

What though there comes a time of pain
  When autumn winds forbode decay;
The days of love are born again,
  That fabled time is far away!

And never seemed the land so fair
  As now, nor birds such notes to sing,
Since first within your shining hair
  I wove the blossoms of the Spring.

III.

SHADOW-LAND.

"THE UNDISCOVERED COUNTRY."

COULD we but know
  The land that ends our dark, uncertain travel,
  Where lie those happier hills and meadows low, —
Ah, if beyond the spirit's inmost cavil,
  Aught of that country could we surely know,
      Who would not go?

     Might we but hear
The hovering angels' high imagined chorus,
  Or catch, betimes, with wakeful eyes and clear,
One radiant vista of the realm before us, —
  With one rapt moment given to see and hear,
      Ah, who would fear?

     Were we quite sure
To find the peerless friend who left us lonely,
  Or there, by some celestial stream as pure,
To gaze in eyes that here were lovelit only, —.
  This weary mortal coil, were we quite sure,
      Who would endure?

"DARKNESS AND THE SHADOW."

WAKING, I have been nigh to Death, —
  Have felt the chillness of his breath
Whiten my cheek and numb my heart,
And wondered why he stayed his dart, —
Yet quailed not, but could meet him so,
As any lesser friend or foe.

But sleeping, in the dreams of night,
His phantom stifles me with fright !
O God ! what frozen horrors fall
Upon me with his visioned pall :
The movelessness, the unknown dread,
Fair life to pulseless silence wed !

And *is* the grave so darkly deep,
So hopeless, as it seems in sleep ?
Can our sweet selves the coffin hold
So dumb within its crumbling mould ?
And is the shroud so dank and drear
A garb, — the noisome worm *so* near ?

Where then is Heaven's mercy fled, —
To quite forget the voiceless dead ?

THE ASSAULT BY NIGHT.

ALL night we hear the rattling flaw,
  The casements shiver with each breath ;
And still more near the foemen draw,
    The pioneers of Death.

Their grisly chieftain comes :
He steals upon us in the night ;
Call up the guards ! light every light !
Beat the alarum drums !

His tramp is at the outer door ;
He bears against the shuddering walls ;
Lo ! what a dismal frost and hoar
Upon the window falls !
Outbar him while ye may !
Feed, feed the watch-fires everywhere, —
Even yet their cheery warmth will scare
This thing of night away.

Ye cannot ! something chokes the grate
And clogs the air within its flues,
And runners from the entrance-gate
Come chill with evil news :
The bars are broken ope !
Ha ! he has scaled the inner wall !
But fight him still, from hall to hall ;
While life remains, there 's hope.

Too late ! the very frame is dust,
The locks and trammels fall apart ;
He reaches, scornful of their trust,
The portals of the heart.
Ay, take the citadel !
But where, grim Conqueror, is thy prey ?
In vain thou 'lt search each secret way,
Its flight is hidden well.

We yield thee, for thy paltry spoils,
This shell, this ruin thou hast made ;

Its tenant has escaped thy toils,
　　Though they were darkly laid.
　　Even now, immortal, pure,
It gains a house not made with hands,
A refuge in serener lands,
　　A heritage secure.

GEORGE ARNOLD.

GREENWOOD, NOVEMBER 13, 1865.

WE stood around the dreamless form
　　Whose strength was so untimely shaken,
Whose sleep not all our love could warm,
　　Nor any dearest voice awaken ;

And while the Autumn breathed her sighs,
　　And dropped a thousand leafy glories,
And all the pathways, and the skies,
　　Were mindful of his songs and stories,

Nor failed to wear the mingled hues
　　He loved, and knew so well to render,
But wooed, — alas, in vain ! — their Muse
　　For one more tuneful lay and tender,

We paused awhile, — the gathered few
　　Who came, in longing, not in duty, —
With eyes that full of weeping grew,
　　To look their last upon his beauty.

Death would not rudely rob that face,
  Nor dim its fine Arcadian brightness,
But gave the lines a clearer grace,
  And sleep's repose, and marble's whiteness.

And, gazing there on him so young,
  We thought of all his ended mission,
The broken links, the songs unsung,
  The love that found no ripe fruition ;

Till last the old, old question came
  To hearts that beat with life around him,
Why Death, with downward torch aflame,
  Had searched our number till he found him ?

Why passed the one who poorly knows
  That blithesome spell for either fortune,
Or mocked with lingering menace those
  Whose pains the final thrust importune ;

Or left the toiling ones who bear
  The crowd's neglect, the want that presses,
The woes no human soul can share,
  Nor look, nor spoken word, confesses.

And from the earth no answer came,
  The forest wore a stillness deeper,
The sky and lake smiled on the same,
  And voiceless as the silent sleeper.

And so we turned ourselves away,
  By earth and air and water chidden,
And left him with them, where he lay,
  A sharer of their secret hidden.

And each the staff and shell again
  Took up, and marched with memories haunted;
But henceforth, in our pilgrim-strain,
  We 'll miss a voice that sweetly chaunted!

THE SAD BRIDAL.

WHAT would you do, my dear one said, —
    What would you do, if I were dead?
If Death should mumble, as he list,
These red lips which now you kist?
What would my love do, were I wed
To that ghastly groom instead;
If o'er me, in the chancel, Death
Should cast his amaranthine wreath, —
Before my eyes, with fingers pale,
Draw down the mouldy bridal veil?
—Ah no! no! it cannot be!
Death would spare their light, and flee,
And leave my love to Life and me!

OCCASIONAL POEMS.

SEVERAL of the earlier productions under this title are **reprinted in an-** swer to frequent requests for copies of them, and in deference to a public sentiment which received them kindly when they first appeared.

.

OCCASIONAL POEMS.

SUMTER.

APRIL 12, 1871.

CAME the morning of that day
　　When the God to whom we pray
Gave the soul of Henry Clay
　　　　To the land ;
How we loved him, living, dying !
But his birthday banners flying
Saw us asking and replying
　　　　Hand to hand.

For we knew that far away,
Round the fort in Charleston Bay,
Hung the dark impending fray,
　　　　Soon to fall ;
And that Sumter's brave defender
Had the summons to surrender
Seventy loyal hearts and tender, —
　　　　(Those were all !)

And we knew the April sun
Lit the length of many a gun, —
Hosts of batteries to the one
  Island crag ;
Guns and mortars grimly frowning,
Johnson, Moultrie, Pinckney, crowning,
And ten thousand men disowning
  The old flag.

O, the fury of the fight
Even then was at its height !
Yet no breath, from noon till night,
  Reached us here ;
We had almost ceased to wonder,
And the day had faded under,
When the echo of the thunder
  Filled each ear !

Then our hearts more fiercely beat,
As we crowded on the street,
Hot to gather and repeat
  All the tale ;
All the doubtful chances turning,
Till our souls with shame were burning,
As if twice our bitter yearning
  Could avail !

Who had fired the earliest gun ?
Was the fort by traitors won ?
Was there succor ?   What was done
  Who could know ?
And once more our thoughts would wander
To the gallant, lone commander,
On his battered ramparts grander
  Than the foe.

Not too long the brave shall wait :
On their own heads be their fate,
Who against the hallowed State
      Dare begin ;
Flag defied and compact riven !
In the record of high Heaven
How shall Southern men be shriven
      For the sin ?

WANTED — A MAN.

BACK from the trebly crimsoned field
    Terrible words are thunder-tost ;
Full of the wrath that will not yield,
    Full of revenge for battles lost !
    Hark to their echo, as it crost
The Capital, making faces wan :
    " End this murderous holocaust ;
Abraham Lincoln, give us a MAN !

" Give us a man of God's own mould,
    Born to marshal his fellow-men ;
One whose fame is not bought and sold
    At the stroke of a politician's pen ;
    Give us the man of thousands ten,
Fit to do as well as to plan ;
    Give us a rallying-cry, and then,
Abraham Lincoln, give us a MAN !

" No leader to shirk the boasting foe,
    And to march and countermarch our brave,

Till they fall like ghosts in the marshes low,
    And swamp-grass covers each nameless grave ;
    Nor another, whose fatal banners wave
Aye in Disaster's shameful van ;
    Nor another, to bluster, **and lie, and rave** ; —
Abraham Lincoln, give us a MAN !

" Hearts are mourning in the North,
    While the sister rivers seek the main,
Red with our life-blood flowing forth, —
    Who shall gather it up again ?
    Though we march to the battle-plain
Firmly as when the strife began,
    Shall all **our offering be in vain ?** —
Abraham Lincoln, give us a MAN !

" Is there never one in all **the land**,
    One on whose might the Cause may lean ?
Are all the common ones so grand,
    And all the titled ones **so mean** ?
    What if your failure may have been
In trying to make good bread from bran,
    From worthless metal a weapon keen ? —
Abraham Lincoln, find us a MAN !

" O, we will follow him to the death,
    Where the foeman's fiercest columns are !
O, we will use our latest breath,
    Cheering **for** every sacred star !
    His to marshal us high and far ;
Ours to battle, as patriots can
    When a Hero leads the Holy War ! —
Abraham Lincoln, give us a MAN ! "

September 8, 1862.

TREASON'S LAST DEVICE.

SONS of New England, in the fray,
  Do you hear the clamor behind your back?
Do you hear the yelping of Blanche, and Tray,
  Sweetheart, and all the mongrel pack?
Girded well with her ocean crags,
  Little our mother heeds their noise;
Her eyes are fixed on crimsoned flags:
  But you — do you hear it, Yankee boys?

Do you hear them say that the patriot fire
  Burns on her altars too pure and bright,
To the darkened heavens leaping higher,
  Though drenched with the blood of every fight;
That in the light of its searching flame
  Treason and tyrants stand revealed,
And the yielding craven is put to shame,
  On Capitol floor or foughten field?

Do you hear the hissing voice, which saith
  That she — who bore through all the land
The lyre of Freedom, the torch of Faith,
  And young Invention's mystic wand —
Should gather her skirts and dwell apart,
  With not one of her sisters to share her fate, —
A Hagar, wandering sick at heart;
  A pariah, bearing the Nation's hate?

Sons, who have peopled the distant West,
  And planted the Pilgrim vine anew,
Where, by a richer soil carest,
  It grows as ever its parent grew,

Say, do you hear, — while the very bells
　　Of your churches ring with her ancient voice,
And the song of your children sweetly tells
　　How true was the land of your fathers' choice, —

Do you hear the traitors who bid you speak
　　The word that shall sever the sacred tie?
And ye, who dwell by the golden Peak,
　　Has the subtle whisper glided by?
Has it crost the immemorial plains,
　　To coasts where the gray Pacific roars
And the Pilgrim blood in the people's veins
　　Is pure as the wealth of their mountain ores?

Spirits of sons who, side by side,
　　In a hundred battles fought and fell,
Whom now no East and West divide,
　　In the isles where the shades of heroes dwell;
Say, has it reached your glorious rest,
　　And ruffled the calm which crowns you there, —
The shame that recreants have confest,
　　The plot that floats in the troubled air?

Sons of New England, here and there,
　　Wherever men are still holding by
The honor our fathers left so fair!
　　Say, do you hear the cowards' cry?
Crouching among her grand old crags,
　　Lightly our mother heeds their noise,
With her fond eyes fixed on distant flags;
　　But you — do you hear it, Yankee boys?

Washington, January 19, 1863.

ABRAHAM LINCOLN.

ASSASSINATED GOOD FRIDAY, 1865.

" FORGIVE them, for they know not what they do ! "
He said, and so went shriven to his fate, —
Unknowing went, that generous heart and true.
  Even while he spoke the slayer lay in wait,
  And when the morning opened Heaven's gate
There passed the whitest soul a nation knew.
  Henceforth all thoughts of pardon are too late ;
They, in whose cause that arm its weapon drew,
  Have murdered Mercy. Now alone shall stand
Blind Justice, with the sword unsheathed she wore.
  Hark, from the eastern to the western strand,
The swelling thunder of the people's roar :
  What words they murmur, — Fetter not her hand !
So let it smite, such deeds shall be no more !

ISRAEL FREYER'S BID FOR GOLD.

FRIDAY, SEPTEMBER 24, 1869.

ZOUNDS ! how the price went flashing through
Wall street, William, Broad street, New !
All the specie in all the land
Held in one Ring by a giant hand —
For millions more it was ready to pay,
And throttle the Street on hangman's-day.
Up from the Gold Pit's nether hell,
While the innocent fountain rose and fell,

Loud and higher the bidding rose,
And the bulls, triumphant, **faced their foes.**
It seemed as if Satan himself were in it :
Lifting it — one per cent a minute —
Through the bellowing broker, **there amid,**
Who made the terrible, final bid !
    High over all, and ever higher,
    Was heard the voice of Israel Freyer, —
A doleful knell in the storm-swept mart, —
" Five millions more ! and for any part
    " I 'll give One Hundred and Sixty ! "

Israel Freyer — the Government Jew —
Good as the best — soaked through and through
With credit gained in the year he sold
Our Treasury's precious hoard of gold ;
Now through his thankless mouth rings out
The leaguers' last and cruellest shout !
Pity the shorts?   Not they, indeed,
While a single rival 's left to bleed !
Down come dealers in silks and hides,
Crowding the Gold Room's rounded sides,
Jostling, trampling each **other's** feet,
Uttering groans in the outer street ;
Watching, with upturned faces pale,
The scurrying index mark its tale ;
    Hearing the bid of Israel Freyer, --
    That ominous voice, would it never tire ?
" Five millions more ! — for any **part,**
(If it breaks your firm, if it cracks your **heart,)**
    I 'll give One Hundred and Sixty ! "

One Hundred and Sixty !   Can't be true !
What will the bears-at-forty do ?

How will the merchants pay their dues ?
How will the country stand the news ?
What 'll the banks — but listen ! hold !
In screwing upward the price of gold
To that dangerous, last, particular peg,
They had killed their Goose with the Golden Egg !
Just there the metal came pouring out,
All ways at once, like a water-spout,
Or a rushing, gushing, yellow flood,
That drenched the bulls wherever they stood !
Small need to open the Washington main,
Their coffer-dams were burst with the strain !
    It came by runners, it came by wire,
    To answer the bid of Israel Freyer,
It poured in millions from every side,
And almost strangled him as he cried, —
    " I 'll give One Hundred and Sixty ! "

Like Vulcan after Jupiter's kick,
Or the aphoristical Rocket's stick,
Down, down, down, the premium fell,
Faster than this rude rhyme can tell !
Thirty per cent the index slid,
Yet Freyer still kept making his bid, —
" One Hundred and Sixty for any part ! "
— The sudden ruin had crazed *his* heart,
Shattered his senses, cracked his brain,
And left him crying again and again, —
Still making his bid at the market's top
(Like the Dutchman's leg that never could stop,)
" One Hundred and Sixty — Five Millions more ! "
Till they dragged him, howling, off the floor.
    The very last words that seller and buyer
    Heard from the mouth of Israel Freyer --

A cry to remember long as they live —
Were, " I 'll take Five Millions more ! I 'll give, —
    I 'll give One Hundred and Sixty ! "

Suppose (to avoid the appearance of evil)
There 's such a thing as a Personal Devil,
It would seem that his Highness here got hold,
For once, of a bellowing Bull in Gold !
Whether bull or bear, it wouldn 't much matter
Should Israel Freyer keep up his clatter
On earth or under it (as, they say,
He is doomed) till the general Judgment Day,
When the Clerk, as he cites him to answer for 't,
Shall bid him keep silence in that Court !
But it matters most, as it seems to me,
That my countrymen, great and strong and free,
So marvel at fellows who seem to win,
That if even a Clown can only begin
By stealing a railroad, and use its purse
For cornering stocks and gold, or — worse —
For buying a Judge and Legislature,
And sinking still lower poor human nature,
The gaping public, whatever befall,
Will swallow him, tandem, harlots, and all !
While our rich men drivel and stand amazed
At the dust and pother his gang have raised,
And make us remember a nursery tale
Of the four-and-twenty who feared one snail.

What 's bred in the bone will breed, you know ;
Clowns and their trainers, high and low,
Will cut such capers, long as they dare,
While honest Poverty says its prayer.
But tell me what prayer or fast can save

Some hoary candidate for the grave,
The market's wrinkled Giant Despair,
Muttering, brooding, scheming there, —
Founding a college or building a church
Lest Heaven should leave him in the lurch!
Better come out in the rival way,
Issue your scrip in open day,
And pour your wealth in the grimy fist
Of some gross-mouthed, gambling pugilist;
Leave toil and poverty where they lie,
Pass thinkers, workers, artists, by,
Your pot-house fag from his counters bring
And make him into a Railway King!
Between such Gentiles and such Jews
Little enough one finds to choose :
Either the other will buy and use,
Eat the meat and throw him the bone,
And leave him to stand the brunt alone.

— Let the tempest come, that's gathering near,
And give us a better atmosphere!

CUBA.

IS it naught?   Is it naught
  That the South-wind brings her wail to our shore,
  That the spoilers compass our desolate sister ?
Is it naught?   Must we say to her, " Strive no more."
  With the lips wherewith we loved her and kissed her ?
With the mocking lips wherewith we said,
  " Thou art the dearest and fairest to us

Of all the daughters the sea hath bred,
  Of all green-girdled isles that woo us ! "
      Is it naught ?

     Must ye wait ?   Must ye wait.
Till they ravage her gardens of orange and palm,
  Till her heart is dust, till her strength is water ?
Must ye see them trample her, and be calm
  As priests when a virgin is led to slaughter ?
Shall they smite the marvel of all lands, —
  The nation's longing, the Earth's completeness, —
On her red mouth dropping myrrh, her hands
  Filled with fruitage and spice and sweetness ?
     Must ye wait ?

     In the day, in the night,
In the burning day, in the dolorous night,
  Her sun-browned cheeks are stained with weeping.
Her watch-fires beacon the misty height : —
  Why are her friends and lovers sleeping ?
" Ye, at whose ear the flatterer bends,
  Who were my kindred before all others, —
Hath he set your hearts afar, my friends ?
  Hath he made ye alien, my brothers,
     Day and night ? "

     Hear ye not ?   Hear ye not
From the hollow sea the sound of her voice ;
  The passionate, far-off tone, which sayeth :
" Alas, my brothers ! alas, what choice, —
  The lust that shameth, the sword that slayeth ?
They bind me ! they rend my delicate locks ;
  They shred the beautiful robes I won me !

My round limbs bleed on the mountain rocks :
　Save me, ere they have quite undone me ! "
　　　Hear ye not ?

　　Speak at last !　Speak at last !
In the might of your strength, in the strength of your right,
　Speak out at last to the treacherous spoiler !
Say : " Will ye harry her in our sight ?
　Ye shall not trample her down, nor soil her !
Loose her bonds ! let her rise in her loveliness, —
　Our virginal sister ; or, if ye shame her,
Dark Amnon shall rue for her sore distress,
　And her sure revenge shall be that of Tamar ! "
　　　Speak at last !

1870.

CRETE.

THOUGH Arkádi's shattered pile
　　Hides her dead without a dirge,
Lo ! where still the mountain isle
　Fronts the angry Moslem surge !
Hers, in old, heroic days,
　Her unfettered heights afar
'Twixt the Grecian Gulf to raise,
　And the torrid Libyan star.

From her bulwarks to the North
　　Stretched the glad Ægæan Sea,
Sending bards and warriors forth
　To the triumphs of the free ;
Ill the fierce invader throve,
　When, from island or from main,

Side by side the Grecians strove :
   Swift he sought his lair again !

Though the Cretan eagle fell,
   And the ancient heights were won,
Freedom's light was guarded well, —
   Handed down from sire to son ;
Through the centuries of shame,
   Ah ! it never wholly died,
But was hid, a sacred flame,
   There on topmost Ida's side.

Shades of heroes Homer sung —
   Wearing once her hundred crowns —
Rise with shadowy swords among
   Candia's smoking fields and towns ;
Not again their souls shall sleep,
   Nor the crescent wane in peace,
Till from every island-keep
   Shines the starry Cross of Greece.

THE OLD ADMIRAL.

GONE at last,
   That brave old hero of the Past !
His spirit has a second birth,
   An unknown, grander life ; —
All of him that was earth
   Lies mute and cold,
   Like a wrinkled sheath and old
Thrown off forever from the shimmering blade
That has good entrance made
   Upon some distant, glorious strife.

" Every broadside swept to death a score."   Page 301.

From another generation,
  A simpler age, to ours Old Ironsides came ;
The morn and noontide of the nation
  Alike he knew, nor yet outlived his fame, —
    O, not outlived his fame !
The dauntless men whose service guards our shore
  Lengthen still their glory-roll
  With his name to lead the scroll,
As a flagship at her fore
  Carries the Union, with its azure and the stars,
Symbol of times that are no more
  And the old heroic wars.

He was the one
Whom Death had spared alone
  Of all the captains of that lusty age,
Who sought the foeman where he lay,
On sea or sheltering bay,
  Nor till the prize was theirs repressed their rage.
They are gone, — all gone :
  They rest with glory and the undying Powers ;
  Only their name and fame and what they saved are ours !

It was fifty years ago,
  Upon the Gallic Sea,
  He bore the banner of the free,
And fought the fight whereof our children know.
  The deathful, desperate fight ! —
  Under the fair moon's light
The frigate squared, and yawed to left and right.
  Every broadside swept to death a score !
Roundly played her guns and well, till their fiery en-
    signs fell,
    Neither foe replying more.

All in silence, when the night-breeze cleared the air,
  Old Ironsides rested there,
Locked in between the twain, and drenched with blood.
  Then homeward, like an eagle with her prey !
  O, it was a gallant fray,
  That fight in Biscay Bay !
Fearless the Captain stood, in his youthful hardihood ;
  He was the boldest of them all,
  Our brave old Admiral !

And still our heroes bleed,
Taught by that olden deed.
  Whether of iron or of oak
The ships we marshal at our country's need,
  Still speak their cannon now as then they spoke ;
Still floats our unstruck banner from the mast
  As in the stormy Past.

Lay him in the ground :
  Let him rest where the ancient river rolls ;
Let him sleep beneath the shadow and the sound
  Of the bell whose proclamation, as it tolls,
Is of Freedom and the gift our fathers gave.
  Lay him gently down :
  The clamor of the town
Will not break the slumbers deep, the beautiful ripe
      sleep
  Of this lion of the wave,
  Will not trouble the old Admiral in his grave.

Earth to earth his dust is laid.
Methinks his stately shade
  On the shadow of a great ship leaves the shore ;
Over cloudless western seas

Seeks the far Hesperides,
  The islands of the blest,
Where no turbulent billows roar, —
    Where is rest.
His ghost upon the shadowy quarter stands
Nearing the deathless lands.
    There all his martial mates, renewed and strong,
    Await his coming long.
    I see the happy **Heroes rise**
    With gratulation in their eyes :
" Welcome, old comrade," Lawrence cries ;
  " Ah, Stewart, tell us of the wars !
    Who win the glory and the scars ?
      How floats the skyey flag, — how many stars ?
    Still speak they of Decatur's name,
    Of Bainbridge's and Perry's fame ?
    Of me, who earliest came ?
Make ready, all :
Room for the Admiral !
    Come, Stewart, tell us of the wars ! "

GETTYSBURG.

WAVE, wave your glorious battle-flags, brave sol-
    diers of the North,
And from the field your arms have won to-day go
    proudly forth !
For now, O comrades dear and leal, — from whom no
    ills could part,
Through the long years of hopes and fears, the nation's
    constant heart, —

Men who have driven so oft the foe, so oft have striven
    in vain,
Yet ever in the perilous hour have crossed his path
    again, —
At last we have our hearts' desire, from them we met
    have wrung
A victory that round the world shall long be told and
    sung !
It was the memory of the past that bore us through
    the fray,
That gave the grand old Army strength to conquer on
    this day !

O now forget how dark and red Virginia's rivers flow,
The Rappahannock's tangled wilds, the glory and the
    woe ;
The fever-hung encampments, where our dying knew
    full sore
How sweet the north-wind to the cheek it soon shall
    cool no more ;
The fields we fought, and gained, and lost ; the low-
    land sun and rain
That wasted us, that bleached the bones of our un-
    buried slain !
There was no lack of foes to meet, of deaths to die no
    lack,
And all the hawks of heaven learned to follow on our
    track ;
But henceforth, hovering southward, their flight shall
    mark afar
The paths of yon retreating hosts that shun the north-
    ern star.

At night, before the closing fray, when all the front
    was still,

We lay in bivouac along the cannon-crested hill.
Ours was the dauntless Second Corps ; and many a
    soldier knew
How sped the fight, and sternly thought of what was
    yet to do.
Guarding the centre there, we lay, and talked with
    bated breath
Of Buford's stand beyond the town, of gallant Rey-
    nold's death,
Of cruel retreats through pent-up streets by murderous
    volleys swept, —
How well the Stone, the Iron, Brigades their bloody
    outposts kept :
'T was for the Union, for the Flag, they perished,
    heroes all,
And we swore to conquer in the end, or even like them
    to fall.

And passed from mouth to mouth the tale of that grim
    day just done,
The fight by Round Top's craggy spur, — of all the
    deadliest one ;
It saved the left : but on the right they pressed us
    back too well,
And like a field in Spring the ground was ploughed with
    shot and shell.
There was the ancient graveyard, its hummocks crushed
    and red,
And there, between them, side by side, the wounded
    and the dead :
The mangled corpses fallen above, — the peaceful dead
    below,
Laid in their graves, to slumber here, a score of years
    ago ;

T

It seemed their waking, wandering shades were asking
    of our slain,
What brought such hideous tumult now where they so
    still had lain !

Bright rose the sun of Gettysburg that morrow morn-
    ing-tide,
And call of trump and roll of drum from height to
    height replied.
Hark ! from the east already goes up the rattling din ;
The Twelfth Corps, winning back their ground, right
    well the day begin !
They whirl fierce Ewell from their front !   Now we of
    the Second pray,
As right and left the brunt have borne, the centre
    might to-day.
But all was still from hill to hill for many a breathless
    hour,
While for the coming battle-shock Lee gathered in his
    power ;
And back and forth our leaders rode, who knew not
    rest or fear,
And along the lines, where'er they came, went up
    the ringing cheer.

'T was past the hour of nooning ; the Summer skies
    were blue ;
Behind the covering timber the foe was hid from view ;
So fair and sweet with waving wheat the pleasant val-
    ley lay,
It brought to mind our Northern homes and meadows
    far away ;
When the whole western ridge at once was fringed
    with fire and smoke ;

Against our lines from sevenscore guns the dreadful
    tempest broke !
Then loud our batteries answer, and far along the crest,
And to and fro the roaring bolts are driven east and
    west ;
Heavy and dark around us glooms the stifling sulphur-
    cloud,
And the cries of mangled men and horse go up beneath
    its shroud.

The guns are still: the end is nigh: we grasp our
    arms anew ;
O now let every heart be stanch and every aim be
    true !
For look ! from yonder wood that skirts the valley's
    further marge,
The flower of all the Southern host move to the final
    charge.
By Heaven ! it is a fearful sight to see their double rank
Come with a hundred battle-flags, — a mile from flank
    to flank !
Tramping the grain to earth, they come, ten thousand
    men abreast ;
Their standards wave, — their hearts are brave, — they
    hasten not, nor rest,
But close the gaps our cannon make, and onward press,
    and nigher,
And, yelling at our very front, again pour in their fire !

Now burst our sheeted lightnings forth, now all our
    wrath has vent !
They die, they wither ; through and through their
    wavering lines are rent.
But these are gallant, desperate men, of our own race
    and land,

Who charge anew, and welcome death, and fight us
    hand to hand :
Vain, vain ! give way, as well ye may — the crimson
    die is cast !
Their bravest leaders bite the dust, their strength is
    failing fast ;
They yield, they turn, they fly the field : we smite them
    as they run ;
Their arms, their colors are our spoil ; the furious fight
    is done !
Across the plain we follow far and backward push the
    fray :
Cheer ! cheer ! the grand old Army at last has won the
    day !

Hurrah ! the day has won the cause ! No gray-clad
    host henceforth
Shall come with fire and sword to tread the highways
    of the North !
'T was such a flood as when ye see, along the Atlantic
    shore,
The great Spring-tide roll grandly in with swelling
    surge and roar :
It seems no wall can stay its leap or balk its wild desire
Beyond the bound that Heaven hath fixed to higher
    mount, and higher ;
But now, when whitest lifts its crest, most loud its bil-
    lows call,
Touched by the Power that led them on, they fall, and
    fall, and fall.
Even thus, unstayed upon his course, to Gettysburg
    the foe
His legions led, and fought, and fled, and might no
    further go.

Full many a dark-eyed Southern girl shall weep her
    lover dead ;
But with a price the fight was ours, — we too have
    tears to shed !
The bells that peal our triumph forth anon shall toll
    the brave,
Above whose heads the cross must stand, the hill-
    side grasses wave !
Alas ! alas ! the trampled grass shall thrive another
    year,
The blossoms on the apple-boughs with each new
    Spring appear,
But when our patriot-soldiers fall, Earth gives them up
    to God ;
Though their souls rise in clearer skies, their forms
    are as the sod ;
Only their names and deeds are ours, — but, for a cen-
    tury yet,
The dead who fell at Gettysburg the land shall not
    forget.

God send us peace ! and where for aye the loved and
    lost recline
Let fall, O South, your leaves of palm, — O North,
    your sprigs of pine !
But when, with every ripened year, we keep the har-
    vest-home,
And to the dear Thanksgiving-feast our sons and
    daughters come, —
When children's children throng the board in the old
    homestead spread,
And the bent soldier of these wars is seated at the head,
Long, long the lads shall listen to hear the gray-beard
    tell

Of those who fought at Gettysburg and stood their
    ground so well :
" 'T was for the Union and the Flag," the veteran
    shall say,
" Our grand old Army held the ridge, and won that
    glorious day ! "

DARTMOUTH ODE.

I.

PRELUDE.

A WIND and a voice from the North !
    A courier-wind sent forth
    From the mountains to the sea :
    A summons borne to me
From halls which the Muses haunt, from hills where
    the heart and the wind are free !

    " Come from the outer throng ! "
    (Such was the burden it bore,)
    " Thou who hast gone before,
    Hither ! and sing us a song,
Far from the round of the town and the sound of the
    great world's roar ! "

    O masterful voice of Youth,
That will have, like the upland wind, its own wild
    way !
O choral words, that with every season rise
Like the warblings of orchard-birds at break of day !
O faces, fresh with the light of morning skies !

No marvel world-worn toilers seek you here,
Even as they life renew, from year to year,
In woods and meadows lit with blossoming May;
But O, blithe voices, that have such sweet power,
Unto your high behest this summer hour
What answer has the poet? how shall he frame his
lay?

II.

THEME.

"WHAT shall my song rehearse?" I said
To a wise bard, whose hoary head
Is bowed, like Kearsarge crouching low
Beneath a winter weight of snow,
But whose songs of passion, joy, or scorn,
Within a fiery heart are born.

"What can I spread, what proper feast
For these young Magi of the East?
What wisdom find, what mystic lore,
What chant they have not heard before?
Strange words of old has every tongue
Those happy cloistered hills among;
For each riddle I divine
They can answer me with nine;
Their footsteps by the Muse are led,
Their lips on Plato's honey fed;
Their eyes have skill to read the page
Of Theban bard or Attic sage;
"For them all Nature's mysteries, —
The deep-down secrets of the seas,
The cyclone's whirl, the lightning's shock,
The language of the riven rock;
They know the starry sisters seven, —

What clouds the molten suns enfold,
And all the golden woof of heaven
Unravelled in their lens behold !
Gazing in a thousand eyes,
So rapt and clear, so wonder-wise,
What shall my language picture, then,
Beyond their wont — that has not reached their ken ?

" What else are poets used to sing,
Who sing of youth, than laurelled fame and love ?
But ah ! it needs no words to move
Young hearts to some impassioned vow,
To whom already on the wing
The blind god hastens.   Even now
Their pulses quiver with a thrill
Than all that wisdom wiser still.
Nor any need to tell of rustling bays,
Of honor ever at the victor's hand,
To them who at the portals stand
Like mettled steeds, — each eager from control
To leap, and, where the corso lies ablaze,
Let out his speed and soonest pass the goal.

"What is there left? what shall my verse
Within those ancient halls rehearse ? "
Deep in his heart my plaint the minstrel weighed,
And a subtle answer made :
" The world that is, the ways of men,
Not yet are glassed within their ken.
Their foster-mother holds them long, —
Long, long to youth, — short, short to age, appear
The rounds of her Olympic Year, —
Their ears are quickened for the trumpet-call.
Sing to them one true song,

Ere from the Happy Vale they turn,
Of all the Abyssinian craved to learn,
And dared his fate, and scaled the mountain-wall
To join the ranks without, and meet what might
    befall."

III.

VESTIGIA RETRORSUM.

GONE the Arcadian age,
When, from his hillside hermitage
Sent forth, the gentle scholar strode
At ease upon a royal road,
And found the outer regions all they seem
    In Youth's prophetic dream.
The graduate took his station then
By right, a ruler among men :
Courtly the three estates, and sure ;
The bar, the bench, the pulpit, pure ;
No cosmic doubts arose, to vex
The preacher's heart, his faith perplex.
Content in ancient paths he trod,
Nor searched beyond his Book for God.
Great virtue lurked in many a saw
And in the doctor's Latin lay ;
Men thought, lived, died, in the appointed way.
Yet eloquence was slave to law,
And law to right : the statesman sought
A patriot's fame, and served his land, unbought,
And bore erect his front, and held his oath in awe.

14

IV.

ÆREA PROLES.

BUT, now, far other days
Have made less green the poet's bays, —
Have less revered the band and gown,
The grave physician's learnéd frown, —
Shaken the penitential mind
That read the text nor looked behind, —
Brought from his throne the bookman down,
Made hard the road to station and renown !
Now from this seclusion deep
The scholar wakes, — as one from sleep,
As one from sleep remote and sweet,
In some fragrant garden-close
Between the lily and the rose,
Roused by the tramp of many feet,
Leaps up to find a ruthless, warring band,
Dust, strife, an untried weapon in his hand !
The time unto itself is strange,
Driven on from change to change,
Neither of past nor present sure,
The ideal vanished nor the real secure.
Heaven has faded from the skies,
Faith hides apart and weeps with clouded eyes ;
A noise of cries we hear, a noise of creeds,
While the old heroic deeds
Not of the leaders now are told, as then,
But of lowly, common men.
See by what paths the loud-voiced gain
Their little heights above the plain :
Truth, honor, virtue, cast away
For the poor plaudits of a day !
Now fashion guides at will

The artist's brush, the writer's quill,
While, for a weary time unknown,
The reverent workman toils alone,
Asking for bread and given but a stone.
Fettered with gold the statesman's tongue;
Now, even the church, among
New doubts and strange discoveries, half in vain
Defends her long, ancestral reign;
Now, than all others grown more great,
That which was the last estate
By turns reflects and rules the age, —
Laughs, scolds, weeps, counsels, jeers, — a jester and a
sage!

V.

ENCHANTMENTS.

HERE, in Learning's shaded haunt,
The battle-fugue and mingled cries forlorn
Softened to music seem, nor the clear spirit daunt;
Here, in the gracious world that looks
From earth and sky and books,
Easeful and sweet it seems all else to scorn
Than works of noble use and virtue born;
Brave hope and high ambition consecrate
Our coming years to something great.
But when the man has stood,
Anon, in garish outer light,
Feeling the first wild fever of the blood
That places self with self at strife
Whether to hoard or drain the wine of life, —
When the broad pageant flares upon the sight,
And tuneful Pleasure plumes her wing
And the crowds jostle and the mad bells ring, —

Then he, who sees the vain world take slow heed
Albeit of his worthiest and best,
And still, through years of failure and unrest,
    Would keep inviolate his vow,
Of all his faith and valor has sore need !
Even then, I know, do nobly as we will,
What we would not, we do, and see not how ;
That which we would, is not, we know not why ;
Some fortune holds us from our purpose still, —
Chance sternly beats us back, and turns our steps
      awry !

VI.

YOUTH AND AGE.

How slow, how sure, how swift,
The sands within each glass,
The brief, illusive moments, pass !
Half unawares we mark their drift
Till the awakened heart cries out, — Alas !
    Alas, the fair occasion fled,
The precious chance to action all unwed !
And murmurs in its depths the old refrain, —
Had we but known betimes what now we know in
      vain !

When the veil from the eyes is lifted
    The seer's head is gray ;
When the sailor to shore has drifted
    The sirens are far away.
Why must the clearer vision,
    The wisdom of Life's late hour,
Come, as in Fate's derision,
    When the hand has lost its power ?

Is there a rarer being,
  Is there a fairer sphere
Where the strong are not unseeing,
  And the harvests are not sere ;
Where, ere the seasons dwindle
  They yield their due return ;
Where the lamps of knowledge kindle
  While the flames of youth still burn ?
O for the young man's chances !
  O for the old man's will !
Those flee while this advances,
  And the strong years cheat us still.

VII.

WHAT CHEER ?

  Is there naught else ? — you say, —
No braver prospect far away ?
No gladder song, no ringing call
Beyond the misty mountain-wall ?
And were it thus indeed, I know
  Your hearts would still with courage glow ;
I know how yon historic stream
  Is laden yet, as in the past,
With dreamful longings on it cast
  By those who saunter from the crown
Of this broad slope, their reverend Academe, —
Who reach the meadowed banks, and lay them down
On the green sward, and set their faces south,
    Embarked in Fancy's shallop there,
And with the current seek the river's mouth,
Finding the outer ocean grand and fair.
    Ay, like the stream's perpetual tide,
Wave after wave each blithe, successive throng

Must join the main and wander far and wide.
To you the golden, vanward years belong !
  Ye need not fear to leave the shore :
  Not seldom youth has shamed the sage
  With riper wisdom, — but to age
  Youth, youth, returns no more !
Be yours the strength by will to conquer fate,
Since to the man who sees his purpose clear,
  And gains that knowledge of his sphere
  Within which lies all happiness, —
  Without, all danger and distress, —
And seeks the right, content to strive and wait,
To him all good things flow, nor honor crowns him
  late.

VIII.

PHAROS.

ONE such there was, that brother elder-born
  And loftiest, — from your household torn
   In the rathe spring-time, ere
His steps could seek their olden pathways here.
   Mourn !
Mourn, for your Mother mourns, of him bereft, —
Her strong one ! he is fallen :
     But has left
  His works your heritage and guide,
Through East and West his stalwart fame divide.
   Mourn, for the liberal youth,
The undaunted spirit whose quintessence rare,
   Fanned by the Norseland air,
Saw flaming in its own white heat the truth
  That Man, whate'er his ancestry,
Tanned by what sun or exiled from what shore,
Hears in his soul the high command, — Be Free !

For him who, at the parting of the ways,
    Disdained the flowery path, and gave
His succor to the hunted Afric slave,
Whose cause he chose nor feared the world's dis-
      praise;
Yet found anon the right become the might,
    And, in the long revenge of time,
Lived to renown and hoary years sublime.
      Ye know him now, your beacon-light!
      Ay, he was fronted like a tower, —
      In thought large-moulded, as of frame;
      He that, in the supreme hour,
Sat brooding at the river-heads of power
With sovereign strength for every need that came!
      Not for that blameless one the place
That opens wide to men of lesser race; —
      Even as of old the votes are given,
And Aristides is from Athens driven;
But for our statesman, in his grander trust
      No less the undefiled, The Just, —
With poesy and learning lightly worn,
And knees that bent to Heaven night and morn, —
For him that sacred, unimpassioned seat,
Where right and wrong for stainless judgment meet
Above the greed, the strife, the party call. —
Henceforth let CHASE'S robes on no base shoulders
    fall!

IX.

ATLANTIS SURGENS.

WELL may your hearts be valiant, — ye who stand
    Within that glory from the past,
And see how ripe the time, how fair the land

In which your lot is cast!
  For us alone your sorrow,
   Ye children of the morrow, —
    For us, who struggle yet, and wait,
    Sent forth too early and too late!
But yours shall be our tenure handed down,
Conveyed in blood, stamped with the martyr's
    crown;
   For which the toilers long have wrought,
   And poets sung, and heroes fought;
   The new Saturnian age is yours,
   That juster season soon to be
On the near coasts (whereto your vessels sail
   Beyond the darkness and the gale),
Of proud Atlantis risen from the sea!
You shall not know the pain that now endures
    The surge, the smiting of the waves,
      The overhanging thunder,
The shades of night which plunge engulféd under
      Those yawning island-caves;
But in their stead for you shall glisten soon
The coral circlet and the still lagoon,
   Green shores of freedom, blest with calms,
And sunlit streams and meads, and shadowy palms:
Such joys await you, in our sorrows' stead;
   Thither our charts have almost led;
Nor in that land shall worth, truth, courage, ask for
    alms.

X.

VALETE ET SALVETE.

O, TRAINED beneath the Northern Star!
Worth, courage, honor, these indeed

Your sustenance and birthright are!
Now, from her sweet dominion freed,
Your Foster Mother bids you speed;
Her gracious hands the gates unbar,
Her richest gifts you bear away,
Her memories shall be your stay:
Go where you will, her eyes your course shall mark
     afar.

June 25, 1873.

HORACE GREELEY.

EARTH, let thy softest mantle rest
  On this worn child to thee returning,
Whose youth was nurtured at thy breast,
  Who loved thee with such tender yearning!
He knew thy fields and woodland ways,
  And deemed thy humblest son his brother:—
Asleep, beyond our blame or praise,
  We yield him back, O gentle Mother!

Of praise, of blame, he drank his fill:
  Who has not read the life-long story?
And dear we hold his fame, but still
  The man was dearer than his glory.
And now to us are left alone
  The closet where his shadow lingers,
The vacant chair,—that was a throne,—
  The pen, just fallen from his fingers.

Wrath changed to kindness on that pen;
  Though dipped in gall, it flowed with honey;
One flash from out the cloud, and then
  The skies with smile and jest were sunny.

14 *   U

Of hate he surely lacked the art,
  Who made his enemy his lover:
O reverend head and Christian heart !
  Where now their like the round world over ?

He saw the goodness, not the taint,
  In many a poor, do-nothing creature,
And gave to sinner and to saint,
  But kept his faith in human nature ;
Perchance he was not worldly-wise,
  Yet we who noted, standing nearer,
The shrewd, kind twinkle in his eyes,
  For every weakness held him dearer.

Alas that unto him who gave
  So much, so little should be given !
Himself alone he might not save
  Of all for whom his hands had striven.
Place, freedom, fame, his work bestowed :
  Men took, and passed, and left him lonely ; —
What marvel if, beneath his load,
  At times he craved — for justice only !

Yet thanklessness, the serpent's tooth,
  His lofty purpose could not alter ;
Toil had no power to bend his youth,
  Or make his lusty manhood falter ;
From envy's sling, from slander's dart,
  That armored soul the body shielded,
Till one dark sorrow chilled his heart,
  And then he bowed his head and yielded.

Now, now, we measure at its worth
  The gracious presence gone forever !

The wrinkled East, that gave him birth,
　Laments with every laboring river;
Wild moan the free winds of the West
　For him who gathered to her prairies
The sons of men, and made each crest
　The haunt of happy household fairies;

And anguish sits upon the mouth
　Of her who came to know him latest:
His heart was ever thine, O South!
　He was thy truest friend, and greatest!
He shunned thee in thy splendid shame,
　He stayed thee in thy voiceless sorrow;
The day thou shalt forget his name,
　Fair South, can have no sadder morrow.

The tears that fall from eyes unused, —
　The hands above his grave united, —
The words of men whose lips he loosed,
　Whose cross he bore, whose wrongs he righted, —
Could he but know, and rest with this!
　Yet stay, through Death's low-lying hollow,
His one last foe's insatiate hiss
　On that benignant shade would follow!

Peace! while we shroud this man of men
　Let no unhallowed word be spoken!
He will not answer thee again,
　His mouth is sealed, his wand is broken.
Some holier cause, some vaster trust
　Beyond the veil, he doth inherit:
O gently, Earth, receive his dust,
　And Heaven soothe his troubled spirit!

　　December 3, 1872.

KEARNY AT SEVEN PINES.

So that soldierly legend is still on its journey, —
  That story of Kearny who knew not to yield!
'T was the day when with Jameson, fierce Berry, and
    Birney,
  Against twenty thousand he rallied the field.
Where the red volleys poured, where the clamor rose
    highest,
  Where the dead lay in clumps through the dwarf oak
    and pine,
Where the aim from the thicket was surest and nigh-
    est, —
  No charge like Phil Kearny's along the whole line.

When the battle went ill, and the bravest were solemn,
  Near the dark Seven Pines, where we still held our
    ground,
He rode down the length of the withering column,
  And his heart at our war-cry leapt up with a bound;
He snuffed, like his charger, the wind of the powder, —
  His sword waved us on and we answered the sign:
Loud our cheer as we rushed, but his laugh rang the
    louder,
  "There 's the devil's own fun, boys, along the whole
    line!"

How he strode his brown steed! How we saw his blade
    brighten
  In the one hand still left, — and the reins in his
    teeth!
He laughed like a boy when the holidays heighten,
  But a soldier's glance shot from his visor beneath.

Up came the reserves to the mellay infernal,
    Asking where to go in, — through the clearing or
        pine ?
" O, anywhere ! Forward ! 'T is all the same, Colonel :
    You 'll find lovely fighting along the whole line ! "

O, evil the black shroud of night at Chantilly,
    That hid him from sight of his brave men and tried !
Foul, foul sped the bullet that clipped the white lily,
    The flower of our knighthood, the whole army's pride !
Yet we dream that he still, — in that shadowy region
    Where the dead form their ranks at the wan drum-
        mer's sign, —
Rides on, as of old, down the length of his legion,
    And the word still is Forward ! along the whole line.

CUSTER.

WHAT ! shall that sudden blade
      Leap out no more ?
  No more thy hand be laid
Upon the sword-hilt, smiting sore ?
    O for another such
    The charger's rein to clutch, —
One equal voice to summon victory,
    Sounding thy battle-cry,
Brave darling of the soldiers' choice !
    Would there were one more voice !

    O gallant charge, too bold !
    O fierce, imperious greed
To pierce the clouds that in their darkness hold

Slaughter of man and steed !
Now, stark and cold,
Among thy fallen braves thou **liest**,
And even with thy blood defiest
The wolfish foe :
But ah, thou liest low,
And all our birthday song is hushed indeed !

Young lion of the plain,
Thou of the tawny mane !
Hotly the soldiers' hearts shall beat,
Their mouths thy death repeat,
Their vengeance seek the trail again
Where thy red doomsmen be ;
But on the charge no more shall stream
Thy hair, — no more thy sabre gleam, —
No more ring out thy battle-shout,
Thy cry of victory !

Not when a hero falls
The sound a world appalls :
For while we plant his cross
There is a glory, even in the loss :
But when some craven heart
From honor dares to part,
Then, then, the groan, the blanching **cheek,**
And men in whispers speak,
Nor kith nor country dare reclaim
From the black depths his name.

Thou, wild young warrior, rest,
By all the prairie winds caressed !
Swift was thy dying pang ;
Even as the war-cry rang

Thy deathless spirit mounted high
And sought Columbia's sky : —
There, to the northward far,
Shines a new star,
And from it blazes down
The light of thy renown !

July 10, 1876.

THE COMEDIAN'S LAST NIGHT.

NOT yet ! No, no, — you would not quote
That meanest of the critic's gags ?
'T was surely not of me they wrote
Those words, *too late the veteran lags :*
'T is not so very late with me ;
I 'm not so old as that, you know,
Though work and trouble — as you see —
(Not years) have brought me somewhat low.
I failed, you say ? No, no, not yet !
Or, if I did, — with such a past,
Where is the man would have me quit
Without one triumph at the last ?

But one night more, — a little thing
To you, — I swear 't is all I ask !
Once more to make the wide house ring, —
To tread the boards, to wear the mask,
To move the coldest as of yore,
To make them laugh, to make them cry,
To be — to be myself once more,
And then, if must be, let me die !

The prompter's bell !   I 'm here, you see :
  By Heaven, friends, you 'll break my heart !
Nat *Gosling's called :* let be, let be, —
  None but myself shall act the part !

———

Yes, thank you, boy, **I 'll take your chair**
  One moment, while I catch my breath.
D' ye hear the noise they 're making there ?
  'T would warm a player's heart in death.
How say you now ?   Whate'er they write,
  We 've put that bitter gibe **to shame ;**
I knew, I knew there burned to-night
  Within my soul the olden flame !
Stand off a bit : that final round, —
  I 'd hear it ere it dies away
The last, last time ! — there 's no more sound :
  So end the player and the play.

The house is cleared.   My senses swim ;
  I shall be better, though, anon, —
One stumbles when the lights are dim, —
  'T is growing late : we must be gone.
Well, braver luck than mine, old friends !
  A little work and fame are ours
While Heaven health and fortune lends,
  And then — the coffin and the flowers !
These scattered garments ? let them lie :
  Some fresher actor (I 'm not vain)
Will dress **anew** the part ; — but I —
  I shall not put them on again.

November 17, 1875.

THE MONUMENT OF GREELEY.

READ AT THE UNVEILING OF THE BUST SURMOUNTING THE
PRINTERS' MONUMENT TO HORACE GREELEY, GREEN-
WOOD CEMETERY, DECEMBER 4, 1876.

ONCE more, dear mother Earth, we stand
   In reverence where thy bounty gave
Our brother, yielded to thy hand,
   The sweet protection of the grave !
Well hast thou soothed him through the years,
   The years our love and sorrow number, —
And with thy smiles, and with thy tears,
   Made green and fair his place of slumber.

Thine be the keeping of that trust ;
   And ours this image, born of Art
To shine above his hidden dust,
   What time the sunrise breezes part
The trees, and with new light enwreathe
   Yon head, — until the lips are golden,
And from them music seems to breathe
   As from the desert statue olden.

Would it were so ! that now we might
   Hear once his uttered voice again,
Or hold him present to our sight,
   Nor reach with empty hands and vain !
O that, from some far place, were heard
   One cadence of his speech returning, —
A whispered tone, a single word,
   Sent back in answer to our yearning !

It may not be ?　What then the spark,
　The essence which illumed the whole
And made his living form its mark
　And outward likeness ?　What the soul
That warmed the heart and poised the head,
　And spoke the thoughts we now inherit ?
Bright force of fire and ether bred, —
　Where art thou now, elusive Spirit ?

Where, now, the sunburst of a love
　Which blended still with sudden wrath
To nerve the righteous hand that strove,
　And blaze in the oppressor's path ?
Fair Earth, our dust is thine indeed !
　Too soon he reached the voiceless portal, —
That whither leads ?　Where lies the mead
　He gained, and knew himself immortal ?

Or, tell us, on what distant star,
　Where even as here are toil and wrong,
With strength renewed he lifts afar
　A voice of aid, a war-cry strong ?
What fruit, this stern Olympiad past,
　Has that rich nature elsewhere yielded,
What conquest gained and knowledge vast,
　What kindred beings loved and shielded !

Why seek to know ? he little sought,
　Himself, to lift the close-drawn veil,
Nor for his own salvation wrought
　And pleaded, ay, and wore his mail ;
No selfish grasp of life, no fear,
　Won for mankind his ceaseless caring,
But for themselves he held them dear, —
　Their birth and shrouded exit sharing.

Not his the feverish will to live
  A sunnier life, a longer space,
Save that the Eternal Law might give
  The boon in common to his race.
Earth, 't was thy heaven he loved, and best
  Thy precious offspring, man and woman,
And labor for them seemed but rest
  To him, whose nature was so human.

Even here his spirit haply longed
  To stay, remembered by our kind,
And where the haunts of men are thronged
  Move yet among them.   Seek and find
A presence, though his voice has ceased,
  Still, even where we dwell, remaining,
With all its tenderest thrills increased
  And all it cared to ask obtaining.

List, how the varied things that took
  The impress of his passion rare
Make answer !   To the roadways look,
  The watered vales, the hamlets fair.
He walks unseen the living woods,
  The fields, the town, the shaded borough,
And in the pastoral solitudes
  Delights to view the lengthening furrow.

The faithful East that cradled him,
  Still, while she deems her nursling sleeps,
Sits by his couch with vision dim ;
  The plenteous West his feast-day keeps ;
The wistful South recalls the ways
  Of one who in his love enwound her,
And stayed her, in the evil days,
  With arms of comfort thrown around her.

He lives wherever men to men
  In perilous hours his words repeat,
Where clangs the forge, where glides the pen,
  Where toil and traffic crowd the street ;
And in whatever time or place
  Earth's purest souls their purpose strengthen,
Down the broad pathway of his race
  The shadow of his name shall lengthen.

" Still with us ! " all the liegemen cry
  Who read his heart and held him dear ;
The hills declare " He shall not die ! "
  The prairies answer " He is here ! "
Immortal thus, no dread of fate
  Be ours, no vain *memento mori :*
Life, Life, not Death, we celebrate, —
  A lasting presence touched with glory.

The star may vanish, — but a ray,
  Sent forth, what mandate can recall ?
The circling wave still keeps its way
  That marked a turret's seaward fall ;
The least of music's uttered strains
  Is part of Nature's voice forever ;
And aye beyond the grave remains
  The great, the good man's high endeavor !

Well may the brooding Earth retake
  The form we knew, to be a part
Of bloom and herbage, fern and brake,
  New lives that from her being start.
Naught of the soul shall there remain :
  They came on void and darkness solely
Who the veiled Spirit sought in vain
  Within the temple's shrine Most Holy.

That, that, has found again the source
  From which itself to us was lent :
The Power that, in perpetual course,
  Makes of the dust an instrument
Supreme ; the universal Soul ;
  The current infinite and single
Wherein, as ages onward roll,
  Life, Thought, and Will forever mingle.

What more is left, to keep *our* hold
  On him who was so true and strong ?
This semblance, raised above the mould
  With offerings of word and song,
That men may teach, in aftertime,
  Their sons how goodness marked the features
Of one whose life was made sublime
  By service for his brother creatures.

And last, and lordliest, his fame, —
  A station in the sacred line
Of heroes that have left a name
  We conjure with, — a place divine,
Since, in the world's eternal plan,
  Divinity itself is given,
To him who lives or dies for Man
  And looks within his soul for Heaven.

NEWS FROM OLYMPIA.[1]

OLYMPIA ? Yes, strange tidings from the city
    Which pious mortals builded, stone by stone,
For those old gods of Hellas, half in pity
    Of their storm-mantled height and dwelling lone, —
Their seat upon the mountain overhanging
    Where Zeus withdrew behind the rolling cloud,
, Where crowned Apollo sang, the phorminx twanging,
    And at Poseidon's word the forests bowed.

      Ay, but that fated day
When from the plain Olympia passed away ;
When ceased the oracles, and long unwept
Amid their fanes the gods deserted fell,
While sacerdotal ages, as they slept,
      The ruin covered well !

The pale Jew flung his cross, thus one has written,
    Among them as they sat at the high feast,
And saw the gods, before that token smitten,
    Fade slowly, while His presence still increased,
Until the seas Ionian and Ægæan
    Gave out a cry that Pan himself was dead,
And all was still : thenceforth no more the pæan,
    No more by men the prayer to Zeus was said.

      Sank, like a falling star,
Hephaistos in the Lemnian waters far ;

---

[1] " One after the other the figures described by Pausanias are dragged
from the earth. Niké has been found ; the head of Kladeos is there ; Myr-
tilos is announced, and Zeus will soon emerge. This is earnest of what may
follow." — *Despatch to the London Times.*

The silvery Huntress fled the darkened sky ;
Dim grew Athene's helm, Apollo's crown ;
Alpheios' nymphs stood wan and trembling by
    When Hera's fane went down.

News ! what news ? Has it in truth then ended,
    The term appointed for that wondrous sleep ?
Has Earth so well her fairest brood defended
    Within her bosom ? Was their slumber deep
Not this our dreamless rest that knows no waking,
    But that to which the years are as a day ?
What ! are they coming back, their prison breaking, —
    These gods of Homer's chant, of Pindar's lay ?

       Are they coming back in might,
Olympia's gods, to claim their ancient right ?
Shall then the sacred majesty of old,
The grace that holy was, the noble rage,
Temper our strife, abate our greed for gold,
       Make fine the modern age ?

Yes, they are coming back, to light returning !
    Bold are the hearts and void of fear the hands
That toil, the lords of War and Spoil unurning,
    Or of their sisters fair that break the bands ;
That loose the sovran mistress of desire,
    Queen Aphrodite, to possess the earth
Once more ; that dare renew dread Hera's ire,
    And rouse old Pan to wantonness of mirth.

       The herald Niké, first,
From the dim resting-place unfettered burst,
Winged victor over fate and time and death !
Zeus follows next, and all his children then ;

Phoibos awakes and draws a joyous breath,
　　And Love returns to men.

Ah, let them come, the glorious Immortals,
　　Rulers no more, but with mankind to dwell,
The dear companions of our hearts and portals,
　　Voiceless, unworshipped, yet beloved right well!
Pallas shall sit enthroned in wisdom's station,
　　Eros and Psyche be forever wed,
And still the primal loveliest creation
　　Yield new delight from ancient beauty bred.

　　Triumphant as of old,
Changeless while Art and Song their warrant hold,
The visions of our childhood haunt us still,
Still Hellas sways us with her charm supreme.
The morn is past, but Man has not the will
　　To banish yet the dream.

LE JOUR DU ROSSIGNOL.

'TWAS the season of feasts, when the blithe birds
　　had met
In their easternmost arbor, an innocent throng,
And they made the glad birthday of each gladder yet,
　　With the daintiest cheer and the rarest of song.

What brave tirra-lirras!   But clear amid all,
　　At each festival held in the favorite haunt,
The nightingale's music would quaver and fall,
　　And surest and sweetest of all was his chant.

At last came the nightingale's fête, and they sought
  To make it the blithefullest tryst of the year,
Since this was the songster that oftenest caught
  The moment's quick rapture, the joy that is near.

But, alas ! half in vain the fine chorus they made ;
  Fresh-plumed and all fluttering, and uttering their
      best,
For silent among them, so etiquette bade,
  To the notes of his praisers sat listening the guest.

Quel dommage ! Must a failure, like theirs, be our
      feast ?
  Must our chorister's voice at his own fête be still ?
While he thinks : " You are kind. May your tribe be
      increased ;
  But at this I can give you *such* odds if I will ! "

What avail, fellow-minstrels, our crotchets and staves,
  Though your tribute, like mine, rises straight from
      the heart,
Unless while the bough on his laurel-bush waves,
  To his own sängerfest the one guest lends his art ?

Whose swift wit like his, with which none dares to vie,
  Whose carol so instant, so joyous and true ?
Sound it cheerly, dear HOLMES, for the sun is still high,
  And we 're glad, as he halts, to be out-sung by you.

15

MERIDIAN.

AN OLD-FASHIONED POEM.

THE TWENTY-FIFTH ANNIVERSARY OF THE YALE CLASS OF 1853.

Inque brevi spatio mutantur sæcla animantum
Et quasi cursores vitai lampada tradunt.
LUCRETIUS, *De Rer. Nat.*, Lib. ii.

I.

THE tryst is kept.   How fares it with each one
At this mid hour, when mariners take the sun
And cast their reckoning? when some level height
Is reached by men who set their strength aright, —
Who for a little space the firm plateau
Tread sure and steadfast, yet who needs must know
Full soon begins the inevitable slide
Down westward slopings of the steep divide.

How stands it, comrades, at this noontide fleet,
When for an hour we gather to the meet?
Like huntsmen, rallied by the winding horn,
Who seek the shade with trophies lightly borne,
Remembering their deeds of derring-do —
What bows were bent, what arrows speeded true.
All, all have striven, and far apart have strayed:
Fling down! fill up the can! wipe off the blade!
Ring out the song! nor care, in this our mood,
What hollow echo mocks us from the wood!

Or is it with us, haply, as with those
Each man of whom the morn's long combat knows?

All veterans now : the bugle's far recall
From the hot strife has sounded sweet to all.
Welcome the rendezvous beneath the elms,
The truce, the throwing down of swords and helms !

Life *is* a battle !   How these sayings trite
Which school-boys write — and know not what they
    write —
In after years begin to burn and glow !
What man is here that has not found it so ?
Who here is not a soldier of the wars,
Has not his half-healed wound, his early scars, —
Has broken not his sword, or from the field
Borne often naught but honor and his shield ?
Ah, ye recruits, with flags and arms unstained,
See by what toil and moil the heights are gained !
Learn of our skirmish lost, our ridges won,
The dust, the thirst beneath the scorching sun ;
Then see us closer draw — by fate bereft
Of men we loved — the firm-set column left.

II.

To me the picture that some painter drew
Makes answer for our past.   His throng pursue
A siren, one that ever smiles before,
Almost in reach, alluring more and more.
Old, young, with outstretched hand, with eager eye,
Fast follow where her wingèd sandals fly,
While by some witchery unto each she seems
His dearest hope, the spirit of his dreams.
Ah, me ! how like those dupes of Pleasure's chase,
Yet how unlike, we left our starting-place !
Is there not something nobler, far more true,
In the Ideal, still before our view,

Upon whose shining course we followed far
While sank and rose the night and morning star?
Ever we saw a bright glance cast behind
Or heard a word of hope borne down the wind, —
As yet we see and hear, and follow still
With faithful hearts and long-enduring will.

In what weird circle has the enchantress led
Our footsteps, so that now again they tread
These walks, and all that on the course befell
Seems to ourselves a shadow and a spell?
Was it the magic of a moment's trance,
A scholar's day-dream?   Have we been, perchance,
Like that bewildered king who dipped his face
In water — while a dervish paused to trace
A mystic phrase — and, ere he raised it, lived
A score of seasons, labored, journeyed, wived
In a strange city, — Tunis or Algiers, —
And, after what had seemed so many years,
Came to himself, and found all this had been
During the palace-clock's brief noonday din?

For here the same blithe robins seem to house
In the elm-forest, underneath whose boughs
We too were sheltered; nay, we cannot mark
The five-and-twenty rings, beneath the bark,
That tell the growth of some historic tree,
Since we, too, were a part of Arcady.
And in our trance, *negari*, should the bell
Speak out the hour, *non potest quin*, 't were well
The upper or the lower room to seek
For Tully's Latin, Homer's rhythmic Greek; —
Yet were it well? ay, brothers, if, alack,
For this one day the shadow might go back!

Ah, no ! with doubtful faces each on each
We look, we speak with altered, graver speech :
The spell is gone ! We know what 't is to wake
From an illusive dream, at morning's break,
That we again are dark-haired, buoyant, young, —
Scanning, once more, our spring-time mates among,
The grand hexameter — that anthem free
Of the pursuing, loud-resounding sea, —
To wake, anon, and know another day
Already speeds for one whose hairs are gray, —
In this swift change to lose a third of life
Lopped by the stroke of Memory's ruthless knife,
And feel, though naught go ill, it is a pain
That youth, lost youth, can never come again !

Were the dream real, or should we idly go
To yonder halls and strive to make it so,
There listening to the voices that rehearse,
Like ours of old, the swift Ionic verse,
What silvery speech could now for us restore
The cadence that we thought to hear once more ?
The low, calm utterance of him who first
Our faltering minds to clearer knowledge nursed, —
The perfect teacher, who endured our raw
Harsh bleatings with a pang we never saw ;
Whose bearing was so apt we scarcely knew,
At first, the wit that lit him through and through,
Strength's surplusage ; nor, after many a day
Had taught us, rated well the heart that lay
Beneath his speech, nor guessed how brave a soul
In that frail body dwelt with fine control :
Alas, no longer dwells ! Time's largest theft
Was that which learning and the world bereft
Of this pure scholar, — one who had been great
In every walk where led by choice or fate,

Were not his delicate yearnings still represt
Obeying duty's every-day behest.
He shrank from note, yet might have worn at ease
The garb whose counterfeit a sad world sees
Round many a dolt who gains, and deems it fame,
One tenth the honor **due to HADLEY's name.**

Too soon the years, gray Time's relentless breed,
Have claimed our Pascal. He is theirs indeed ;
Yet three remain of the ancestral mould,
Abreast, like them who kept the bridge of old :
The true, large-hearted man so many found
A helpful guardian, stalwart, sane, and sound ;
And he, by sure selection upward led,
Whom now we reverence as becomes the Head, —
The sweet polemic, pointing shafts divine
With kindly satire, — latest of the **line**
That dates from godly Pierson. No less dear,
And more revered with each unruffled year,
That other Grecian : he who stands aside
Watching the streams that gather and divide.
Alcestis' love, the Titan's deathless will,
We read of in his text, and drank our fill
At Plato's spring. Now, from his sacred shade,
Still on the outer world his hand is laid
In use and counsel. Whom the nation saw
Most fit for Heaven could best expound Earth's law.

His wise, kind eyes behold — nor are they loth —
The larger scope, the quarter-century's growth :
How blooms the Mother with unwrinkled brow
To whom her wandering sons, returning now,
Come not alone, but bring their sons to prove
That children's children have a share of love.

Through them she proffers us a second chance ;
With their young eyes we see her hands advance
To crown the sports once banished from her sight ;
With them we see old wrong become the right,
Tread pleasant halls, a healthy life behold
Less stinted than the cloister-range of old —
When the last hour of morning sleep was lost
And prayer was sanctified by dusk and frost,
And hungry tutors taught a class unfed
That a full stomach meant an empty head.
For them a tenth Muse, Beauty, here and there
Has touched the landmarks, making all more fair ; —
We knew her not, save in our stolen dreams
Or stumbling song, but now her likeness gleams
Through chapel aisles, and in the house where Art
Has builded for her praise its shrines apart.

Now the new Knowledge, risen like a sun,
Makes bright for them the hidden ways that none
· Revealed to us ; or haply would dethrone
The gods of old, and rule these hearts alone
From yonder stronghold.   By unnumbered strings
She draws our sons to her discoverings, —
Traces the secret paths of force, the heat
That makes the stout heart give its patient beat,
Follows the stars through æons far and free
And shows what forms have been and are to be.

Such things are plain to these we hither brought,
More strange and varied than ourselves were taught ;
But has the iris of the murmuring shell
A charm the less because we know full well
Sweet Nature's trick ?   Is Music's dying fall
Less finely blent with strains antiphonal

Because within a harp's quick vibratings
We count the tremor of the spirit's wings ?
There is a path by Science yet untrod
Where with closed eyes we walk to find out **God !**
Still, still, the unattained ideal lures,
The spell evades, the splendor yet endures ;
False sang the poet, — there is no good in rest,
And Truth still **leads us to a deeper quest.**

III.

But Alma Mater, with her mother-eyes
Seeing us graver grown if not more wise, —
She calls us back, dear comrades — ah, how dear,
And dearer than when each to each was near !
Time thickens blood !   Enough to know that one
Our classmate was and is, and is her son ; —
She looks unto the East, the South. the West,
Asking, " Now who have kept my maxims best ?
Who have most nearly held within their grasp
The fluttering robe that each essayed to clasp ? "
Can ye not answer, brothers, even as I,
That still in front the vision seems to fly. —
More light and fleet her shining footsteps burn,
And speed the most when most she seems to turn ?
And some have fallen, fallen from our band
Just as we thought to see them lay the hand
Upon her scarf : we know their precious names,
Their **hearts, their** work, **their sorrows, and their**
          fames.
Few gifts the brief years brought them, yet how few
Fell to the living as the lots we drew !
But some, who most were baffled, later found
Capricious Fortune's arms a moment wound
About them ; some, who sought her on one **side,**
Beheld her reach them by a compass wide.

What then is Life? or what Success may be
Who, who can tell? who for another see?
From those, perchance, that closest seem to hold
Her love, her strength, her laurels, or her gold,
In this meridian hour she far has sped
And left them but her phantom mask instead.

A grave, sweet poet in a song has told
Of one, a king, who in his palace old
Hung up a bell; and placed its cord anear
His couch, — that thenceforth, when the court should
    hear
Its music, all might know the king had rung
With his own hand, and that its silver tongue
Gave out the words of joy he wished to say,
" I have been wholly happy on this day ! "
Joy's full perfection never to him came ;
Voiceless the bell, year after year the same,
Till, in his death-throes, round the cord his hand
Gathered — and there was mourning in the land.

I pray you, search the wistful past, and tell
Which of you all could ring the happy bell !
The treasure-trove, the gifts we ask of Fate,
Come far apart, come mildewed, come too late.
What says the legend? " All that man desires
Greatly at morn he gains ere day expires ; "
But Age craves not the fruits that gladden Youth, —
It sits among its vineyards, full of ruth,
Finding the owner's right to what is best
Of little worth without the seeker's zest.

Yet something has been gained. Not all a waste
The light-winged years have vanished in their haste,

Howbeit their gift was scant of what we thought,
So much we thought not of they slowly wrought !
Not all a waste the insight and the zeal
We gathered here : these surely make for weal ;
The current sets for him who swims upbuoyed
By the trained skill, with all his arts employed.
Coy Fortune may disdain our noblest cares,
The good she gives at last comes unawares : —
Long, long in vain, — with patience, worth, and love, —
To do her task the enchanted princess strove,
Till in the midnight pitying fairies crept
Unraveling the tangle while she slept.

This, then, the boon our Age of Wisdom brings, —
A knowledge of the real worth of things :
How poor, how good, is wealth ; how surely fame
And beauty must return to whence they came,
Yet not for this less beautiful and rare —
It is their evanescence makes them fair
And worth possession. Ours the age still strong
With passions, that demand not curb nor thong ;
And ours the age not old enough to set
Youth's joys above their proper worth, nor yet
So young as still to trust its empery more
Than unseen hands which lead to fortune's door.
For most have done the best they could, and all
The reign of law has compassed like a wall ;
Something accrued to each, and each has seen
A Power that works for good in life's demesne.
In our own time, to many a masquerade
The hour has come when masks aside were laid :
We 've seen the shams die out, the poor pretense
Cut off at last by truth's keen instruments,
The ignoble fashion wane and pass away, —

The fine return a second time, to stay, —
The knave, the quack, and all the meaner brood,
Go surely down, by the strong years subdued,
And, in the quarter-century's capping-race,
Strength, talent, honor, take and hold their place.

More glad, you say, the song I might have sung
In the free, careless days when all were young!
Now, long deferred, the sullen stroke of time
Has given a graver key, a deeper chime,
That the late singer of this strain might prove
Himself less keen for honors, more for love,
And in the music of your answer find
The charms that life to further action bind.
The Past is past; survey its course no more;
Henceforth our glasses sweep the further shore.
Five lustra, briefer than those gone, remain,
And then — a white-haired few shall meet again,
Lifting their heads that long have learned to droop,
And hear some sweeter minstrel of our group.
But stay! which one of us, alone, shall dine
At the Last Shadowy Banquet of the line?
Who knows? who does not in his heart reply
" It matters not, so that it be not I."

TRANSLATIONS.

THE DEATH OF AGAMEMNON.

TRANSLATIONS.

———◆———

I. THE DEATH OF AGAMEMNON.

FROM HOMER.

[*Odyssey*, XI., 385–456.]

ODYSSEUS IN HADES.

AFTERWARD, soon as the chaste Persephone
  hither and thither   385
Now had scattered afar the slender shades of the
  women,
Came the sorrowing ghost of Agamemnon Atreides;
Round whom thronged, besides, the souls of the others
  who also
Died, and met their fate, with him in the house of Aigisthos.
He, then, after he drank of the dark blood, instantly
  knew me, —   390
Ay, and he wailed aloud, and plenteous tears was shedding,
Toward me reaching hands and eagerly longing to
  touch me ;
But he was shorn of strength, nor longer came at his
  bidding

That great force which once abode in his pliant mem-
  bers.
Seeing him thus, I wept, and my heart was laden with
  pity,   395
And, uplifting my voice, in wingéd words I addressed
  him :
  "King of men, Agamemnon, thou glorious son of
    Atreus,
Say, in what wise did the doom of prostrate death over-
  come thee ?
Was it within thy ships thou wast subdued by Poseidon
Rousing the dreadful blast of winds too hard to be
  mastered,   400
Or on the firm-set land did banded foemen destroy thee
Cutting their oxen off, and their flocks so fair, or, it
  may be,
While in a town's defence, or in that of women, con-
  tending ?"
  Thus I spake, and he, replying, said to me straight-
    way :
" Nobly-born and wise Odysseus, son of Laertes,   405
Neither within my ships was I subdued by Poseidon
Rousing the dreadful blast of winds too hard to be mas-
  tered,
Nor on the firm-set land did banded foemen destroy
  me, —
Nay, but death and my doom were well contrived by
  Aigisthos,
Who, with my curséd wife, at his own house bidding me
  welcome,   410
Fed me, and slew me, as one might slay an ox at the
  manger !
So, by a death most wretched, I died ; and all my com-
  panions

Round me were slain off-hand, like white-toothed swine
    that are slaughtered
Thus, when some lordly man, abounding in power and
    riches,
Orders a wedding - feast, or a frolic, or mighty ca-
    rousal.   415
Thou indeed hast witnessed the slaughter of number-
    less heroes
Massacred, one by one, in the battle's heat; but with
    pity
All thy heart had been full, if thou hadst seen what I
    tell thee, —
How in the hall we lay among the wine-jars, and
    under
Tables laden with food ; and how the pavement, on all
    sides,   420
Swam with blood ! And I heard the dolorous cry of
    Kassandra,
Priam's daughter, whom treacherous Klytaimnestra
    anear me
Slew ; and upon the ground I fell in my death-throes,
    vainly
Reaching out hands to my sword, while the shameless
    woman departed,
Nor did she even stay to press her hands on my eye-
    lids,   425
No, nor to close my mouth, although I was passing to
    Hades.
O, there is naught more dire, more insolent than a
    woman
After the very thought of deeds like these has pos-
    sessed her, —
One who would dare to devise an act so utterly shame-
    less,

Lying in wait to slay her wedded lord.   I bethought
me,   430
Verily, home to my children and servants giving me
welcome
Safe to return ; but she has wrought for herself con-
fusion,
Plotting these grievous woes, and for other women here-
after,
Even for those, in sooth, whose thoughts are set upon
goodness."
 Thus he spake, and I, in turn replying, addressed
him :   435
" Heavens ! how from the first has Zeus the thunderer
hated,
All for the women's wiles, the brood of Atreus !   What
numbers
Perished in quest of Helen, — and Klytaimnestra, the
meanwhile,
Wrought in her soul this guile for thee afar on thy
journey."
 Thus I spake, and he, replying, said to me straight-
way :   440
" See that thou art not, then, like me too mild to thy
helpmeet ;
Nor to her ear reveal each secret matter thou knowest,
Tell her the part, forsooth, and see that the rest shall
be hidden.
Nathless, not unto thee will come such murder, Odys-
seus,
Dealt by a wife ; for wise indeed, and true in her pur-
pose,   445
Noble Penelope is, the child of Ikarios.   Truly,
She it was whom we left, a fair young bride, when we
started

Off for the wars ; and then an infant lay at her bosom,
One who now, methinks, in the list of men must be
    seated, —
Blest indeed ! ah, yes, for his well - loved father, re-
    turning,   450
Him shall behold, and the son shall clasp the sire, as is
    fitting.
Not unto me to feast my eyes with the sight of my off-
    spring
Granted the wife of my bosom, but first of life she be-
    reft me.
Therefore I say, moreover, and charge thee well to
    remember,
Unto thine own dear land steer thou thy vessel in
    secret,   455
Not in the light ; since faith can be placed in woman
    no longer."

II. THE DEATH OF AGAMEMNON.

FROM AISCHYLOS.

I.

[AISCHYLOS, *Agamemnon*, 1266–1318.[1]]

CHORUS — KASSANDRA — AGAMEMNON.

CHORUS.

O WRETCHED woman indeed, and O most wise,
    Much hast thou said ; but if thou knowest well
Thy doom, why, like a heifer, by the Gods
Led to the altar, tread so brave of soul ?

[1] Text of Paley.

KASSANDRA.

There's no escape, O friends, the time is full.

CHORUS.

Nathless, the last to enter gains in time.

KASSANDRA.

The day has come; little I make by flight.

CHORUS.

Thou art bold indeed, and of a daring spirit !

KASSANDRA.

Such sayings from the happy none hath heard.

CHORUS.

Grandly to die is still a grace to mortals.

KASSANDRA.

Alas, my sire, — thee and thy noble brood !
(She starts back from the entrance.)

CHORUS.

How now ?   What horror turns thee back again ?

KASSANDRA.

Faugh ! faugh !

CHORUS.

Why such a cry ?   There's something chills thy soul !

KASSANDRA.

The halls breathe murder, — ay, they drip with blood.

CHORUS.

How ?   'T is the smell of victims at the hearth.

KASSANDRA.

Nay, but the exhalation of the tomb !

CHORUS.

No Syrian dainty, this, of which thou speakest.

KASSANDRA (*at the portal*).

Yet will I in the palace wail my own
And Agamemnon's fate !   Enough of life !
Alas, O friends !
Yet not for naught I quail, not as a bird
Snared in the bush : bear witness, though I die,
A woman's slaughter shall requite my own,
And, for this man ill-yoked, a man shall fall !
Thus prays of you a stranger, at death's door.

CHORUS.

Lost one, I rue with thee thy foretold doom !

KASSANDRA.

Once more I fain would utter words, once more, —
'T is my own threne !   And I invoke the Sun,
By his last beam, that my detested foes
May pay no less to them who shall avenge me,
Than I who die an unresisting slave !

(She enters the palace.)

CHORUS.

Of Fortune was never yet enow
To mortal man ; and no one ever
Her presence from his house would sever
And point, and say, " Come no more nigh ! "
Unto our King granted the Gods on high

That Priam's towers should bow,
And homeward, crowned of Heaven, hath he come ;
But now if, for the ancestral blood that lay
At his doors, he falls, — and the dead, that cursed his
　　home,
　　He, dying, must in full requite, —
What manner of man is one that would not pray
　　To be born with a good attendant Sprite ?

　　　　　　(An outcry within the palace.)

AGAMEMNON.

Woe 's me !　I am stricken a deadly blow within !

CHORUS.

Hark !　Who is 't cries " a blow " ?　Who meets his
　　death ?

AGAMEMNON.

Woe 's me ! again ! a second time I am stricken !

CHORUS.

The deed, methinks, from the King's cry, is done.
Quick, let us see what help may be in counsel !

2.

[*Agamemnon,* 1343–1377.]

Enter KLYTAIMNESTRA, *from the Palace.*

KLYTAIMNESTRA.

Now, all this formal outcry having vent,
I shall not blush to speak the opposite.
How should one, plotting evil things for foes,

Encompass seeming friends with such a bane
Of toils ? it were a height too great to leap ?
Not without full prevision came, though late,
To me this crisis of an ancient feud.
And here, the deed being done, I stand— even where
I smote him ! nor deny that thus I did it,
So that he could not flee nor ward off doom.
A seamless net, as round a fish, I cast
About him, yea, a deadly wealth of robe ;
Then smote him twice ; and with a double cry
He loosed his limbs ; and to him fallen I gave
Yet a third thrust, a grace to Hades, lord
Of the underworld and guardian of the dead.
So, falling, out he gasps his soul, and out
He spurts a sudden jet of blood, that smites
Me with a sable rain of gory dew, —
Me, then no less exulting than the field
In the sky's gift, while bursts the pregnant ear !
Things being thus, old men of Argos, joy,
If joy ye can ; — I glory in the deed !
And if 't were seemly ever yet to pour
Libation to the dead, 't were most so now ;
Most meet that one, who poured for his own home
A cup of ills, returning, thus should drain it !

CHORUS.

Shame on thy tongue ! how bold of mouth thou art
That vauntest such a speech above thy husband !

KLYTAIMNESTRA.

Ye try me as a woman loose of soul ;
But I with dauntless heart avow to you
Well knowing — and whether ye choose to praise or
      blame

I care not — this is Agamemnon ; yea,
My husband ; yea, a corpse, of this right hand,
This craftsman sure, the handiwork !   Thus stands it.

3.

[*Agamemnon*, 1466-1507.]

CHORUS — SEMI-CHORUS — KLYTAIMNESTRA.

CHORUS.

Woe !   Woe !
King !   O how shall I weep for thy dying ?
    What shall my fond heart say anew ?
Thou in the web of the spider art lying,
    Breathing out life by a death she shall rue.

SEMI-CHORUS.

Alas ! alas for this slavish couch !   By a sword
    Two-edged, by a hand untrue,
Thou art smitten, even to death, my lord !

KLYTAIMNESTRA.

Thou sayest this deed was mine alone ;
    But I bid thee call me not
The wife of Agamemnon's bed ;
'T was the ancient fell Alastor[1] of Atreus' throne,
    The lord of a horrid feast, this crime begot,
Taking the shape that seemed the wife of the dead, —
        His sure revenge, I wot,
A victim ripe hath claimed for the young that bled.

[1] The Evil Genius, the Avenger.

SEMI-CHORUS.

Who shall bear witness now, —
Who of this murder, now, thee guiltless hold?
How sayest thou? How?
Yet the fell Alastor may have holpen, I trow:
Still is dark Ares driven
Down currents manifold
Of kindred blood, wherever judgment is given,
And he comes to avenge the children slain of old,
And their thick gore cries to Heaven!

CHORUS.

Woe! Woe!
King! O how shall I weep for thy dying?
What shall my fond heart say anew?
Thou in the web of the spider art lying,
Breathing out life by a death she shall rue!

SEMI-CHORUS.

Alas! alas for this slavish couch! By a sword
Two-edged, by a hand untrue,
Thou art smitten, even to death, my lord!

KLYTAIMNESTRA.

Hath he not subtle Atè brought
Himself, to his kingly halls?
'T was on our own dear offspring, — yea,
On Iphigeneia, wept for still, he wrought
The doom that cried for the doom by which he falls.
O, let him not in Hades boast, I say,
For 't is the sword that calls,
Even for that foul deed, his soul away!

16

LATER POEMS.

LATER POEMS.

THE SONGSTER.

A MIDSUMMER CAROL.

I.

WITHIN our summer hermitage
    I have an aviary, —
'T is but a little, rustic cage,
That holds a golden-winged Canary, —
A bird with no companion of his kind.
      But when the warm south-wind
      Blows, from rathe meadows, over
      The honey-scented clover,
I hang him in the porch, that he may hear
The voices of the bobolink and thrush,
      The robin's joyous gush,
The bluebird's warble, and the tunes of all
Glad matin songsters in the fields anear.
      Then, as the blithe responses vary,

And rise anew, and fall,
In every hush
He answers them again,
With his own wild, reliant strain,
As if he breathed the air of sweet Canary.

II.

Bird, bird of the golden wing,
Thou lithe, melodious thing!
Where hast thy music found?
What fantasies of vale and vine,
Of glades where orchids intertwine,
Of palm-trees, garlanded and crowned,
And forests flooded deep with sound, —
What high imagining
Hath made this carol thine?
By what instinct art thou bound
To all rare harmonies that be
In those green islands of the sea,
Where thy radiant, wildwood kin
Their madrigals at morn begin,
Above the rainbow and the roar
Of the long billow from the Afric shore?

Asking other guerdon
None, than Heaven's light,
Holding thy crested head aright,
Thy melody's sweet burden
Thou dost proudly utter,
With many an ecstatic flutter
And ruffle of thy tawny throat
For each delicious note.
— Art thou a waif from Paradise,

In some fine moment wrought
By an artist of the skies,
Thou winged, cherubic Thought?

Bird of the amber beak,
Bird of the golden wing !
Thy dower is thy carolling;
Thou hast not far to seek
Thy bread, nor needest wine
To make thine utterance divine;
Thou art canopied and clothed
And unto Song betrothed !
In thy lone aërial cage
Thou hast thine ancient heritage;
There is no task-work on thee laid
But to rehearse the ditties thou hast made ;
Thou hast a lordly store,
And, though thou scatterest them free,
Art richer than before,
Holding in fee
The glad domain of·minstrelsy.

III.

Brave songster, bold Canary !
Thou art not of thy listeners wary,
Art not timorous, nor chary
Of quaver, trill, and tone,
Each perfect and thine own ;
But renewest, shrill or soft,
Thy greeting to the upper skies,
Chanting thy latest song aloft
With no tremor or disguise.
Thine is a music that defies

The envious rival near ;
Thou hast no fear
Of the day's vogue, the scornful critic's sneer.

Would, O wisest bard, that now
I could cheerly sing as thou !
Would I might chant the thoughts which on me throng
For the very joy of song !
Here, on the written page,
I falter, yearning to impart
The vague and wandering murmur of my heart,
Haply a little to assuage
This human restlessness and pain,
And half forget my chain :
Thou, unconscious of thy cage,
Showerest music everywhere ;
Thou hast no care
But to pour out the largesse thou hast won
From the south-wind and the sun ;
There are no prison-bars
Betwixt thy tricksy spirit and the stars.

When from its delicate clay
Thy little life shall pass away,
Thou wilt not meanly die,
Nor voiceless yield to silence and decay ;
But triumph still in art
And act thy minstrel-part,
Lifting a last, long pæan
To the unventured empyrean.
— So bid the world go by,
And they who list to thee aright,
Seeing thee fold thy wings and fall, shall say :
" The Songster perished of his own delight ! "

CRABBED AGE AND YOUTH.

OUT, out, Old Age! aroint ye!
  I fain would disappoint ye,
Nor wrinkled grow and learned
Before I am inurned.
Ruthless the Hours and hoary,
That scatter ills before ye!
Thy touch is pestilential,
Thy lays are penitential;
With stealthy steps thou stealest
And life's hot tide congealest;
Before thee vainly flying
We are already dying.
Why must the blood grow colder,
And men and maidens older?
Bring not thy maledictions,
Thy grewsome, grim afflictions, —
Thy bodings bring not hither
To make us blight and wither.
When this thy frost hath bound us,
All fairer things around us
Seem Youth's divine extortion
In which we have no portion.
" Fie, Senex!" saith a lass now,
" What need ye of a glass now?
Though flowers of May be springing
And I my songs am singing,
Thy blood no whit the faster
Doth flow, my ancient Master!"
Age is by Youth delighted,
Youth is by Age affrighted;

Blithe sunny May and joysome
Still finds December noisome.
Alack! a guest unbidden,
Howe'er our feast be hidden,
Doth enter with the feaster
And make a Lent of Easter!
I would thou wert not able
To seat thee at our table;
I would that altogether
From this thy wintry weather,
Since Youth and Love must leave us,
Death might at once retrieve us.
Old wizard, ill betide ye!
I cannot yet abide ye!

Ah, Youth, sweet Youth, I love ye!
There 's naught on Earth above ye!
Thou purling bird uncaged
That never wilt grow aged,
To whom each day is giving
Increase of joyous living!
Soft words to thee are spoken,
For thee strong vows are broken,
All loves and lovers cluster,
To bask them in thy lustre.
Ah, girlhood, pout and dimple,
Half hid beneath the wimple!
Ah, boyhood, blithe and cruel,
Whose heat doth need no fuel,
No help of wine and spices
And frigid Eld's devices!
All pleasant things ye find you,
And to your sweet selves bind you.
For you alone the motion

Of brave ships on the ocean ;
All stars for you are shining,
All wreaths your foreheads twining ;
All joys, your joys decreeing,
Are portions of your being, —
All fairest sights your features,
Ye selfish, soulful creatures !
Sing me no more distiches
Of glory, wisdom, riches ;
Tell me no beldame's story
Of wisdom, wealth, and glory !
To Youth these are a wonder, —
To Age a corpse-light under
The tomb with rusted portal
Of that which seemed immortal.
I, too, in Youth's dear fetter,
Will love my foeman better, —
Ay, though his ill I study, —
So he be young and ruddy,
Than comrade true and golden,
So he be waxen olden.
Ah, winsome Youth, stay by us !
I prithee, do not fly us !
Ah, Youth, sweet Youth, I love ye !
There 's naught on Earth above ye !

STANZAS FOR MUSIC.

(FROM AN UNFINISHED DRAMA.)

THOU art mine, thou hast given thy word ;
  Close, close in my arms thou art clinging ;
 Alone for my ear thou art singing
A song which no stranger hath heard :

But afar from me yet, like a bird,
Thy soul, in some region unstirred,
   On its mystical circuit is winging.

Thou art mine, I have made thee mine own ;
 . Henceforth we are mingled forever :
   But in vain, all in vain, I endeavor —
Though round thee my garlands are thrown,
And thou yieldest thy lips and thy zone —
To master the spell that alone
   My hold on thy being can sever.

Thou art mine, thou hast come unto me !
   But thy soul, when I strive to be near it —
   The innermost fold of thy spirit —
Is as far from my grasp, is as free,
As the stars from the mountain-tops be,
As the pearl, in the depths of the sea,
.   From the portionless king that would wear it.

THE FLIGHT OF THE BIRDS.

WHITHER away, Robin,
   Whither away?
Is it through envy of the maple-leaf,
 Whose blushes mock the crimson of thy breast,
   Thou wilt not stay ?
The summer days were long, yet all too brief
 The happy season thou hast been our guest :
   Whither away?

"The blast is chill, yet in the upper sky
    Thou still canst find the color of thy wing."   Page 373.

Whither away, Bluebird,
Whither away?
The blast is chill, yet in the upper sky
Thou still canst find the color of thy wing,
The hue of May.
Warbler, why speed thy southern flight? ah, why,
Thou too, whose song first told us of the Spring?
Whither away?

Whither away, Swallow,
Whither away?
Canst thou no longer tarry in the North,
Here, where our roof so well hath screened thy nest?
Not one short day?
Wilt thou — as if thou human wert — go forth
And wanton far from them who love thee best?
Whither away?

HYPATIA.

'T IS fifteen hundred years, you say,
Since that fair teacher died
In learnéd Alexandria
By the stone altar's side : —
The wild monks slew her, as she lay
At the feet of the Crucified. ·

Yet in a prairie-town, one night,
I found her lecture-hall,
Where bench and dais stood aright,
And statues graced the wall,
And pendent brazen lamps the light
Of classic days let fall.

A throng that watched the speaker's face,
  And on her accents hung,
Was gathered there : the strength, the grace
  Of lands where life is young
Ceased not, I saw, with that blithe race
  From old Pelasgia sprung.

No civic crown the sibyl wore,
  Nor academic tire,
But shining skirts, that trailed the floor
  And made her stature higher ;
A written scroll the lecturn bore,
  And flowers bloomed anigh her.

The wealth her honeyed speech had won
  Adorned her in our sight ;
The silkworm for her sake had spun
  His cincture, day and night ;
With broider-work and Honiton
  Her open sleeves were bright.

But still Hypatia's self I knew,
  And saw, with dreamy wonder,
The form of her whom Cyril slew
  (See Kingsley's novel, yonder)
Some fifteen centuries since, 't is true,
  And half a world asunder.

Her hair was coifed Athenian-wise,
  With one loose tress down-flowing ;
Apollo's rapture lit her eyes,
  His utterance bestowing, —
A silver flute's clear harmonies
  On which a god was blowing.

Yet not of Plato's sounding spheres,
  And universal Pan,
She spoke ; but searched historic years,
  The sisterhood to scan
Of women, — girt with ills and fears, —
  Slaves to the tyrant, Man.

Their crosiered banner she unfurled,
  And onward pushed her quest
Through golden ages of a world
  By their deliverance blest : —
At all who stay their hands she hurled
  Defiance from her breast.

I saw her burning words infuse
  A warmth through many a heart,
As still, in bright successive views,
  She drew her sex's part ;
Discoursing, like the Lesbian Muse,
  Of work, and song, and art.

Why vaunt, I thought, the past, or say
  The later is the less ?
Our Sappho sang but yesterday,
  Of whom two climes confess
Heaven's flame within her wore away
  Her earthly loveliness.

So let thy wild heart ripple on,
  Brave girl, through vale and city !
Spare, of its listless moments, one
  To this, thy poet's ditty ;
Nor long forbear, when all is done,
  Thine own sweet self to pity.

The priestess of the Sestian **tower,**
　Whose knight the sea swam over,
Among her votaries' gifts no flower
　Of heart's-ease could discover :
She died, but in no evil hour,
　Who, dying, clasped her lover.

The rose-tree has its perfect life
　When the full rose is blown ;
Some height of womanhood the wife
　Beyond thy dream has known ;
Set not thy head and heart at strife
　To keep thee from thine own.

Hypatia ! **thine essence rare**
　The rarer joy should merit :
Possess thee of that common share
　Which lesser souls inherit :
All gods to thee their garlands bear, —
　Take **one from Love and wear it !**

THE HEART OF NEW ENGLAND.

O LONG are years of waiting, when lovers' hearts
　　are bound
By words that hold in life and death, and last the half-
　　world round ;
Long, long for him who wanders far and strives with
　　all his main,
But crueller yet for her who bides at home and hides
　　her pain !
　　And lone are the homes of New England.

'T was in the mellow summer I heard her sweet reply;
The barefoot lads and lassies a-berrying went by;
The locust dinned amid the trees; the fields were high
    with corn;
The white-sailed clouds against the sky like ships were
    onward borne:
    And blue are the skies of New England.

Her lips were like the raspberries; her cheek was soft
    and fair,
And little breezes stopped to lift the tangle of her hair;
A light was in her hazel eyes, and she was nothing
    loth
To hear the words her lover spoke, and pledged me
    there her troth;
    And true is the word of New England.

When September brought the golden-rod, and maples
    burned like fire,
And bluer than in August rose the village smoke and
    higher,
And large and red among the stacks the ripened pump-
    kins shone, —
One hour, in which to say farewell, was left to us alone;
    And sweet are the lanes of New England.

We loved each other truly! hard, hard it was to part;
But my ring was on her finger, and her hair lay next
    my heart.
"'T is but a year, my darling," I said; "in one short
    year,
When our Western home is ready, I shall seek my
    Katie here";
    And brave is the hope of New England.

I went to gain a home for her, and in the Golden State
With head and hand I planned and toiled, and early
 worked and late ;
But luck was all against me, and sickness on me lay,
And ere I got my strength again 't was many a weary
 day ;
 And long are the thoughts of New England.

And many a day, and many a month, and thrice the
 rolling year,
I bravely strove, and still the goal seemed never yet
 more near.
My Katie's letters told me that she kept her promise
 true,
But now, for very hopelessness, my own to her were few ;
 And stern is the pride of New England.

But still she trusted in me, though sick with hope
 deferred ;
No more among the village choir her voice was sweetest
 heard ;
For when the wild northeaster of the fourth long winter
 blew,
So thin her frame with pining, the cold wind pierced
 her through ;
 And chill are the blasts of New England.

At last my fortunes bettered, on the far Pacific shore,
And I thought to see old Windham and my patient love
 once more ;
When a kinsman's letter reached me : " Come at once,
 or come too late !
Your Katie's strength is failing ; if you love her, do not
 wait :
 Come back to the elms of New England."

O, it wrung my heart with sorrow! I left all else
    behind,
And straight for dear New England I speeded like the
    wind.
The day and night were blended till I reached my boy-
    hood's home,
And the old cliffs seemed to mock me that I had not
    sooner come;
      And gray are the rocks of New England.

I could not think 't was Katie, who sat before me there
Reading her Bible — 't was my gift — and pillowed in
    her chair.
A ring, with all my letters, lay on a little stand, —
She could no longer wear it, so frail her poor, white
    hand!
      But strong is the love of New England.

Her hair had lost its tangle and was parted off her
    brow;
She used to be a joyous girl, — but seemed an angel
    now, —
Heaven's darling, mine no longer; yet in her hazel eyes
The same dear love-light glistened, as she soothed my
    bitter cries:
      And pure is the faith of New England.

A month I watched her dying, pale, pale as any rose
That drops its petals one by one and sweetens as it
    goes.
My life was darkened when at last her large eyes
    closed in death,
And I heard my own name whispered as she drew her
    parting breath;
      Still, still was the heart of New England.

It was a woful funeral the coming sabbath-day ;
We bore her to the barren hill on which the graveyard
    lay,
And when the narrow grave was filled, and what we
    might was done,
Of all the stricken group around I was the loneliest
    one ;
    And drear are the hills of New England.

I gazed upon the stunted pines, the bleak November
    sky,
And knew that buried deep with her my heart hence-
    forth would lie ;
And waking in the solemn nights my thoughts still
    thither go
To Katie, lying in her grave beneath the winter snow ;
    And cold are the snows of New England.

THE DISCOVERER.

I HAVE a little kinsman
    Whose earthly summers are but three,
And yet a voyager is he
Greater than Drake or Frobisher,
Than all their peers together !
He is a brave discoverer,
And, far beyond the tether
Of them who seek the frozen Pole,
Has sailed where the noiseless surges roll.
    Ay, he has travelled whither
A winged pilot steered his bark
Through the portals of the dark,

Past hoary Mimir's well and tree,
　　Across the unknown sea.

Suddenly, in his fair young hour,
Came one who bore a flower,
And laid it in his dimpled hand
　　With this command:
" Henceforth thou art a rover!
Thou must make a voyage far,
Sail beneath the evening star,
And a wondrous land discover."
— With his sweet smile innocent
　　Our little kinsman went.

Since that time no word
From the absent has been heard.
　　Who can tell
How he fares, or answer well
What the little one has found
Since he left us, outward bound?
Would that he might return!
Then should we learn
From the pricking of his chart
How the skyey roadways part.
Hush! does not the baby this way bring,
　　To lay beside this severed curl,
　　　Some starry offering
　　Of chrysolite or pearl?

　　　Ah, no! not so!
We may follow on his track,
　　But he comes not back.
　　And yet I dare aver
He is a brave discoverer

Of climes his elders do not know.
He has more learning than appears
On the scroll of twice three thousand years,
More than in the groves is taught,
Or from furthest Indies brought ;
He knows, perchance, how spirits fare, —
What shapes the angels wear,
What is their guise and speech
In those lands beyond our reach, —
    And his eyes behold
Things that shall never, never be to mortal hearers told.

SISTER BEATRICE.

A LEGEND FROM THE "SERMONES DISCIPULI" OF JEAN HEROLT, THE DOMINICAN, A. D. 1518.

A CLOISTER tale, — a strange and ancient thing
    Long since on vellum writ in gules and or :
And why should Chance to me this trover bring
    From the grim dust-heap of forgotten lore,
And not to that gray bard still measuring
    His laurelled years by music's golden score,
Nor to some comrade who like him has caught
The charm of lands by me too long unsought ?

Why not to one who, with a steadfast eye,
    Ingathering her shadow and her sheen,
Saw Venice as she is, and, standing nigh,
    Drew from the life that old, dismantled queen ?
Or to the poet through whom I well descry
    Castile, and the Campeador's demesne ?

Or to that eager one whose quest has found
Each place of long renown, the world around ;

Whose foot has rested firm on either hill, —
 The sea-girt height where glows the midnight **sun,**
And wild Parnassus ; whose melodious skill
 Has left no song untried, no wreath unwon ?
Why not to these ? Yet, since by Fortune's will
 This quaint task given **me** I must not shun,
My verse shall render, fitly as it may,
An old church legend, meet for Christmas Day.

Once on a time (so read the monkish pages),
 Within a convent — that doth still abide
Even as it stood in those devouter ages,
 Near a fair city, by the highway's side —
There dwelt a sisterhood of them **whose** wages
 Are stored in heaven : **each** a virgin bride
Of Christ, and **bounden meekly to endure**
In faith, and works, **and chastity most pure.**

A convent, and within a summer-land,
 Like that of Browning and Boccaccio !
Years since, my greener fancy would have planned
 Its station thus : it should have had, I trow,
A square and flattened bell-tower, that might stand
 Above deep-windowed buildings long and low,
Closed all securely by a vine-clung wall,
And shadowed on one side **by cypress tall.**

Within the gate, a garden **set** with care :
 Box-bordered plots, where peach and almond trees
Rained blossoms on the maidens walking there,
 Or rustled softly in the summer breeze ;

Here were sweet jessamine and jonquil rare,
 And arbors meet for pious talk at ease ;
There must have been a dove-cote too, I know,
Where white-winged birds like spirits come and go.

Outside, the thrush and lark their music made
 Beyond the olive-grove at dewy morn ;
By noon, cicalas, shrilling in the shade
 Of oak and ilex, woke the peasant's horn ;
And, at the time when into darkness fade
 The vineyards, from their purple depths were borne
The nightingale's responses to the prayer
Of those sweet saints at vespers, meek and fair.

Such is the place that, with the hand and eye
 Which are the joy of youth, I should have painted.
Say not, who look thereon, that 't is awry —
 Like nothing real, by rhymesters' use attainted.
Ah well ! then put the faulty picture by,
 And help me draw an abbess long since sainted.
Think of your love, each one, and thereby guess
The fashion of this lady's beauteousness.

For in this convent Sister Beatrice,
 Of all her nuns the fairest and most young,
Became, through grace and special holiness,
 Their sacred head, and moved, her brood among,
Dévote d'âme et fervente au service ;
 And thrice each day, their hymns and Aves sung,
At Mary's altar would before them kneel,
Keeping her vows with chaste and pious zeal.

Now in the Holy Church there was a clerk,
 A godly-seeming man (as such there be

Whose selfish hearts with craft and guile are dark),
　Young, gentle-phrased, of handsome mien and free.
His passion chose this maiden for its mark,
　Begrudging heaven her white chastity,
And with most sacrilegious art the while
He sought her trustful nature to beguile.

Oft as they met, with subtle hardihood
　He still more archly played the traitor's part,
And strove to wake that murmur in her blood
　That times the pulses of a woman's heart ;
And in her innocence she long withstood
　The secret tempter, but at last his art
Changed all her tranquil thoughts to love's desire,
Her vestal flame to earth's unhallowed fire.

So the fair governess, o'ermastered, gave
　Herself to the destroyer, yet as one
That slays, in pity, her sweet self, to save
　Another from some wretched deed undone ;
But when she found her heart was folly's slave,
　She sought the altar which her steps must shun
Thenceforth, and yielded up her sacred trust,
Ere tasting that false fruit which turns to dust.

One eve the nuns beheld her entering
　Alone, as if for prayer beneath the rood,
Their chapel-shrine, wherein the offering
　And masterpiece of some great painter stood, —
The Virgin Mother, without plume or wing
　Ascending, poised in rapt beatitude,
With hands crosswise, and intercession mild
For all who crave her mercy undefiled.

17

There Beatrice — poor, guilty, desperate maid —
　Took from her belt the convent's blessed keys,
And with them on the altar humbly laid
　Her missal, uttering such words as these
(Her eyes cast down, and all her soul afraid) :
　"O dearest mistress, hear me on my knees
Confess to thee, in helplessness and shame,
I am no longer fit to speak thy name.

" Take back the keys wherewith in constancy
　Thy house and altar I have guarded well !
No more may Beatrice thy servant be,
　For earthly love her steps must needs compel.
Forget me in this sore infirmity
　When my successor here her beads shall tell."
This said, the girl withdrew her as she might,
And with her lover fled that selfsame night ;

Fled out, and into the relentless world
　Where Love abides, but Love that breedeth Sorrow,
Where Purity still weeps with pinions furled,
　And Passion lies in wait her all to borrow.
From such a height to such abasement whirled
　She fled that night, and many a day and morrow
Abode indeed with him for whose embrace
She bartered heaven and her hope of grace.

O fickle will and pitiless desire,
　Twin wolves, that raven in a lustful heart
And spare not innocence, nor yield, nor tire,
　But youth from joy and life from goodness part ;
That drag an unstained victim to the mire,
　Then cast it soiled and hopeless on the mart !
Even so the clerk, once having dulled his longing,
A worse thing did than that first bitter wronging.

The base hind left her, ruined and alone,
    Unknowing by what craft to gain her bread
In the hard world that gives to Want a stone.
    What marvel that she drifted whither led
The current, that with none to heed her moan
    She reached the shore where life on husks is fed,
Sank down, and, in the strangeness of her fall,
Among her fellows was the worst of all !

Thus stranded, her fair body, consecrate
    To holiness, was smutched by spoilers rude,
And·entered all the seven fiends where late
    Abode a seeming angel, pure and good.
What paths she followed in such woful state,
    By want, remorse, and the world's hate pursued,
Were known alone to them whose spacious ken
O'erlooks not even the poor Magdalen.

After black years their dismal change had wrought
    Upon her beauty, and there was no stay
By which to hold, some chance or yearning brought
    Her vagrant feet along the convent-way ;
And half as in a dream there came a thought
    (For years she had not dared to think or pray)
That moved her there to bow her in the dust
And bear no more, but perish as she must.

Crouched by the gate she waited, it is told,
    Brooding the past and all of life forlorn,
Nor dared to lift her pallid face and old
    Against the passer's pity or his scorn ;
And there perchance had ere another morn
    Died of her shame and sorrows manifold,
But that a portress bade her pass within
For solace of her wretchedness or sin.

To whom the lost one, drinking now her fill
　　Of woe that wakened memories made more drear,
Said, " Was there not one Beatrice, until
　　Some time now gone, that was an abbess here ? "
" That was ? " the other said.　" Is she not still
　　The convent's head, and still our mistress dear ?
Look ! even now she comes with open hand,
The purest, saintliest lady in the land ! "

And Beatrice, uplifting then her eyes,
　　Saw her own self (in womanhood divine,
It seemed) draw nigh, with holy look and wise,
　　The aged portress leaving at a sign.
Even while she marvelled at that strange disguise,
　　There stood before her, radiant, benign,
The blessed Mother of Mercy, all aflame
With light, as if from Paradise she came !

From her most sacred lips, upon the ears
　　Of Beatrice, these words of wonder fell :
" Daughter, thy sins are pardoned ; dry thy tears,
　　And in this house again my mercies tell,
For, in thy stead, myself these woful years
　　Have governed here and borne thine office well.
Take back the keys : save thee and me alone
No one thy fall and penance yet hath known ! "

Even then, as faded out that loveliness,
　　The abbess, looking down, herself descried
Clean-robed and spotless, such as all confess
　　To be a saint and fit for Heaven's bride.
So ends the legend, and ye well may guess
　　(Who, being untempted, walk in thoughtless pride)
God of his grace can make the sinful pure,
And while earth lasts shall mercy still endure.

SEEKING THE MAY-FLOWER.

THE sweetest sound our whole year round —
   'T is the first robin of the spring !
The song of the full orchard choir
     Is not so fine a thing.

Glad sights are common : Nature draws
   Her random pictures through the year,
But oft her music bids us long
     Remember those most dear.

To me, when in the sudden spring
   I hear the earliest robin's lay,
With the first trill there comes again
     One picture of the May.

The veil is parted wide, and lo,
   A moment, though my eyelids close,
Once more I see that wooded hill
     Where the arbutus grows.

I see the village dryad kneel,
   Trailing her slender fingers through
The knotted tendrils, as she lifts
     Their pink, pale flowers to view.

Once more I dare to stoop beside
   The dove-eyed beauty of my choice,
And long to touch her careless hair,
     And think how dear her voice.

My eager, wandering hands assist
  With fragrant blooms her lap to fill,
And half by chance they meet her own,
    Half by our young hearts' will.

Till, at the last, those blossoms won, —
  Like her, so pure, so sweet, so shy, —
Upon the gray and lichened rocks
    Close at her feet I lie.

Fresh blows the breeze through hemlock-trees,
  The fields are edged with green below ;
And naught but youth and hope and love
    We know or care to know !

Hark ! from the moss-clung apple-bough,
  Beyond the tumbled wall, there broke
That gurgling music of the May, —
    'T was the first robin spoke !

I heard it, ay, and heard it not, —
  For little then my glad heart wist
What toil and time should come to pass,
    And what delight be missed ;

Nor thought thereafter, year by year
  Hearing that fresh yet olden song,
To yearn for unreturning joys
    That with its joy belong.

HAWTHORNE

HARP of New England song,
  That even in slumber tremblest with the touch
 Of poets who like the four winds from thee waken
All harmonies that to thy strings belong, —
Say, wilt thou blame the younger hands too much
  Which from thy laurelled resting-place have taken
Thee, crowned-one, in their hold ? There is a name
  Should quicken thee ! No carol Hawthorne sang,
Yet his articulate spirit, like thine own,
        Made answer, quick as flame,
  To each breath of the shore from which he sprang,
  And prose like his was poesy's high tone.

        By measureless degrees
Star follows star throughout the rounded night.
  Far off his path began, yet reached the near
Sweet influences of the Pleiades, —
A portion and a sharer of the light
  That shall so long outlast each burning sphere.
Beneath the shade and whisper of the pines
  Two youths were fostered in the Norseland air ;
One found an eagle's plume, and one the wand
        Wherewith a seer divines :
  Now but the Minstrel lingers of that pair, —
  The rod has fallen from the mage's hand.

        Gray on thy mountain height,
More fair than wonderland beside thy streams,
  Thou with the splendors twain of youth and age,

This was the son who read thy heart aright,
Of whom thou wast beholden in his dreams, —
  The one New-Englander! Upon whose page
Thine offspring still are animate, and move
  Adown thy paths, a quaint and stately throng:
Grave men of God who made the olden law,
        Fair maidens, meet for love, —
  All living types that to the coast belong
    Since Carver from the prow thy headland saw.

        What should the master be
Who to the world New-England's self must render,
  Her best interpreter, her very own?
How spake the brooding Mother, strong and tender,
Back-looking through her youth betwixt the moan
  Of forests and the murmur of the sea?
"Thou too," she said, "must first be set aside
  To keep my ancient vigil for a space, —
Taught by repression, by the combating
        With thine own pride of pride,
  An unknown watcher in a lonely place
    With none on whom thine utterance to fling."

        But first of all she fed
Her heart's own favorite upon the store
  Of precious things she treasures in her woods,
Of charm and story in her valleys spread.
For him her whispering winds and brooks that pour
  Made ceaseless music in the solitudes;
The manifold bright surges of her deep
  Gave him their light. Within her voice's call
She lured him on, by roadways overhung
        With elms, that he might keep
  Remembrance of her legends as they fall
    Her shaded walks and gabled roofs among.

Within the mists she drew,
Anon, his silent footsteps, as her own
Were led of old, until he came to be
An eremite, whose life the desert knew,
And gained companionship in dreams alone.
The world, it seemed, had naught for such **as he,** —
For one who in his heart's deep wilderness
Shrunk darkling, and, whatever wind might blow,
Found no quick use for potent hands and fain,
No chance that **might express**
To human-kind the thoughts which moved him so.
— O, **deem** not those long years were quite in vain!

For his was the brave soul
Which, touched with fire, dwells not on whatsoever
Its outer senses hold in their intent,
But, sleepless even in sleep, must gather toll
Of dreams which pass like **barks upon the river**
And make each vision Beauty's instrument ;
That from its own love Love's delight can tell,
And from its own grief guess the shrouded Sorrow ;
From its own joyousness of Joy can sing ;
That can predict so well
From its own dawn the lustre of to-morrow,
The whole flight from the flutter of the wing.

And his the gift which sees
A revelation and a tropic sign
In the lone passion-flower, and can discover
The likeness of the far Antipodes,
Though but a leaf **is stranded from the brine ;**
His the fine spirit which is so true a lover
Of sovran Art, that all the becks of life
Allure it not until the work be wrought.

Nay, though the shout and smoke of combat rose,
      He, through the changeful strife,
  Eternal loveliness more closely sought,
    And Beauty's changeless law and sure repose.

        Was it not well that one —
One, if no more — should meditate aloof,
  Though not for naught the time's heroic quarrel,
From what men rush to do and what is done.
He little knew to join the web and woof
  Whereof slow Progress weaves her rich apparel,
But toward the Past half longing turned his head.
  His deft hand dallied with its common share
Of human toil, nor sought new loads to lift,
      But held itself, instead,
  All consecrate to uses that make fair,
    By right divine of his mysterious gift.

        How should the world discern
The artist's self, save through the fine creation
  Of his rare moment ? How, but from his song,
The unfettered spirit of the minstrel learn ?
Yet on this one the stars had set the station
  Which to the chief romancer should belong :
Child of the Beautiful ! whose regnant brow
  She made her canopy, and from his eyes
Looked outward with a steadfast purple gleam.
      Who saw him marvelled how
  The soul of that impassioned ray could lie
    So calm beyond, — unspoken all its dream.

      What sibyl to him bore
The secret oracles that move and haunt ?
  At night's dread noon he scanned the enchanted glass,

Ay, and himself the warlock's mantle wore,
Nor to the thronging phantoms said Avaunt,
  But waved his rod and bade them rise and pass;
Till thus he drew the lineaments of men
  Who fought the old colonial battles three,
Who with the lustihood of Nature warred
            And made her docile, — then
Wrestled with Terror and with Tyranny,
    Twin wardens of the scaffold and the sword.

          He drew his native land,
The few and rude plantations of her Past,
  Fringed by the beaches of her sounding shore;
Her children, as he drew them, there they stand;
There, too, her Present, with an outline cast
  Still from the shape those other centuries wore.
Betimes the orchards and the clover-fields
  Change into woods o'ershadowing a host
That winds along the Massachusetts Path;
          The sword of Standish shields
  The Plymouth band, and where the lewd ones boast
    Stern Endicott pours out his godly wrath.

          Within the Province House
The ancient governors hold their broidered state, —
  Still gleam the lights, the shadows come and go;
Here once again the powdered guests carouse,
The masquerade lasts on, the night is late.
  Thrice waves a mist-invoking wand, and lo,
What troubled sights! What summit bald and steep
  Where stands a ladder 'gainst the accursed tree?
What dark processions thither slowly climb?
          Anon, what lost ones keep
  Their midnight tryst with forms that evil be,
    Around the witch-fire in the forest grim!

Clearly the master's plan
Revealed his people, even as they were,
  The prayerful elder and the winsome maid,
The errant roisterer, the Puritan,
Dark Pyncheon, mournful Hester, — all are there.
  But none save he in our own time so laid
His summons on man's spirit; none but he,
  Whether the light thereof were clear or clouded,
Thus on his canvas fixed the human soul,
    The thoughts of mystery,
  In deep hearts by this mortal guise enshrouded,
    Wild hearts that like the church-bells ring and toll.

    Two natures in him strove
Like day with night, his sunshine and his gloom.
  To him the stern forefathers' creed descended,
The weight of some inexorable Jove
Prejudging from the cradle to the tomb;
  But therewithal the lightsome laughter blended
Of that Arcadian sweetness undismayed
  Which finds in Love its law, and graces still
The rood, the penitential symbol worn, —
    Which sees, beyond the shade,
  The Naiad nymph of every rippling rill,
    And hears quick Fancy wind her wilful horn.

    What if he brooded long
On Time and Fate, — the ominous progression
  Of years that with Man's retributions frown, —
The destinies which round his footsteps throng, —
Justice, that heeds not Mercy's intercession, —
  Crime, on its own head calling vengeance down, —
Deaf Chance and blind, that, like the mountain-slide
  Puts out Youth's heart of fire and all is dark !

What though the blemish which, in aught of earth,
    The maker's hand defied,
Was plain to him, — the one evasive mark
    Wherewith Death stamps us for his **own at** birth !

    Ah, none the less we know
He felt the imperceptible fine thrill
    With which the waves of being palpitate,
Whether in ecstasy of joy or woe,
And saw **the strong divinity of Will**
    Bringing to halt the stolid tramp of Fate;
Nor from **his work was ever absent quite**
    The presence which, o'ercast it as we may,
Things far beyond our reason can suggest :
    There was a drifting light
In Donatello's cell, — a fitful ray
    Of sunshine came to hapless **Clifford's breast.**

    Into such blossom brake
Our northern hedge, that neither morta. sadness
    Nor the drear thought of lives that strive and fail,
Nor any hues its sombre leaves might take
From clouded **skies, could overcome** its gladness
    Or in the **blessing of its shade** prevail.
Fresh sprays **it** yielded them of Merry Mount
    For wedding wreaths; blithe Phœbe with the sweet
Pure flowers her promise to her lover gave :
    Beside **it, from** a fount
Where Pearl and Pansie plashed **their innocent feet,**
    A brook ran on and kissed **Zenobia's grave.**

    Silent and dark the spell
Laid on **New** England by the frozen North ;
    Long, long the months, — and yet **the Winter ends,**

The snow-wraiths vanish, and rejoicing well
The dandelions from the grass leap forth,
  And Spring through budding birch and willow sends
Her wind of Paradise.   And there are left
  Poets to sing of all, and welcome still
The robin's voice, the humble-bee's wise drone;
     Nor are we yet bereft
  Of one whose sagas ever at his will
    Can answer back the ocean, tone for tone.

     But he whose quickened eye
Saw through New England's life her inmost spirit, —
  Her heart, and all the stays on which it leant, —
Returns not, since he laid the **pencil by**
  Whose mystic touch none other shall inherit !
What though its work unfinished lies ?   Half-bent
The rainbow's arch fades out in upper **air;**
  The shining cataract half-way down the height
Breaks **into mist**; the haunting strain, that fell
     On listeners unaware,
  Ends incomplete, but through the starry night
    The ear still waits for what it did not tell.

ALL IN A LIFETIME.

THOU shalt have sun and shower **from heaven**
    above,
  Thou shalt have flower and thorn from earth below,
Thine shall be foe to hate and friend to love,
  Pleasures that others gain, the ills they know, —
      And all in a lifetime.

Hast thou a golden day, a starlit night,
  Mirth, and music, and love without alloy?
Leave no drop undrunken of thy delight:
  Sorrow and shadow follow on thy joy.
                'T is all in a lifetime.

What if the battle end and thou hast lost?
  Others have lost the battles thou hast won;
Haste thee, bind thy wounds, nor count the cost:
  Over the field will rise to-morrow's sun.
                'T is all in a lifetime.

Laugh at the braggart sneer, the open scorn, —
  'Ware of the secret stab, the slanderous lie:
For seventy years of turmoil thou wast born,
  Bitter and sweet are thine till these go by.
                'T is all in a lifetime.

Reckon thy voyage well, and spread the sail, —
  Wind and calm and current shall warp thy way;
Compass shall set thee false, and chart shall fail;
  Ever the waves will use thee for their play.
                'T is all in a lifetime.

Thousands of years agone were chance and change,
  Thousands of ages hence the same shall be;
Naught of thy joy and grief is new or strange:
  Gather apace the good that falls to thee!
                'T is all in a lifetime!

THE SKULL IN THE GOLD DRIFT.

WHAT ho ! dumb jester, cease to grin and mask it !
    Grim courier, thou hast stayed upon the road !
Yield up the secret of this battered casket,
    This shard, where once a living soul abode !
What dost thou here ? how long hast lain imbedded
    In crystal sands, the drift of Time's despair ;
Thine earth to earth with aureate dower wedded,
    Thy parts all changed to something rich and rare ?

Voiceless thou art, and yet a revelation
    Of that most ancient world beneath the new ;
But who shall guess thy race, thy name and station,
    Æons and æons ere these bowlders grew ?
What alchemy can make thy visage liker
    Its untransmuted shape, thy flesh restore,
Resolve to blood again thy golden ichor,
    Possess thee of the life thou hadst before ?

Before ! And when ? What ages immemorial
    Have passed since daylight fell where thou dost sleep !
What molten strata, ay, and flotsam boreal,
    Have shielded well thy rest, and pressed thee deep !
Thou little wist what mighty floods descended,
    How sprawled the armored monsters in their camp,
Nor heardest, when the watery cycle ended,
    The mastodon and mammoth o'er thee tramp.

How seemed this globe of ours when thou didst scan it ?
    When, in its lusty youth, there sprang to birth

All that has life, unnurtured, and the planet
  Was paradise, the true Saturnian Earth !
Far toward the poles was stretched the happy garden ;
  Earth kept it fair by warmth from her own breast ;
Toil had not come to dwarf her sons and harden ;
  No crime (there was no want) perturbed their rest.

How lived thy kind ? Was there no duty blended
  With all their toilless joy, — no grand desire ?
Perchance as shepherds on the meads they tended
  Their flocks, and knew the pastoral pipe and lyre ;
Until a hundred happy generations,
  Whose birth and death had neither pain nor fear,
At last, in riper ages, brought the nations
  To modes which we renew who greet thee here.

How stately then they built their royal cities,
  With what strong engines speeded to and fro ;
What music thrilled their souls ; what poets' ditties
  Made youth with love, and age with honor glow !
And had they then their Homer, Kepler, Bacon ?
  Did some Columbus find an unknown clime ?
Was there an archetypal Christ, forsaken
  Of those he died to save, in that far time ?

When came the end ? What terrible convulsion
  Heaved from within the Earth's distended shell ?
What pent-up demons, by their fierce repulsion,
  Made of that sunlit crust a sunless hell ?
How, when the hour was ripe, those deathful forces
  In one resistless doom o'erwhelmed ye all ;
Ingulfed the seas and dried the river courses,
  And made the forests and the cities fall !

Ah me! with what a sudden, dreadful thunder
  The whole round world was split from pole to pole !
Down sank the continents, the waters under,
  And fire burst forth where now the oceans roll;
Of those wan flames the dismal exhalations
  Stifled, anon, each living creature's **breath,**
Dear life was driven from its utmost stations,
  And seethed beneath the smoking pall of death !

Then brawling leapt full height yon helméd giants ;
  The proud Sierras on the skies laid hold ;
Their watch and ward have bidden time defiance,
  Guarding thy grave amid the sands of gold.
Thy kind was then **no more !   What untold ages,**
  Ere Man, renewed from **earth** by slow degrees,
Woke to the strife he now with Nature wages
  O'er ruder lands and more tempestuous seas.

How poor the gold, that made thy burial splendid,
  Beside one single annal of thy race,
One implement, one fragment that attended
  Thy life — which now has left not even a trace !
From the soul's realm awhile recall thy spirit,
  See how the land is spread, how flows the main,
The tribes that in thy stead **the** globe inherit,
  Their grand unrest, their eager joy and pain.

Beneath our feet a thousand ages moulder,
  Grayer our skies than thine, the winds more chill ;
Thine the young world, and ours the hoarier, colder,
  But Man's unfaltering heart is dauntless still.
And yet — and yet like thine his solemn **story ;**
  Grope where he will, transition lies before ;
We, too, must pass ! our wisdom, works, and glory
  In turn shall yield, and change, and be no more.

SONG FROM A DRAMA.

I KNOW not if moonlight or starlight
    Be soft on the land and the sea, —
I catch but the near light, the far light,
    Of eyes that are burning for me ;
The scent of the night, of the roses,
    May burden the air for thee, Sweet, —
'T is only the breath of thy sighing
    I know, as I lie at thy feet.

The winds may be sobbing or singing,
    Their touch may be fervent or cold,
The night-bells may toll or be ringing, —
    I care not, while thee I enfold !
The feast may go on, and the music
    Be scattered in ecstasy round, —
Thy whisper, " I love thee ! I love thee !"
    Hath flooded my soul with its sound.

I think not of time that is flying,
    How short is the hour I have won,
How near is this living to dying,
    How the shadow still follows the sun ;
There is naught upon earth, no desire,
    Worth a thought, though 't were had by a sign !
I love thee ! I love thee ! bring nigher
    Thy spirit, thy kisses, to mine.

.

THE SUN-DIAL.

" Horas non numero nisi serenas."

ONLY the sunny hours
　　Are numbered here, —
No winter-time that lowers,
　　No twilight drear.
But from a golden sky
　　When sunbeams fall,
Though the bright moments fly, —
　　They 're counted all.

My heart **its transient woe**
　　Remembers not!
The ills of **long ago**
　　Are half forgot ;
But Childhood's round of bliss,
　　Youth's tender thrill,
Hope's whisper, Love's first kiss, —
　　They haunt me **still** !

Sorrows are everywhere,
　　Joys — all too few !
Have we not had our **share**
　　Of pleasure too ?
No Past the glad heart cowers,
　　No memories dark ;
Only the sunny hours
　　The dial mark.

MADRIGAL.

DORUS TO LYCORIS, WHO REPROVED HIM FOR INCONSTANCY.

WHY should I constant be?
The bird in yonder tree,
This leafy summer,
Hath not his last year's mate,
Nor dreads to venture fate
With a new-comer.

Why should I fear to sip
The sweets of each red lip?
In every bower
The roving bee may taste
(Lest aught should run to waste)
Each fresh-blown flower.

The trickling rain doth fall
Upon us one and all;
The south-wind kisses
The saucy milkmaid's cheek,
The nun's, demure and meek,
Nor any misses.

Then ask no more of me
That I should constant be,
Nor eke desire it;
Take not such idle pains
To hold our love in chains,
Nor coax, nor hire it.

Be all things in thyself, —
A sprite, a tricksy elf,
　　Forever changing,
So that thy latest mood
May ever bring new food
　　To Fancy ranging.

Forget what thou wast first,
And as I loved thee erst
　　In soul and feature,
I 'll love thee out of mind
When each new morn shall find
　　Thee a new creature.

WITH A SPRIG OF HEATHER.

TO THE LADY WHO SENT ME A JAR OF HYMETTIAN HONEY.

LADY, had the lot been mine
　　That befell the sage divine,
Near Hymettus to be bred,
And in sleep on honey fed,
I would send to you, be sure,
Rhythmic verses — tuneful, pure,
Such as flowed when Greece was young,
And the Attic songs were sung ;
I would take your little jar,
Filled with sweetness from afar, —
Brown as amber, bright as gold,
Breathing odors manifold, —
And would thank you, sip by sip,
With the classic honeyed lip.
But the gods did not befriend

Me in childhood's sleep, nor send,
One by one, their laden bees,
That I now might sing at ease
With the winsome voice and word
In this age too seldom heard.
(Had they the Atlantic crost,
Half their treasure had been lost!)
Changed the time, and gone the art
Of the glad Athenian heart.
Take you, then, in turn, I pray,
For your gift, this little spray, —
Heather from a breezy hill
That of Burns doth whisper still.
On the soil where this was bred
The rapt ploughman laid his head,
Sang, and looking to the sky
Saw the Muses hovering nigh.
From the air and from the gorse
Scotland's sweetness took its source ; —
Precious still your jar, you see,
Though its honey stays with me.

THE LORD'S-DAY GALE.

BAY ST. LAWRENCE, AUGUST, 1873.

IN Gloucester port lie fishing craft, —
   More stanch and trim were never seen :
They are sharp before and sheer abaft,
   And true their lines the masts between.
Along the wharves of Gloucester Town
Their fares are lightly handed down,
   And the laden flakes to landward lean.

Well know the men each cruising-ground,
　And where the cod and mackerel be ;
Old Eastern Point the schooners round
　And leave Cape Ann on the larboard lee :
Sound are the planks, the hearts are bold,
That brave December's surges cold
　On Georges' shoals in the outer sea.

And some must sail to the banks far north
　And set their trawls for the hungry cod, —
In the ghostly fog grope back and forth
　By shrouded paths no foot hath trod;
Upon the crews the ice-winds blow,
The bitter sleet, the frozen snow, —
　Their lives are in the hand of God !

New England ! New England !
　Needs sail they must, so brave and poor,
Or June be warm or Winter storm,
　Lest a wolf gnaw through the cottage-door !
Three weeks at home, three long months gone,
While the patient goodwives sleep alone,
　And wake to hear the breakers roar.

The Grand Bank gathers in its dead, —
　The deep sea-sand is their winding-sheet ;
Who does not Georges' billows dread
　That dash together the drifting fleet ?
Who does not long to hear, in May,
The pleasant wash of Saint Lawrence Bay,
　The fairest ground where fishermen meet ?

There the west wave holds the red sunlight
　Till the bells at home are rung for nine :

Short, short the watch, and calm the night ;
   The fiery northern streamers shine ;
The eastern sky anon is gold,
And winds from piny forests old
   Scatter the white mists off the brine.

The Province craft with ours at morn
   Are mingled when the vapors shift ;
All day, by breeze and current borne,
   Across the bay the sailors drift ;
With toll and seine its wealth they **win,** —
The dappled, **silvery spoil come in**
   Fast as their hands can haul and lift.

New England ! New England !
   Thou lovest well thine ocean main !
It spreadeth its **locks among thy rocks,**
   And long against thy heart **hath lain ;**
Thy ships upon its bosom ride
And feel the heaving **of** its tide;
   To thee its secret speech is **plain.**

Cape Breton and Edward Isle between,
   In strait and gulf the schooners lay ;
The sea was all at peace, I ween,
   The night before that August day ;
Was never a Gloucester skipper there,
But thought **erelong,** with **a right** good **fare,**
   To sail **for home from Saint Lawrence Bay.**

New England ! New England !
   Thy giant's love was turned to **hate !**
The winds control his fickle soul,
   And in his wrath **he** hath no mate.

18

Thy shores his angry scourges tear,
And for thy children in his care
    The sudden tempests lie in wait.

The East Wind gathered all unknown, —
    A thick sea-cloud his course before ;
He left by night the frozen zone
    And smote the cliffs of Labrador ;
He lashed the coasts on either hand,
And betwixt the Cape and Newfoundland
    Into the Bay his armies pour.

He caught our helpless cruisers there
    As a gray wolf harries the huddling fold ;
A sleet — a darkness — filled the air,
    A shuddering wave before it rolled :
That Lord's-day morn it was a breeze, —
At noon, a blast that shook the seas, —
    At night, — a wind of Death took hold !

It leapt across the Breton bar,
    A death-wind from the stormy East !
It scarred the land, and whirled afar
    The sheltering thatch of man and beast ;
It mingled rick and roof and tree,
And like a besom swept the sea,
    And churned the waters into yeast.

From Saint Paul's light to Edward Isle
    A thousand craft it smote amain ;
And some against it strove the while,
    And more to make a port were fain :
The mackerel-gulls flew screaming past,

And the stick that bent to the noonday blast
  Was split by the sundown hurricane.

Woe, woe to those whom the islands pen !
  In vain they shun the double capes :
Cruel are the reefs of Magdalen ;
  The Wolf's white fang what prey escapes ?
The Grin'stone grinds the bones of some,
And Coffin Isle is craped with foam ; —
  On Deadman's shore are fearful shapes !

O, what can live on the open sea,
  Or moored in port the gale outride ?
The very craft that at anchor be
  Are dragged along by the swollen tide !
The great storm-wave came rolling west,
And tossed the vessels on its crest :
  The ancient bounds its might defied !

The ebb to check it had no power ;
  The surf ran up an untold height ;
It rose, nor yielded, hour by hour,
  A night and day, a day and night ;
Far up the seething shores it cast
The wrecks of hull and spar and mast,
  The strangled crews, — a woful sight !

There were twenty and more of Breton sail
  Fast anchored on one mooring-ground ;
Each lay within his neighbor's hail
  When the thick of the tempest closed them
    round :
All sank at once in the gaping sea, —
Somewhere on the shoals their corses be,
  The foundered hulks, and the seamen drowned.

On reef and bar our schooners drove
  Before the wind, before the swell ;
By the steep sand-cliffs their ribs were stove, —
  Long, long, their crews the tale shall tell !
Of the Gloucester fleet are wrecks threescore ;
Of the Province sail two hundred more
  Were stranded in that tempest fell.

The bedtime bells in Gloucester Town
  That Sabbath night rang soft and clear ;
The sailors' children laid them down, —
  Dear Lord ! their sweet prayers couldst thou hear ?
'T is said that gently blew the winds ;
The goodwives, through the seaward blinds,
  Looked down the bay and had no fear.

New England ! New England !
  Thy ports their dauntless seamen mourn ;
The twin capes yearn for their return
  Who never shall be thither borne ;
Their orphans whisper as they meet ;
The homes are dark in many a street,
  And women move in weeds forlorn.

And wilt thou quail, and dost thou fear ?
  Ah, no ! though widows' cheeks are pale,
The lads shall say : " Another year,
  And we shall be of age to sail ! "
And the mothers' hearts shall fill with pride,
Though tears drop fast for them who died
  When the fleet was wrecked in the Lord's-Day gale.

L'ENVOI.

AD VATEM.

WHITTIER ! the Land that loves thee, she whose
        child
Thou art, — and whose uplifted hands thou long
Hast stayed with song availing like a prayer, —
She feels a sudden pang, who gave thee birth
And gave to thee the lineaments supreme
Of her own freedom, that she could not make
Thy tissues all immortal, or, if to change,
To bloom through years coeval with her own;
So that no touch of age nor frost of time
Should wither thee, nor furrow thy dear face,
Nor fleck thy hair with silver. Ay, she feels
A double pang that thee, with each new year,
Glad Youth may not revisit, like the Spring
That routs her northern Winter and anew
Melts off the hoar snow from her puissant hills.
She could not make thee deathless ; no, but thou,
Thou sangest her always in abiding verse
And hast thy fame immortal — as we say
Immortal in this Earth that yet must die,
And in this land now fairest and most young
Of all fair lands that yet must perish with it.
Thy words shall last : albeit thou growest old,
Men say ; but never old the poet's soul
Becomes ; only its covering takes on

A reverend splendour, as in the misty fall
Thine own auroral forests, ere at last
Passes the spirit of the wooded dell.
And stay thou with us long; vouchsafe us long
This brave autumnal presence, ere the hues
Slow fading, — ere the quaver of thy voice,
The twilight of thine eye, move men to ask
Where hides the chariot, — in what sunset vale,
Beyond thy chosen river, champ the steeds
That wait to bear thee skyward? Since we too
Would feign thee, in our tenderness, to be
Inviolate, excepted from thy kind,
And that our bard and prophet best-beloved
Shall vanish like that other: him that stood
Undaunted in the pleasure-house of kings,
And unto kings and crownéd harlots spake
God's truth and judgment. At his sacred feet
Far followed all the lesser men of old
Whose lips were touched with fire, and caught from him
The gift of prophecy; and thus from thee,
Whittier, the younger singers, — whom thou seest
Each emulous to be thy staff this day, —
What learned they? righteous anger, burning scorn
Of the oppressor, love to humankind,
Sweet fealty to country and to home,
Peace, stainless purity, high thoughts of heaven,
And the clear, natural music of thy song.

THE END

www.ingramcontent.com/pod-product-compliance
Lightning Source LLC
Chambersburg PA
CBHW020857130726
47900CB00014B/944